Praise for Eoin C Macken's debut
Kingdom of Scars

"Quite brilliant. An edgy coming of age story which never flags."
Sue Leonard, *Irish Examiner*

"Imbues his first book with a cinematic quality . . ."
Deirdre Reynolds, *Independent.ie*

"Evocative, stand out, Macken has a natural flair for the descriptive . . ." Michael Doherty, *RTÉ Guide*

"Spectacular debut fiction – a novel of fear, uncertainty and the constant need to fit in . . ." Bleach House Library

"A gritty story about growing up, friendship and betrayal that perfectly captures the confusion and longings of teenage years, this crossover novel will appeal to adults as well as teen readers . . ."
Sarah Webb, *Irish Independent*

"Eoin Macken's writing bristles and prickles with authentic purpose. *Kingdom of Stars* feels both epic and intimate simultaneously." Eoghan McDermott, *2FM*

"A wonderful first novel from a new talent: rich, absorbing and gritty. One to watch for the future." Jim Fitzpatrick, Artist

Hunter and the Grape

EOIN C MACKEN

WARD
RIVER
PRESS

Published 2017
by Ward River Press
123 Grange Hill, Baldoyle
Dublin 13, Ireland
www.wardriverpress.com

A catalogue record for this book is available from the British Library.

1

ISBN 978-1-78199-9127

Printed by CPI, Mackeys, UK

www.wardriverpress.com

About the author

Eoin C Macken studied Psychology in UCD, Dublin, before pursuing an acting, writing and film-making career. He is best known for his roles in BBC's hit show *Merlin* as Gwaine, the lead role of TC Callahan in the hit NBC/Sony/Netflix prime-time show *The Night Shift*, and opposite Milla Jovovich in *Resident Evil 6*.

Eoin was the cinematographer on the international award-winning *Charlie Casanova* for Terry McMahon, and on Mark O'Connor's Galway Film Fleadh success *Stalker*. He wrote and directed the FrightFest Film Festival Premiering Horror Film *The Inside*, an acclaimed indie horror that was released across the UK, USA and Australia, and *Leopard* (originally titled *Cold*) which premiered in the Galway Film Fleadh in 2014 before a USA release in 2016, starring Jack Reynor, Tom Hopper and himself.

His debut novel, *Kingdom of Scars*, was nominated for an Irish Book Award for best debut novel amdist numerous plaudits and excellent reviews, and is also available with Poolbeg Press.

Acknowledgements

I was told by my mother that I could become a writer if that's what I wanted to do. I didn't believe her, but she insisted. She gave me the belief in everything that I do, and her support has always been unwavering. Without her I wouldn't be doing what I am today.

To Anya, the most incredible person I've met and my best friend, who encouraged me to read the words on the page out loud, which allowed me to hear the flaws and improve upon them.

Thanks again to Paula and Poolbeg for having the faith in this, my second book, and to my wonderful editor Gaye Shortland, who has a knack for improving everything.

Thanks to Caroline Grace Cassidy and Louise O'Neill who read my early drafts and convinced me that what I had written was good enough for print.

To my fantastic manager Stephanie Comer and agent Kat Gosling, who never stop pushing and supporting me.

To my sisters Freya and Niamh, just for being them – never change!

To Robert and Sophie in Madrid – hope you guys enjoy this one.

Dedication

This book is dedicated to everybody who has fallen in love, wants to fall in love, and to everybody who forays on an adventure out into the world to become something more than they could have expected.

And to my late father, James Macken. I discovered after he had passed away that he had written an unfinished novel, and I am always surprised and inspired by everything that he has done and who he was. I can only aspire to be the man I hope makes him proud.

Prologue

His boots cast puffy sprays of dirt up into the air. The sun was raw on his back, at its midday peak, and forced him to pull his jacket high up on his neck to protect the skin. He was taking the longer route to the bus depot in an effort to avoid the Walgreens where he was due to report for work in an hour. Making a clean break without anybody knowing. He didn't know any other way of doing it. There was no other way. He turned down a small alleyway, ignoring the growls of a chained dog. Every inch of these streets was familiar, having wandered them for hours alone every year since as far back as he could remember. He was thirsty but his water bottle was buried deep in his backpack and he didn't want to stop. There was a finality about leaving a place, that called for continual movement. If he hesitated he might not have the strength to start again.

It was a full five-mile walk from his mother's house to where the bus picked up passengers on its journey to Los Angeles. He never called it his house anymore. He used to

1

once, but it had become a shelter his body had inhabited, nothing more. The bus depot was ahead and he instinctively slowed his pace, searching for any familiar faces. There was nobody else there. He was early. When you were leaving a place it was best not to be late and fall at the first hurdle. He double-checked the time and once satisfied that he was still on track sat on the ground, leaning against a small wall on the other side of the street from the bus depot.

Cat wondered what would happen when he didn't show up for work. Not very much. Marsha would scream a few times, her fat ass jiggling wildly, until the effort was too much and she was satisfied that she had made enough of a show of displeasure. Then they would continue as normal, expecting him to turn up later. When he didn't, he would have a black mark against his name on the employee board and would be expected in the next day. When he didn't show tomorrow she might make a phone call to the house, which would make no difference as he would be long gone by then. Marsha might scream his name in anger, to prove something to herself and mock him maybe, but that was it. Then he would be forgotten about.

A girl wandered into view, searching for something. She was lighter on her feet than her frame suggested, drifting across the ground like the wind, but the sun was at her back and he couldn't make out her face. He turned his attention away from her and focused on his boots. They were the only thing he owned that he was proud of. Old and battered but holding together gamely, original buckles sternly keeping their shape.

"Is this where the bus goes to Phoenix?"

Her voice was soft and gentle, the question almost

rhetorical. She stood a few feet away from him, keeping her distance. There was something wary about how she leaned into her hip, oversized shorts loose against her body. The sun still flared behind, casting her face in shadow.

"Yeah."

"Thanks."

"Sure."

He figured that was the end of the conversation but she moved closer and sat down on the ground, mimicking his position. She sat like that in silence, not doing anything but leaning back against the same wall, feet outstretched. For some reason it annoyed him. He turned his head to her.

"The bus is arriving on the other side of the street."

"Oh. OK."

She made no movement to get up. He kept looking at her.

"So you might want to wait on that side."

"Are you getting it to Phoenix?"

"Yeah."

"Why?"

Cat didn't want to tell her, so he didn't reply. She smiled at him and stayed where she was, not blinking. He looked at her carefully. Her eyes were too big for her face and that annoyed him. When he didn't answer she finally lost interest and began picking at a torn nail on her left thumb. He was about to get up and wait on the other side but something stopped him.

So Cat sat there, recently turned eighteen, and waited for the bus to take him to Los Angeles and leave Albuquerque behind.

Cat was not actually called Cat. His full name was John Thomas Lennon Jones. A drunken uncle had begun calling him Catherine years ago at a family gathering because it was amusing and it had stuck, mercifully shortened to Cat by his mother to make it more respectable. The only positive effect she had on his life.

He put his hand inside his jacket on impulse, searching for the comforting feeling of dollar bills, checking that the girl didn't notice. The bundle was still there. He pressed the money between his fingers. He had rolled the three hundred and sixteen dollars tightly, wrapping an elastic band around to keep them secure, and placed them in a secret pocket on the inside of his jacket. This money was the only way that he could follow Sophie Durango and he was damned if he was going to lose it without finding her first.

One

He needed to piss so he got to his feet and hopped onto the wall. The girl's eyes followed him, landing on his backpack.

"You forgot your backpack?"

Cat turned to her.

"I'll only be a moment."

"Do you want me to keep watch over it?"

"What? Yeah, sure."

She nodded to him and focused her gaze on the bag as if challenging it to move. Cat felt self-conscious about peeing now so he walked farther away than he needed to. Sometimes when he was uncomfortable he found it hard to pee so he closed his eyes and pictured Sophie Durango in his mind.

She was the reason he was leaving. She had been an alluring presence when she'd walked into the store, intimidatingly welcome.

Her hair was auburn, or the sunny side of brown, and she had a delicate complexion which made her hard features almost handsome. Dark eyes dominated her face, their brown depths shrouding her thoughts. Cat had been patiently counting out the change to an elderly woman when she sashayed up to the check-out, sweaty hair stuck to her face, crinkled blouse loose, and tight shorts holding her ass up. He had seen her out of the corner of his eye and immediately dropped the coins all over the register. The elderly woman gave him a conciliatory smile, her own hands quivering in mid-air. Sophie had barely noticed as Cat scraped the coins back into his sweating palms and she had drifted over to the other check-out which was now free. The lady wanted it all in dimes and fives for parking and Cat was so flustered that he had miscounted the change twice. Sophie had paid for her juice box and cigarettes and he watched in dismay as she floated away while the elderly woman asked him to count the change out a third time. Grimacing, he had politely begun, but then made the decision that changed everything, pushing the coins into the woman's hand and striding out the door.

She was nowhere to be seen. The parking lot was empty at this time of day, the sun beating down hard. It was an ugly day, roughly hot and uncomfortable, not a day to fall in love. He scanned the lot frantically, scouring the perimeter. He had all but given up, turning back to face the supermarket in defeat when he saw her. She was walking out of the shadows at the side of the building, hiking her shorts back up over her hips as she ambled away. The lewdness of having peed so brazenly at the back of the building made her seem even more exotic and alluring. She walked across the lot without a glance towards him. He stood there as his shirt slowly stuck to his sweaty skin and watched her move. She opened the juice box with her teeth, drank the entire contents and tossed it to the side with delicious nonchalance. He had to follow her. So he did.

She stopped walking at the exact moment that he reached her but if she had been aware of his presence she hid it well, lighting a cigarette as she turned and looked at him. He hadn't said anything but simply watched her inhale deeply. Her head was tilted to the side, like a lazy predator, her mouth acutely aware of how she inhaled and exhaled, expertly teasing him.

Grasping the initiative had never been part of Cat's skill-set but he reached into his pocket, pulled out a crumpled discount voucher and shoved it unceremoniously into her hand.

"You forgot your discount voucher. You get free stuff."

He sounded like one of those idiots on a bad television commercial but she arched an eyebrow, the one closest to him from the angle of her face and smiled. He would never forget what she had said to him.

"You wanna get high and make out?" she pouted.

His hand was wet where he had peed on it a little. He shook it off and wiped his hand on the grass at his feet. He wasn't sure how long he had been standing there but his lower back hurt a little.

The girl was where he had left her. It occurred to him that maybe he shouldn't have trusted her, but his money was in his jacket and that was the most important thing. She didn't take her eyes off his backpack until he was seated beside it. Then she looked at him like an eager puppy searching for affirmation of a good deed.

"You're back," she said.

"Yep."

"You shouldn't pee in people's gardens."

He felt uncomfortable at being judged.

"Thanks for telling me."

"Nobody tried to steal your backpack. I'm not surprised – there's not very much in it."

Cat looked at her sharply, her innocent eyes rolling at him.

"You looked in my bag?"

"Sure. I needed to make sure that there weren't any drugs in it. If the cops or anybody came by and there were drugs and the bag was in my possession then I'd be in trouble."

"But why would I leave a bag with drugs in it with you?"

She shrugged to indicate that wasn't any of her business and turned her attention to a little book that had appeared in her hands. It had no cover and the pages were faded and torn. She was immediately engrossed. Cat shook his head, checked his bag to make sure that she hadn't taken anything, and settled back against the wall to wait for the bus.

After a few minutes she looked up at him casually. There was a languid way about her, as if she was perpetually underwater.

"I'm hungry. Do you want to get something to eat? I also need to pee and I'm not doing it in a garden."

"I'm fine. I'm gonna wait for the bus."

"Oh, the bus already came and left."

Cat looked at her, incredulous.

"What?"

"It came when you were peeing. You were gone for a long time. I thought you had realised."

"No. I – what – why didn't you shout for me?"

"I didn't want to disturb you. It's rude."

Cat's scowled. He had spaced out a bit thinking about Sophie Durango but his instinct was still to blame the girl.

"Why didn't you get on the bus then?"

"I didn't want to leave your bag on the street. You asked me to keep an eye on it and I don't break promises. Besides, there's another one in a few hours."

"How do you know?"

"I know all the timetables. It's only a bus – there's plenty of them. Want to get something to eat?"

Cat didn't know how he wanted to respond but then she stood lithely to her feet, a heavy figure yet surprisingly graceful, and looked quizzically at him. He shook his head. There was no chance that he was going anywhere with this strange girl. He had sandwiches and Oreos in his bag anyway.

She mashed her lips together in what appeared to be disappointment and turned away. He watched her for a few moments as she walked away, then sat back against the wall to wait.

Two

She held out a burger to him with a shy smile. The gesture irritated Cat. He didn't want her to be nice to him or be friendly, it made him uncomfortable.

"I didn't spit in it."

"I know that."

"No, you don't. I might have."

The thought seemed to amuse her.

"But you didn't?"

"No."

"I'm not hungry, thanks."

Cat shook his head and she made a face like she wished she had spat on it. She sat down in the same spot as before, a few feet away from him against the wall, and stuffed the burger into her canvas bag.

Cat watched her from the corner of his eye as she took out her book again and began reading, it looked like she was still on the same page. Her brow furrowed. Something about the book was bothering her.

She seemed to feel his gaze upon her and drew her eyes up to meet his but he looked away.

"Do you read?" she asked.

"Sure."

"Me too. Well, sort of, I think."

"Cool."

Cat was silent. He was getting hungry and wanted to have his snacks but, after refusing her offer of the burger, he didn't want her to see him eating. He resolved to wait until he was on the bus to avoid her judgement. He wished that she wasn't here.

She seemed to be waiting for something from him so he turned to her, indicating the book.

"Is the book any good?"

"Yeah."

Silence.

"What's it about?"

Her eyes widened and her face quivered like jelly. Her voice dropped to a whisper and she mumbled something that he couldn't make out.

"What?"

"I ... I don't know." She wouldn't meet his eye and her voice was soft. "It's in French. I don't know what it's about." Her cheeks reddened.

Cat smiled, convinced that she was joking, but as her face flushed her eyes became watery and he knew that she was serious.

"Then why are reading it?"

"I found it in a parking lot a while ago and I kept it. It makes me feel good to have a book in French. It seems important. I like looking at the words – it calms me when I'm confused. I like to imagine what the words mean and what the story is in a different place from where I am."

She looked up at him, eyes wide and imploring some sort of validation.

She was so earnest that it almost made him smile but he didn't want to upset her. He dipped his head and nodded.

"I understand."

"You do?"

Fuck, he had said too much. She was staring at him.

The rumble of the approaching bus saved him. He scrambled to his feet, and determinedly raced across the street in front of the bus so that it had to stop. He didn't look behind to check if the girl was following on, but paid his fare and walked down the aisle, searching for an empty seat. There was a double free near the back and he took the window-seat gladly. Anxiety at leaving Albuquerque momentarily gripped him. Then there was a movement to his right. She was standing there, head tilted. She wanted to take the seat next to him. He nodded. What else could he do?

The bus started off again, dragging its bulk painfully along the road. Cat pressed his face against the glass and watched his world slowly melt away. The girl sat beside him, body curled into itself, staring at the book in her hands, then without warning she let her head drop forward and fell asleep.

The bus trundled along the freeway, an older model that reeked of rust and fleshy indiscretion, hard sun creasing its interior. The girl groaned in her sleep, turning her head to nuzzle into his shoulder, a small sliver of spittle escaping onto his leather jacket. Cat didn't care – it might even clean it.

Sophie Durango. The name had a nice ring to it. He

rolled the words around his mouth for a while, savouring the taste. The rolling motion of the bus was gentle and his eyes began to close.

He awoke suddenly with his head smacking against the glass window. The bus was moving over an uneven dirt track, and shaking violently. The girl was holding her head in her hands and squeezing her temples roughly, a pale-yellow pool of vomit at her feet. Her fingers were speckled with flecks of vomit that mingled in her hair. The bus abruptly stopped. The jerk was so unexpected that Cat slipped forward, right foot sliding out into the vomit, knee hitting the seat in front and forehead slicing into the exposed ashtray on the back of the seat. It hurt like hell.

The bus had stopped in what appeared to be the middle of the desert. Everybody got up off their seats and filtered off in a very systematic manner. Cat stayed where he was.

The girl got up, turned back to him.

"We have to get off."

He shook his head, so she waited a moment, then filed off. He watched through the window as everybody milled around in vague confusion, then began leaving in small pods. The girl stayed on the road, along with an old man burnished with sour indifference and glasses as thick as his finger. They exchanged a few words, and she sat down on the brittle grass, curling her feet underneath her ass and running her hands through her hair a few times. Her eyes looked up at him as the bus began pulling off.

The smell of the vomit was overpowering and, with the entire bus now empty, Cat decided to change his seat. His shoe was slick with vomit so when he stood up he lost his footing, stumbling across the aisle. The bus stopped abruptly for a second time and Cat was thrown forward again, cursing loudly. The driver's face filled the front mirror, gesticulating wildly. Cat ignored him and made himself comfortable on the new seat.

The shadow of the driver loomed over him.

"Get off the bus."

"What?"

"You heard me. It's broken. This journey is cancelled – you have to get off."

"Where am I supposed to go?"

"Another will come."

"When?"

"It'll come when it comes."

The driver grabbed Cat's shoulder and forced him off and into the searing heat of the New Mexican desert.

For a few moments he simply stood there as the bus trundled into the distance. He was abandoned in the middle of nowhere. Squinting back against the sunlight he could make out the vague shapes of the girl and the old man sitting on the ground. He took off his jacket and reluctantly made his way towards them.

The girl acknowledged him with a cheery smile, but the old man either didn't care or didn't notice. Cat stood quietly, the sun burning the back of his neck, and nobody spoke. He didn't know how long he had been asleep or where they were but he figured that they knew something that he didn't so he eventually sat down beside them.

A while passed without anybody saying anything or moving. There was a patient acceptance to their vigil that made him uncomfortable. Standing up to stretch his back, he felt the girl's eyes upon him so he turned to acknowledge her. She had a kind docile face like a young farmyard animal, married into a conversely weathered exterior. Soft eyes behind stern lids. He decided that he could trust her even if he could still see some of the dried vomit in the ends of her hair.

Her brow furrowed, considering something of the gravest importance. When she spoke her words were pronounced and definite, as if each syllable held great significance for the world and needed absolute clarity.

"Are you going to wait for the next bus tomorrow?"

"Tomorrow?"

"The next bus doesn't come until tomorrow, the same time as this one. If it comes. That's why we're waiting."

"Do they not send a replacement bus?"

"Not usually. It's happened to me before many times. You just have to wait."

Cat had no interest in waiting overnight on the side of the road for the next bus. The girl suddenly looked doubtful about what she had said. Casting a surreptitious glance at the old man sitting inches from her, she bit her lip. There was more vomit in her hair than Cat had initially thought.

"I'm not staying," the old man announced.

He had a powerful voice for such a frail figure, but kept staring ahead, unable or unwilling to look at either of them. His glasses appeared too heavy to encourage comfortably turning his head. He didn't stir a muscle or make any movement that would indicate that he was going anywhere though. Maybe he thought he was already walking but his mind was playing tricks on him.

Cat took off one shoe, picked at the curved railings of his toenails and waited. The girl watched him curiously, then pretended that she wasn't.

Three

There was the low drone of an approaching car. Maybe two hours had passed. The old man heard it at the same time and struggled to rise. Cat instinctively reached forward to help him but his hand was batted away contemptuously. Cat stepped back and watched him heroically stagger to his feet. He was standing at the precise moment that an old pickup truck arrived in front of them, the tires scattering dust up into the dry air.

The old man clambered into the truck without a word and when he was settled he turned his face to them through the cab window.

"Are you getting in?"

It was a rhetorical question. There didn't seem any reason to not get in. The cabin only had space for one more so Cat duly clambered into the open back of the truck as the girl got into the front. The shell of the truck was boiling hot from the sun and uncomfortable on the skin but at least he was going somewhere.

"Are you comfortable?" the old man's voice bellowed out as the truck rumbled off into the future, the exact same words as Sophie Durango had said to him when they were smoking.

"Are you comfortable?" Her voice was melted peaches. She was staring, searching for his reaction. "Your shirt is soaked in sweat – it can't be comfortable?"

"It's OK," he lied.

"It's hot – just take it off and let it dry."

She smiled like it was an order, so he slipped off his shirt, acutely aware of the nakedness of his skin so close to her. She licked the papers of the joint one last time, rolled the end tight and then placed it in her mouth ready to smoke. The empty desert billowed out in front of them from the roof of her car where they had pulled over. The isolation was soothing. She lit the joint, inhaled deeply and then passed it to him.

"How old are you?"

"Seventeen. You?"

"Same."

He nodded as if that information really meant anything and imagined what she looked like naked. He tilted his head away from her so she couldn't read his thoughts.

"You live here?" she asked.

"Yeah. My entire life."

He said that proudly but immediately felt ignorant for having been in one place his whole life.

"That's cool."

He nodded, even though he knew that it wasn't cool. He felt that he should ask her something.

"You're not from around here?"

"No."

That was all she gave him: No.

They sat there and smoked in silence, the vastness of the desert around them becoming ever more captivating the more stoned they got.

She looked at him.

"You wanna make out now?"

Her lips were invitingly half open. Peaches.

"You wanna get out now?"

He blinked.

The old man's voice abruptly ground into the soft features of Sophie Durango and he focused on the harsh brown landscape.

The truck had rolled to a sedate stop outside a squat square building surrounded by deep red desert. The red brick was gaudy and hard on the eye, with dust rolling off the walls. The old man got out first and helped the girl out like she was a misguided hound. Cat sat up on his haunches, trying to figure out what to do, the image of Sophie Durango's lips blurring his thoughts. The house was befriended by ragged trees on one side and errant smoke drifted from the chimney. An air of desolate calm hung in the air, mixed with spices and burnt cooking oil.

Cat lifted himself off the truck gingerly, the blood in his legs uncoiling aggressively, and he stumbled a little when his left foot hit the ground. The driver of the truck caught him by the arm to break his fall. Cat looked at the strong fingers firmly gripping his naked skin before he could bring himself to stare into the gnarled face of the tall man holding him up. He had dark hooded eyes which flanked ugly expressionless features. Cat's gaze didn't waver but he felt an uncomfortable knot twist about his belly. The tall man let go of his arm and Cat waited until he had disappeared inside the house before rubbing the redness off his skin where his fingers had bitten deep.

"What's your name?"

The girl was staring at him intently. He didn't answer immediately. She didn't seem to be in any rush so they stood there in silence until he finally responded. Sometimes that happened: he needed time to force his mouth to work – his brain liked the silence.

"Cat."

His voice felt weak and sore. It was always awkward saying just one word without any lead in – the vocal cords needed a gentle warm-up before such naked pronouncement.

"Like a cat?"

"What?"

"Your name is 'Cat' – like a cat?"

He nodded sourly without any desire to follow in the direction of this conversation. It never failed to frustrate him. The girl who had a French book but couldn't understand French was mocking him like everybody else.

"Do you like cats?"

Her question caught him by surprise and he looked at her for any trace of mirth but she was serious.

"Why?"

"Well, if you didn't like cats then I wouldn't understand why you would call yourself after one so you must like them."

"I didn't decide on my name – it was given to me."

"Oh. I chose my own name."

She shrugged her shoulders in such a matter-of-fact manner that he felt like an idiot for not having picked his own name, or for still using Cat. He had never really thought that he shouldn't.

She looked at him for a moment longer then wandered inconclusively into the house. He didn't know what to do. Should he go inside or wait until he was invited? The thought occurred to him that maybe he should just leave. He could probably hitchhike somewhere if he got back onto the main road. He turned on his heel to leave but her voice drew him back before he had taken a single step forward.

"There's soup inside. And coffee."

She was standing in the doorway with complete confidence that he was going to come inside. He found himself obeying.

"Do you like coffee?" she asked.

"Sure."

"Everybody likes coffee. I don't."

She went inside and he followed. The inside of the house was spartan and clearly built by hand – just one room. The ceiling beams were roughly hewn with deep cuts where an axe had cleaved unsuccessfully. The floor was concrete and felt cold through his boots. The walls were naked. The old man was sitting on the only chair, while the girl sat down on a scruffy rug opposite. She seemed comfortable with strangers. Trusting. The only other furniture in the room was a low-lying bed and a rudimentary kitchen in the corner.

Cat sat down on the floor near the girl.

A pot of soup was bubbling on the stove and the tall man was stirring it methodically. Then he stopped and ladled out three thick helpings of soup into three waiting bowls, into which he thrust three spoons. He picked up all three bowls with some dexterity and turned to face them, his face souring a little when he saw Cat – as if he had expected him to disappear. There were only three bowls but now there were four of them. Cat immediately regretted coming inside. The tall man stepped up to him, then thrust a bowl of steaming vegetable soup at his face. The hooded eyes stared down at him and he took the bowl carefully, nodding his thanks. The tall man gave no indication of caring, handed out the other two bowls and walked outside.

The three began to eat in strained silence as the sound of the truck starting up and driving away filled the room. Cat found himself straining to hear the vehicle fade into the distance until he couldn't anymore.

The girl didn't look at him. She concentrated on carefully consuming the soup.

The sound of eating filled the small room.

"What's your name?" he prompted.

Her eyes flickered with joy, and she opened her mouth, pausing to suck in air.

"Star."

"Star?"

"Yes. Star."

She smiled breathlessly.

"It's a nice name."

"I chose it myself."

"I believe you."

Star adjusted her seating position shyly and focused on her soup. Cat waited but there was nothing more forthcoming.

The old man was watching him silently.

"How do you two know each other?"

"We don't," she said. "We just sat down together after the bus left us. I don't even know his name."

This thought seemed to delight her. The old man looked at her and grimaced kindly through a mouthful of sloppy soup. She smiled back at him but didn't say anything else. The old man didn't offer his name.

Cat finished his soup and put the empty bowl down on the floor, hating the scraping sound the ceramic made on the concrete.

They sat like that, with the scraping of spoon on bowl the only sound. Then there was the unmistakable hum of the truck approaching and Cat got to his feet, deciding that he didn't want to be sitting submissively on the ground when the tall man arrived back. He wasn't sure why he felt that but he did.

Four

The tall man was staring at Cat coldly from across the room. The old man had begun plying him with questions the moment his lips had touched a whiskey. His eyes sparkled with amusement as he probed.

"You're going to Los Angeles for a girl you met once?"

Cat squirmed a little. It sounded stupid when said out loud.

"Yes. Well, we spent the day together."

"That's the stupidest thing I've ever heard."

"She was perfect."

"Every girl is perfect for a day."

The old man's mouth curled up in a mocking smirk. Cat decided that he didn't like him very much, but the tall man was hovering in the corner protectively so Cat played nice. The tall man's hooded eyes hadn't left Cat's face since he had come back.

"Well, this girl is different," Cat heard himself say.

The old man laughed so hard that he began to cough

violently. The tall man strode forward and held him still until the fit had passed, all the time glaring accusingly at Cat as if it was his fault.

Star was quiet, observing everything with the perplexed air of a child with too many options.

"Are you staying?" the tall man's voice was quiet with soft violence.

He still held the old man in his arms as if letting him go would cause him to collapse into pieces.

"I don't know," Cat answered slowly.

He really didn't. He wished he had stayed on the side of the road now. The tall man's face twitched with annoyance.

"I don't have a spare bed."

"I can see that."

The tall man stared at him, as if by agreeing Cat was denouncing him in some manner.

"But if I could stay until the next bus tomorrow I would appreciate that. Can you drop me back to the bus tomorrow?"

He looked at Star, who finally piped up, the mention of the bus seemingly reminding her of why she was here.

"I need to get the bus too," she said brightly.

The old man tried to speak but began aggressively coughing again and his aide held him as before. He wanted to say something however and struggled until he was free. Then he crawled over to Cat, still coughing sporadically, and looked him in the eye.

The tall man was visibly displeased and Cat made sure not to turn away from the old man's coughing and spittle.

"What's her name?" he prodded, voice hoarse.

"Who?"

"The … girl." He had to force the words out painfully in between bouts of grating coughs.

Cat would have felt bad for him if he hadn't already decided that he was an asshole.

"Sophie. Sophie Durango."

The old man considered the name, whispering it on his lips, close enough for Cat to taste his breath.

"Not a good name."

Star nodded her head in agreement, or maybe she had already been doing that.

"Why?"

"It's heavy. Too clinical." Cough. "No air. There needs to be air in a name. Now 'Star', that's a name."

Star smiled at him eagerly. She just wanted affection.

"A name doesn't mean anything," Cat countered.

"A name means everything," the old man said.

"Well, I like her name."

The old man smirked. "Of course you do."

Then he began coughing again, worse than before so that drops flew into Cat's face. The tall man moved swiftly to his side, picked him up like a spindly baby and carried him to the bed. For such a big man he was surprisingly gentle. His hands curled around the limbs with great ownership and he stayed cradling him until the coughing stopped. The tall man then lay down beside him and they both quickly fell asleep.

When he was younger Cat remembered seeing two men sleep in the same bed together. His uncle and a distant cousin. He had always remembered how uncomfortable it had seemed, neither man fully sure of how to occupy the shared space in their drunken state. He had been fascinated by it but hadn't thought about it for a long time until now. The tall man and the old man had done this many times, judging by their comfort. It was caring, in much the same way a person might curl up with their dog. A need that would never be quite satisfactory but lessened the loneliness.

Star was looking at him. He finally looked back at her and smiled awkwardly. He wasn't quite sure what to do. She was sitting on the only rug and the cold of the floor had seeped into his bones.

"We should probably get to sleep," he said.

"Do you like my name?" She examined him for his answer.

"Sure."

"Do you think that my name would make somebody want to travel across the country to find me?"

"I would expect so."

This answer seemed to satisfy her, so she moved over on the rug and indicated the extra space there. There didn't seem to be any other option so he moved over. They awkwardly lay on their backs, then searched for a mutually comfortable position. She curled away from him onto her side. They were so close that their bodies were nearly touching and he could see the flecks of vomit still in her hair. He had an urge to pluck them out.

Star wasn't asleep yet. She spoke in an excited whisper over her shoulder, as if doing a bad thing in school.

"If you could change your name, what would you change it to?"

"I don't know."

"You should. Everybody should know."

"Maybe I like my name."

"No."

That was all she said: No. Then silence. Stated something and then left it up to him to decipher.

He couldn't sleep now until he knew more – this obsession with names was vexing.

"Why should I know what different name to take if forced to?"

"You wouldn't be forced. It would be a choice."

"Why?"

"My name gives me freedom. I chose my name because it was what I wanted. So I make my own choices now. I think."

She suddenly seemed unsure. She turned to him, eyes intense and uncertain.

"Do you really like my name?"

"I already said that I did."

"You might have been lying."

"I wasn't."

She closed her eyes and turned back away from him. He was cold so he moved closer to her and she froze up. Cat didn't want her to think that he was trying to mess with her so he let her move away even though it created a gap between them which was replaced with cold stale air.

He was pretty sure that she fell asleep before he did but he couldn't be sure. He just wanted to dream about Sophie Durango. They had curled up awkwardly together after they had sex the first time, but then they had been naked, the air had been warm and he had that content buzzing in his body that an orgasm brings. He suddenly felt hard and hoped that Star wouldn't notice, so he moved his hips as far from her as possible and tried to sleep.

When he woke up the next morning the old man was dead.

Five

Cat had seen rage before. His older brother had a temper that transcended his concept of violence. He had terrorised Cat and the family with an unnatural vigour until eventually, and perhaps mercifully, he aggravated the wrong person in a bar and his resulting anger had landed him in jail. Nobody had mourned his absence. When he had gotten out he had promptly disappeared and Cat hadn't seen him since. Nobody mentioned him. It was strange but he never questioned it. People wanted to forget him. So watching the tall man hammer his fists into the wall with such force that the air trembled didn't much bother him. If the tall man turned his pain in his direction then he might feel differently.

Star didn't appear to have been exposed to such pure aggression however. Either that or she had hidden any such memories in a box deep in her soul. Her little body shivered with each punch that the tall man threw and her eyes were stretched wide enough to break. Cat tried to pull her outside gently but her body was stiff with fear. Immobile. Eventually he put his hand over her eyes which calmed her sufficiently so that he could lead her outside.

It was early, the dawn still figuring out its movements. Once outside, Star maybe forgot what had just happened. She seemed happy again. Cat took out a cigarette and offered her one which she accepted. He didn't often smoke but he had bought some for the journey. It seemed the right thing to do.

She rested her head against him.

"I like mornings," she said simply.

Cat nodded. He could still hear the grunts of the tall man expending the last of his energy. He wondered how long it would take.

"I liked him. He was a nice old man," she continued.

"You didn't know him."

"I still liked him. He had a nice voice. I guess we'll go to the funeral now."

Cat hadn't thought of that. The idea seemed absurd.

"I have to get the bus."

"Oh, we won't be able to drive anywhere today."

This was probably true and it startled Cat. He couldn't really ask the tall man for a ride to the bus stop on the morning when his friend had just died. Fuck.

"I can't stay here."

"He might need us."

"Do you even know his name?"

"No."

Cat finished his cigarette and flicked it out into the surrounding dust at just the same moment that the tall man walked outside. His eyes were softer now, the rage dissipated into something approaching acceptance. He watched the butt fly through the air, waited for it to land, then stepped forward to pick it up. Cat wished that he had thrown it further to look more like a man.

Retrieving the cigarette, the tall man walked back and stood beside the two of them silently. Cat figured that he should say something.

"Sorry about the old man," he mumbled.

The tall man nodded. Cat wanted to reach out and put his hand on his shoulder to comfort him but he didn't.

He had awoken groggily beside Star, who was sitting up like a startled rabbit, fixated on the tall man. He was sitting on the edge of the bed, staring at his old comrade. The old man wasn't moving, and his chest was still. Star had arisen and begun to walk over but the tall man's voice had halted her.

"He's dead."

Then the rage had begun.

Cat couldn't even be certain that he *was* dead. Maybe he was just in a deep sleep, or could be revived. He was accepting the judgement of a potential lunatic. The middle of a rage was a bad time to question the veracity of his judgement, he had reasoned.

And now they were standing in silence on the porch.

He became aware that the tall man was speaking. His voice was so low that it was part vibration. Cat strained to understand.

"... he looked after me. He wasn't my father, just my friend. The only friend I've ever had. He understood me. I don't know how to live now ..."

It would have been dramatic if not for the complete calm emanating now from the tall man. His shoulders slumped deeper into himself and he appeared half of a person, withering before their very eyes.

Then Star did something which Cat didn't really understand. She put her hand on his cheek and turned his face towards her. Then she kissed him slowly. It was a deep kiss. A loving kiss. The tall man responded reluctantly at first but Star was insistent. Then she was in his lap, and his hands were clutching her body with feral need. Not desire, just need. Tears began to roll down his eyes and Star kissed them off his face.

They were clearly engrossed in each other so Cat took his cue and went the only place that he could – back inside.

He remembered when he had first entered Sophie Durango. She had been warm and delightful. It wasn't even sexy – it was just the most comforting feeling he had ever experienced. He felt whole, and for the first time in his life felt like a real person who could decide on his own destiny. Then it was over.

She had kissed him on the nose after, like you would kiss an eager puppy. He hadn't minded. She had taken his virginity and all he cared about at that point was finding the right moment to tell her that he loved her. If she wanted to pat his ass and stroke his hair then that was fine with him as long as she loved him back. He hadn't found the moment to tell her that though, but that's why he was on this journey.

The presence of the old man's body filled the air like a weight. Cat looked everywhere around the room, searching for something interesting, anywhere but where the dead body lay. But he had to see for himself if he was really dead.

He walked to the bed, keeping his eyes on the floor, taking one step at a time. He couldn't explain why but it felt more respectful that way.

The old man was definitely dead. His face bore the

translucent pallor of death and his lips were cracked. The biggest giveaway was his eyes. They stared up at Cat accusingly, the lids pulled back harshly against the frame of his sockets. Old dry wizened eyes. Wherever Cat moved the eyes seemed to follow – it was illusory but Cat was unnerved. He wanted to close the eyes, but he felt that doing so might upset the tall man in some way that he didn't understand so he just stood, waiting for the correct time to pass before he stepped away.

There was a sound behind him and Star walked in. That was his cue. He moved away from the death and faced her. Star had that proud look of somebody who has done a good deed and wants the world to know. Her voice was huskier than before and her cheeks were reddened. She was almost attractive like that.

"He's feeling better now. He'll be OK."

Cat nodded. Of course he was. Any time a man was kissed like that by a woman, any depression would ease off his soul and drift into the ether with his breath. It was in a few minutes, when that elation had passed, that Cat would worry about him again. Worry about himself more like. He felt an urge to leave.

Star was still staring at him.

"He is going to drive us to the bus. He wants to be alone with his friend. He is going to bury him later. He doesn't like us enough to let us join him." Her voice was dusky.

"Of course not, that makes sense." Cat silently thanked the heavens.

Star continued gravely, as if to a congregation. "I told him that you would give him money."

"Why would you do that?"

"Cos that's what people do when somebody dies."

"No, they don't!" he countered.

"Yes, they do – a dowry, I think it's called."

"That's when people get married."

"Oh."

Star was momentarily uncertain, now that Cat had questioned her, cheeks pale again, a mottled cream.

"We should give him some money anyway. He just lost somebody."

Cat was about to argue when the tall man entered the room. He walked straight up to Cat without a word and put out his hand. His eyes were hooded again, no longer defeated but ready to take on the world if necessary. Cat knew that there some moments in life where it was best just to accept the inevitable and get on with it. He reluctantly reached into the stash in his pocket, and carefully separated the money blindly using his fingers to draw out one bill. He hoped it was a $20 or even a $10. It was a $50. His heart sank. The tall man took it wordlessly, then turned on his heel and walked out the door. Star followed proudly.

The sound of the engine startled Cat and he realised what was happening. In his eagerness to get out of the wretched place he stumbled, knee smacking off the concrete and twisting him so that he fell to the ground, facing the old man. He swore that he could hear a chuckling deep laughter but he was so frazzled it could have just been his own grunting pain. He got to his feet quickly before the truck drove off without him.

He didn't feel comfortable sitting up front so he hopped into the back again. He had a feeling the tall man would resent his presence in the cab.

Six

"Why do you do that?"

Sophie Durango was talking to him. He still needed to take a few moments to process that every time it happened.

"Do what?"

"That silence before you speak?"

"Oh. I dunno." Cat felt uncomfortable answering out loud.

"I think you must be very smart."

He wasn't, but she didn't know that yet, maybe he would never let her know. He smiled, and drifted into contented silence again.

"I guess," he said then, "people never listen to me much."

"I'm listening now."

"Yes. Why?"

"Because you're cute."

He felt his cheeks redden and took the joint just for something to occupy his hands. A deep drag hit him hard, filling his face until it felt like it was floating away from his body. Nothing really mattered that much when you were sitting on the roof of a car in the middle of the desert with a beautiful girl.

It was probably the greatest moment of his life thus far. He was smiling so hard his face hurt a little.

Sophie Durango stared at him, a playful smile flickering across her elfin features. She was sort of strange to look at from a certain angle, odd quirky ears, pointed chin, but all together she was perfect. A painting. An oddly perfect painting.

"Do you like staring at me?"

Caught. He coughed and looked away quickly, arm slipping on the car bonnet so that he fell back, skin pressing against the hot metal. He yelped in pain and jerked away so that his arm shot out and smacked Sophie Durango in the face. The joint flew in the air and landed on his naked chest, burning him. He flicked the sizzling butt off his skin instinctively, regretting it the moment the little red barrel of satisfaction flew to the dirt below. He was breathing heavily. He looked apologetically at his goddess.

Sophie Durango wore a poker face. Then an intoxicating dirty railroad laugh jumped from her belly.

Cat was hurt. Was she laughing at him? Her body trembled, tender muscles quivering in the sun. He began to slide off to retrieve the joint but she grabbed him and before he could argue pressed her lips on the burn mark on his skin. He gasped. Her lips were soft, wet and cool.

She kissed his belly gently, then slowly ran her tongue along the crevices of his skin, tasting the salt of his sweat. He shivered involuntarily. He was fixated on the shimmering tussocks of the crown of her head when she leant back and looked at him, eyes wide and coy, mouth *slightly askew in that sexy way only women know how to do.*

He swallowed, mouth dry. Sophie Durango sat up and slowly, agonisingly, lifted her shirt up over her head.

She wasn't wearing a bra.

The truck had stopped moving and the tall man was staring at him over the side. His hooded eyes looked darker than before. Behind him Star waved encouragingly.

"This is our stop," she said.

Cat nodded, doing his best to avoid catching the tall man's eye. Once he had landed on solid ground shame filled him. This man had taken him into his home, had just lost his best friend, and had now helped him back on his way. He may have taken some of his money, but he was a human in grief, he deserved more.

Cat turned to him, gripped his shoulder and affected his most compassionate face.

"I'm sorry about your friend. Thanks."

The tall man opened his mouth, twisted his lips a little, then spat at Cat's feet. The spittle turned in the dirt, making a small cocoon of angry saliva.

"No, you're not," he said simply.

The tall man turned on his heel, boot twisting the earth, and stepped into the truck. Then he was gone.

Cat was surprised. Was he that easy to read or was the tall man far more astute than he thought? Did he feel compassion or was it fake? He was uncertain.

Star's voice twinkled behind him.

"I liked him. He's sad and angry but I liked him."

Cat looked at Star with reluctant patience, as you would at your grandmother's pet dog that was constantly walking into the glass patio doors.

"Do you dislike anybody, Star?"

"No."

"Surely there is somebody that you don't like?"

For a brief moment Star's eyes darkened, but then the cloud passed.

"I like everybody I meet – there's some good in all of them."

Cat bit his tongue. Shaking the tension from his shoulders, he looked around. They were back where they had first got into the truck and he hadn't known where that was the first time. He began to wish that he'd left Albuquerque at least once before in his life. Although so far everything looked exactly the same.

Star was looking down the road dubiously.

"What's wrong?" Cat asked.

"I'm not sure."

"Tell me?"

"Well, this road leads to Alamogordo." She pointed at a sign.

Cat scowled. They were supposed to be on the road to Las Cruces, he knew that at least. From there the bus would carry on to Phoenix via Tucson, before a bus change would apparently take them directly to Los Angeles. Alamogordo wasn't completely off the beaten track but it was enough off the way that they would have to hitch from there to Las Cruces, or at least back on the main highway.

"I don't think the bus ever goes this way."

Star became more and more certain until she was visibly cheered by being aware of something.

"Yes, it doesn't go this way. No, no, we won't get a bus from here."

Cat had only left home less than 24 hours and he had already found himself lost, going the wrong direction and shorn of a heavy part of his finances. This wasn't going the way that he had planned. It was 18 miles to Alamagordo according to the sign.

"You want to walk?" She seemed excited by the prospect.

"We probably should."

"I like walking."

"Of course you do."

They fell into an easy step, walking for minutes without talking. The sun was already beating down, hard on their heads. Cars sporadically flew past them but none paid any attention to Cat's half-hearted thumb.

Star enjoyed his futile attempts to flag down a passing vehicle.

"You're strange."

That was not something that Cat expected her to utter about him. He was caught off guard, then a little insulted.

"Why?"

"You don't talk much. I find people who don't talk much to be strange."

"The man back there, he didn't talk much."

She considered that a moment.

"That didn't matter because I knew what he was thinking. I don't know what you're thinking."

Cat was going to ask how she knew that, but decided against it.

"Tell me what you're thinking right now?" she asked.

The sun was getting hot against the back of his neck, and his old backpack wasn't distributing the weight evenly against his back so he stopped to put a shirt over his head and move his bag around until it was comfortable again.

Star waited patiently.

"Tell me?" she asked again.

"I'm not sure."

"How can you not be sure?"

"I'm just not sure. I'm not thinking anything."

"Everybody is thinking something. All the time. We never stop thinking, even when we are sleeping."

Stare seemed particularly proud of that last statement. She had clearly been told that before and was now eager to impart her limited knowledge to the world. If it would listen.

"Well, I'm not thinking anything."

"I'm not going to stop asking until you tell me."

"Fuck. Fine. I'm thinking how much I hate walking."

Star was silent – evidently that wasn't as interesting as she was hoping. Her pace flagged for a second and just when Cat noticed and began to turn to her she bounded up alongside him again with a self-satisfied grin.

"I don't believe you. You're lying to me because you're afraid to tell me what you're really thinking in case I won't like it."

"Well, maybe, that could be true."

"Is it something that would upset me?"

"No."

"Really?"

Fuck. She was grating on his nerves. She stared at him with her big worried cow eyes and he felt guilty.

"I'm just thinking about you, and why you were on the bus?"

"Oh."

"Yeah. I want to know where you're going?"

Star held his gaze for a minute, something dark flickering behind those docile eyes, then they glazed over again.

"Maybe I'll tell you later."

She smiled coyly and began walking faster. He couldn't win with this girl. For some reason her reticence made her momentarily attractive and he had to pull his eyes off the shapely ass that swayed in front of him. She wasn't conventionally attractive but there was something comforting about her. He was thinking about holding her soft body against his when she suddenly turned to him, catching his eyes on her ass.

"It's OK, I won't tell anybody. Most guys like my ass."

Cat nodded. It was more likely tiredness, hunger and approaching heat stroke that momentarily made her attractive to him. She was like every girl he'd seen before. There was no way that she could compare to Sophie Durango anyway. And once one girl won your heart no other girl could ever compare.

However, to prove her point Star stuck her ass out and waddled like a little duck for a moment. Definitely not sexy. She looked over her shoulder for affirmation.

"Very hot," Cat heard himself mutter.

Star winked at him and began walking normally again.

A car sped past at such pace that the wind flew into their faces and he had to protect his eyes from the flecks of dirt that flew into the air. His mouth was dry, much like when Sophie Durango had lifted her top off. She had such beautiful breasts.

Seven

Sophie Durango's breasts challenged him. They were soft cocoons of joy that melted in his hands. She watched his complete focus on her mounds, gently probing them to confirm that they were real. He rolled her left nipple between his forefinger and thumb, then looked up for approval. She duly opened her mouth a little and gave him a suitable moan. Content that he wasn't hurting her he carried on with his examination, almost forgetting the sexuality involved in the process.

Sophie Durango finally grew bored with his molestations and pushed his right hand down the front of her shorts. He gasped and tried to pull away but she refused, clamping her thighs tightly around his hand until he accepted and began a new exploration.

He was Columbus, uncertain of his direction or destination but secure in the certainty of his mission. Sophie Durango was going to guide him through his first real sexual experience and he was a submissive passenger.

She began humping his hand, losing herself in the moment. He clamped hard on her breast, fearful of letting it go. It must have been painful but it appeared she didn't mind, caught up in the joy in her sex.

Finally she let out a sharp squeal, and Cat grabbed her tight, afraid that he had hurt her. She slumped against his chest and he held her cautiously.

"Are you OK?" he asked.

When she looked up at him, her eyes were clouded, voice deep and husky.

"What, honey?"

"Did I hurt you?"

She smiled then. The smile that was printed in his mind.

"Oh no. You have the hands of an angel."

"I always wanted to be an angel."

Star was babbling, unaware that he was in a completely different space.

"What?" he replied tersely.

Star stopped talking, taken aback by his tone. He internally reproached himself.

"I was only saying ..." Her voice trailed off quietly.

Fuck. This was a constant effort with her. He backtracked.

"I didn't mean that, Star – sorry, I was thinking."

"About what?"

"I dunno."

"Were you thinking about angels?"

Cat smiled a little, and Star was encouraged, waving her arms into small patterns in the air.

"You were, I knew it. You like angels too."

"Everybody likes angels."

"Who is your favourite angel?"

"I don't have a favourite."

"Why not?"

"It never occurred to me that I should."

Star was stumped. She had nothing else to say.

Cat smiled at her again and she blushed. It felt nice. She was fucking weird but he liked her, even though he wasn't sure why. He had a fleeting thought that he might be sad to see her go.

"Let's talk about spirit animals," she continued.

No. He would be positively thrilled to see the back of her. Sophie Durango wouldn't have asked that.

"Let's not."

"Then tell me what you're always thinking about – it seems important …"

She stared at him, eyes locked onto his. She was more perceptive than he gave her credit for.

Cat shook his head and picked up the pace. Midday was behind them and they were still 8 miles from the town. At this rate it would be dark before they got there.

Star quickened her pace to match his and played a game by matching their strides. He found himself playing along, trailing one foot then the next in an attempt to catch her out but she was quick and never missed a step.

"You're good at this," he noted dryly.

"Yep."

"Have you done it before?"

"Yep."

Star was concentrating too hard to talk much. He should have thought of this sooner – all she needed was a little distraction.

"If I stop talking will you tell me what you're thinking?"

She was incessant. He began to half jog but again she kept pace with him.

"Stop, stop, stop!"

He turned back to find her suddenly limping dramatically.

"What's wrong with your leg?"

"Oh, nothing. I just want to stop."

He admittedly needed a break, so without losing that air of reluctance he sat down beside her in the dirt. There weren't half as many cars on the road as he would have expected. He had figured that they would have hitched a ride by now. The scrub was dry and dusty – he would have to wipe his pants down.

Tiredness overtook him and he stretched out backwards, head in the dirt, the warm sun comforting against his face.

Star stopped rubbing her leg and leant over him, playing with her shadow across his face, then she blew on his forehead.

"Tell me what's so special that you can think about it all day long?"

Cat didn't open his eyes.

"How do you know it's the same thing?"

"You always have the same smile when you're thinking it."

"You're very observant."

"I know. Now tell me. Tell me or I'll spit on you."

She began hocking up saliva dramatically and he turned his face.

"OK, fine."

"Yes! I win."

She sat up, crossing her legs as if expecting a sermon.

He sat up. His back hurt.

"I was thinking about that girl."

"Sophie Durango?"

"Yes."

"The one that you told us about?"

"Yes."

"In Los Angeles."

"Yes."

"And?"

"And what?"

"That it? You're still thinking about the same girl?"

"Yes. That is why I'm walking with you, to get a bus, to get to Los Angeles, to meet her, like I told you before."

She blew her cheeks out and looked out at the horizon. She seemed disappointed.

Cat examined her. "What?" he ventured.

"Oh, nothing. It just seems boring. I thought that you might have some other thoughts. The same girl all the time. Boring."

"Boring? Because I'm in love?"

"You love her?"

"Well. Sure."

"How do you know?"

Her eyes blazed at him. How did he know? Cat suddenly felt stupid. His cheeks burnt and he looked away. How did Star make him feel like he knew nothing? Star picked at some dry grasses at her feet, splitting them in half. She was waiting for his response. He wasn't going to give it to her. He stood up.

"Let's get moving. I'm hungry and we still have a while to go."

Star put one of the grasses in her mouth and chewed it. He looked down at her. She didn't move. Finally she spoke, but her voice was low and she kept her eyes on the ground.

"Can I come to Los Angeles with you?"

"What? Why?"

She shrugged her shoulders sadly.

"Does there have to be a reason?"

Fuck. Now what was he going to do? He wanted to tell her no, that it was a bad idea but she seemed so lost and forlorn, chewing on dry grass. He felt she needed him to say yes.

"Well, maybe. Let's talk about it when we get to Alamagordo."

This seemed to satisfy her for now, even though they both knew it wouldn't for very long. Her body shook a little and she clambered to her feet but wouldn't meet his eye.

They began walking, Star remaining just behind him. His feet were tired now, he was getting a blister. If he ignored the pain maybe it didn't exist. Like everything else that happened in the last few days. He knew precisely how to block out pain or memories that he didn't want.

Eight

"Has anybody ever tried to kill you?"

"No."

"What would you do if they did?"

"I don't know."

"I used to pretend that there was somebody trying to kill me."

"Why?"

Cat looked at her and Star suddenly seemed doubtful. She scuffed her feet as she walked as if the dust held a hidden secret.

"I don't know," she said finally.

Cat continued walking. Star didn't seem to like the silence. At first it had appeared that she wasn't much of a talker, but now there a constant edge to her. Something was bothering her and to avoid thinking about it she filled the dead air with ramblings.

"I think because it would make me feel important," she continued.

"That somebody was trying to kill you."

"Yeah. It's a big deal to kill somebody. So they would have to really want to do it. They would have to think about me a lot …"

Her voice trailed off. They were 3 miles from Alamagordo. The sun was heavy in the sky, being dragged into the horizon by the dusk. Cat's legs were sore. He didn't work out much, had always hated gym class and now he was paying for it. Star didn't seem bothered by the walking. They could see the town in the distance, rearing its nondescript head quietly above the desert.

They walked in silence for another few hundred yards. Cat could feel the tension emanating from Star's little body.

Then she stopped to fiddle with her shoe, searching for an intruding stone. Not finding one, she sat down on the ground anyway, took off both her flat shoes, worn from long use, then her socks and wiggled her toes in the air. She closed her eyes.

"I like the air on my toes."

"I can see that."

Cat waited silently. He hadn't spent this much time with one person in a very long time, certainly never by choice. He was getting agitated – there was nothing romantic about being forced into somebody's company.

Star continued stretching her toes until, finally satiated, she ritualistically dressed her feet, got up, brushed herself down and began walking.

Cat duly followed.

"We're almost at Alamagordo."

"Yeah."

"Have you ever swum in the sea?"

Cat hesitated. He couldn't swim. He had never liked the

water. Star was holding herself more upright now as she walked. As if she was imitating royalty.

"No. Have you?"

"Yes. When I was young. I don't remember it much. It was salty. But there were waves. I liked the waves. And it seemed to stretch forever into the distance, like you never knew where it would take you. I liked that. "

A car approached and Cat turned to face it and stuck his thumb out hopefully. The car began to slow down and he smiled. Even hitching the final 3 miles would be a blessing. The car slowed right down until it upon them, then a face leaned out of the window and sneered at them.

"Go fuck yourselves, losers!"

The face, maybe a few years older than Cat, gurned into an ugly grimace and chattering laughter spilled out of the back. Then the engine revved and the car raced away.

Cat and Star watched without saying a word. For some reason that rejection knocked them both. There was something hurtful about being mocked by a stranger. If it had never slowed down it would have been OK, but this way made it personal.

The sun had almost dipped beyond the horizon. It would be dark soon. Just 2 miles.

They continued on their trek and Star automatically filled in the silence.

"What I liked most about the waves was how it felt when they hit your body. It was always different. The sea is much stronger than it looks."

"I'll bet."

"You could never tell how big each wave would be. You had to just hang on and try to keep your feet on the sand."

Star was chattering nervously. Her hands were clenched,

gripping the knuckles between her fingers. If she felt pain she didn't make any noise.

Cat realised that he still had no idea where Star was going.

"Star?"

"Yeah."

"You're not from Albuquerque?"

"No."

"So why were you there, and where are you going?"

She stared at him, big eyes wider than the horizon. Her lips were wet and they weren't symmetrical, lopsided slightly to the left, or maybe that was how she tensed her face in confusion. She stopped walking, brow furrowed, eyes unblinking. There was something that she didn't want to tell him. For the first time he was truly interested in her.

A car ground to a halt beside them but neither of them noticed. Then a sweet voice rang out.

"You kids need a lift?"

Cat looked over his shoulder. A woman's face peered over the rolled-down window of an old Volvo. Floppy red hair framed her tiny face which was dominated by huge sunglasses and small red lips. Her voice was high-pitched but friendly.

Star broke the eye contact with Cat, waved and walked over. It had been the perfect deflection for her.

"Yes, please."

"OK, kids."

Cat ambled over. Star settled herself into the front passenger seat and faced the little woman happily.

The woman was probably in her fifties, almost bird-like, everything about her small and delicate. She sat supported behind by two cushions to help her short legs reach the pedals. Her nails were painted red like her lips and she wore a colourful flowing blue-gold gown – there was no other description that would do her dress justice.

Cat was just getting into the back of the car as Star began talking, awe in her voice.

"Your dress is beautiful. You are so pretty."

"Oh, thank you, dear. Yes, I do like this dress. I only usually wear it on special occasions."

"It looks very nice on you."

"I know."

They giggled at the shared joke and then the little woman offered her hand which Star took delightedly.

"I'm Candica."

"Candice?"

"No. Candic-A."

"Oh, I like that. I'm Star."

"What a lovely name. Nice to meet you, Star."

Candica turned back to Cat, her little head swivelling like a bird's. Her neck was thin and when she stretched out her arm Cat could see little blue veins crisscrossing her pale skin like many confused tributaries.

"What's your name, young man? I'm Candica."

"Cat."

Her hand was cold and was covered completely by Cat's. She momentarily seemed embarrassed at touching his skin, then turned away and focused again on Star, rubbing her hand on her dress as she did.

Cat shook his head and settled into the seat, leaning against his backpack. It would be a short journey.

"So where are you guys going?"

Star opened her mouth but before she could respond Candica continued talking, pulling out onto the road as she did, the Volvo roaring into life. She quickly hit 60 mph, keeping the window open so that she had to scream out every word.

"I'm going to meet my niece. I haven't seen her yet. But I hear she's very beautiful. Everybody tells me that she has the same eyes as me, and the same lips. I was very beautiful when I was younger. All the boys wanted me. I was – oh, I was glamorous! And much like yourself, sweetie – I had class. She has the same hair too. Mine is going a little grey but I cover it up so you would never notice. I never thought that I would go grey but it happens, sweetie, it does, almost without you noticing. It hasn't gone grey 'down there' yet, thank holy of holies, but it will eventually, it all does eventually."

Cat closed his eyes and let the babble drift over him. Soon he would be in Alamagordo and then tomorrow he could get the bus to Los Angeles and find Sophie Durango. He could feel an ulcer on the inside of his lip. He'd get ulcers sometimes when he was tired or stressed. He liked them. He'd dig his teeth into the middle of the ulcer until it hurt so much that his eyes watered and he wanted to scream. Then he would relax, and the numbness that took over the quick release of pain was wonderful. He ran his tongue over the ridges of the invading sore and determined that by tomorrow it would be painful enough to be worth biting. He hoped that it would stay – sometimes they came and went overnight which was frustrating.

"How old is your niece?" Star finally asked.

"Oh, she's twenty-two today. It's her twenty-second birthday – that's a big one. How exciting."

"She's twenty-two? And you've never seen her before?"

"No, sweetie. No. That's why I'm wearing my best dress."

"Why haven't you seen her before?"

Star looked confused and concerned at the same time, her features uncertain how to align.

Candica pursed her lips and furrowed her brow as if a perfectly reasonable question was an affront to her credibility.

"Families are very complicated things, Star. Maybe you wouldn't understand."

"Oh, I know all about complicated families."

"Well, mine is more complicated than most."

"Maybe."

They drove in silence for a few minutes, the miles to Alamagordo quickly turning into yards. They were almost inside the little town when Candica abruptly pulled into a gas station. She turned to them both and smiled brightly.

"Could you spare me some money for gas, kids?"

Cat wasn't expecting that.

"You offered us the lift."

"And I was hoping that you would offer me some money in exchange. That's how America works, kid. Our great country was founded on capitalism and barter."

Cat was too tired to argue and pulled out a few single dollar bills, handing four of them over to Candica. She looked at the money with thinly veiled disgust, adjusted the giant sunglasses on her nose, then smiled tightly.

"Well, good luck with where you're going, kids."

Star clapped her hands in disappointment.

"Oh, we never told you our story and where we're going!"

Candica waved her little hand at her dismissively.

"Oh, it's OK, sweetie, I don't mind."

Star was momentarily stunned, then she slipped out of the car and Cat followed.

"Bye, kids."

Candica's sweet voice drifted into the air after them as she revved the old Volvo and shot back out onto the street with unnecessary aplomb, not even bothering to get any gas.

Cat and Star watched her go, then shared a little smile.

"She was odd," Star said.

Cat bit his tongue and nodded.

Star looked at him, as if awaiting his direction.

"Now what do we do?" she asked.

It was late. There were no buses at this hour. The gas station was empty. Cat looked up and down the street for some activity. A few hundred yards away there was a bar with some bodies outside smoking.

Cat wanted a drink. It was easy to get served underage in bars in Albuquerque – he couldn't imagine that Alamagordo would be any different.

"I want a burger and a drink."

"Where?"

Cat had already started walking.

"But I don't like bars!" Star shouted after him.

He glanced back. She bounced on her heels a couple of times, then followed.

Nine

The group of stragglers ignored Cat as he approached, focused on devouring their cigarettes. The bar was surprisingly packed inside.

After a few moments of hesitation outside where she bounced on her heels again, Star followed. It was a small building and bodies pressed against her uncomfortably. She made herself physically smaller by sucking in her belly and crunching her shoulders in on themselves to pass by with as little physical contact as possible. This made it worse and she quickly found herself surrounded on all sides. She couldn't see past the clot of bodies in front of her.

Cat wondered if they would serve him a drink – not that it mattered much. He had no idea how old Star was – she had that indeterminate aura about her. Maybe he should just ask somebody where to go for the bus. Or for a motel for the night. He didn't want to spend any of his money but he was tired and needed to sleep. The heaving smell of alcohol and sweat was intoxicating and he held himself tall to appear older, lifting up onto his toes to give him an extra inch. He never looked back for Star, focused on blending in.

A few feet behind him Star was being pushed from side to side like a pinball. Feet scraped her ankles and she felt afraid. She looked for Cat but couldn't see him. It was too dark and she was too small to see above anybody.

"*Cat! CAT!*" she yelled above the noise.

He had disappeared. Her voice felt small.

"*Cat? Wait for me!*" She began to panic. She hated crowds and felt like she was suffocating. Her chest began to contract and she couldn't breathe.

"I'll be your cat," a voice replied.

She turned to the owner of the voice and found herself facing a man with darkly cut eyes, but these were silt like a feral cat not roughly hewn like the mountains of the tall man's eyes. The intensity of his gaze made her uncomfortable and she forgot about how tight her chest was.

"I'm fine."

"Yes, you are. So how about it?"

"How about what?"

His hands curled around her waist aggressively and she felt fingers grip her hips. She leaned away but he dipped his body into hers.

"I don't think so." Her voice felt smaller than usual.

"Then let me persuade you."

The dark-eyed man took her arm and smoothly guided her through the melee to the bar. Despite being manhandled, she felt there was something comforting in how easily he parted the crowd. He was strong. Powerful. It momentarily made her less afraid of being alone. Then his hand went to her ass and he pressed her against the bar.

She squirmed but it was no use – he was too big. When he spoke his voice was against her ear, sending tremors through her spine.

"What will the Cat Lady drink?"

Star was mute. She stared into the mirror above the bar, searching desperately for Cat and avoiding the face hovering beside her own. He was lost. She was alone again.

"I don't want a drink. I want to leave."

"Well, that's a shame."

"Is it?"

"Yes. Because I don't want you to leave."

The dark-eyed man's hand dropped again, cupping her ass.

She jerked against the bar and fell back into his grip.

"Please stop."

Her voice was a whisper and she knew that he wasn't listening. His hands began to roam freely over her body now. She was pressed on all sides by bodies, the bar, the smell of stale beer, sticky sweat, smoky breath. The music was loud and overpowering. Nothing was right.

Then Cat was beside her.

His face was tense, the muscles strained tightly across his delicate bones. He was a good-looking kid with kind eyes. He looked even better now. There was a fleeting moment of doubt there but then he blinked and it was gone. She trusted his eyes.

"Star? You alright?" He spoke calmly.

Star shook her head. The dark-eyed man noticed Cat for the first time and saw that he wasn't leaving. He indicated for him to disappear but Cat stood his ground, trying to gain the courage to confront this assailant. He could just leave now. Be done with Star, wash his hands of her and make away for Los Angeles. He wanted to. It felt like the best thing to do. Star could fend for herself and she wasn't his responsibility. Sophie Durango was. He was sure Star would be fine.

Except that he wasn't sure. His gut tumbled.

The dark-eyed man was glowering at him with eyes like hot coals. Star was visibly afraid.

"Fuck off, kid," he growled.

"Take your hands off my friend."

Cat's voice was much stronger than he had expected, deeper too. Emboldened, he put his hand on the dark-eyed man's shoulder.

Big mistake.

All Cat knew next was pain. A sledgehammer to his head with all the force that ever existed. His world tilted. The lights in the dark bar were too bright for his eyes and he closed them. The world turned in on itself as he sank to his knees and hit the floor. Star screamed and people turned. She kept screaming, face reddening.

"Fuck this shit," said the dark-eyed man. He marked his departure with a slap on Star's ass, then melted into the crowd which quickly lost interest. Nobody noticed or cared that Cat was on the ground.

Knees and hips knocked into him as he tried to rise but he couldn't feel anything anymore. He was numb.

Star bent down to her saviour and lifted him to his feet as best she could.

His eyes were wet and blurred, he couldn't see anything. He wanted to sleep. He felt hands upon his face. Was it Star? Maybe it was Sophie Durango. He kissed her hands as they passed his face. They tasted like a girl's hands should. Like Sophie Durango's hands had tasted when she had stroked his face and left her finger in his mouth. He sucked on her palm, tasting the salt, dirt and skin. It was perfect.

Sophie Durango had fucked him. He hadn't fucked her. He was part of the sexual experience almost by default. It was beautiful.

Her naked body on top of his, pants around his ankles, ass burning as his skin stuck to the hot metal of the car. This was movie sex. She came before he did. He didn't know how to. Then he did without warning.

It almost hurt and when she collapsed on top of him he wanted to cry. Cat instinctively knew that if he cried she would like it. But then he didn't feel like crying anymore so he wrapped his exhausted arms around her like a floppy toy. After a moment she pressed her face against his, nose to nose. Her eyes sparkled with something he could never know.

"I like you."

"I like you too."

"Cool."

"Cool."

It felt nice to agree with her.

They dressed slowly even though he wanted to ask her to stay naked forever. To study her. The desert was empty and didn't pry, a friendly voyeur. He was certain that she would oblige him, but it was enough to know that she would do it so he didn't ask. Instead he watched her out of the corner of his eye as he pulled on his own clothes. She didn't ask him to keep his top off and though it was still hot he put it on anyway.

She lit another cigarette and lay on the dirt, hair splayed out in all directions like a split melon. Her eyes were closed, the lids browning in the sun. She was wearing fake eyelashes. He had seen something about them on television and on the side of her left eye they were peeling a little. He didn't know what to do so he just stood there awkwardly until she had finished the cigarette. She didn't offer him any. Finally she turned her head to him.

"How do you feel?"

"Fine."

"For your first time?"

"How do you know it was my first time?"

"Wasn't it?"

"Yes."

"Then how can it just be 'fine'?"

"It was better than fine."

"So how do you feel?"

"Like I'm in love."

Star was kissing him. Not romantically, but with care.

Kissing his cheeks, his forehead, his eyes. He had a large cut running down his temple to his cheek, where he had smacked his head against the floor. She was kissing it tenderly and he was mumbling to her incoherently.

He pushed her off, more roughly than he had meant but she lifted his hands away and continued. Like a small dog, cleaning his wound. His body was weak, he had no energy.

They were outside the bar, sitting against the wall. It was colder out here. They had been sweating inside and now they both shivered. He tried to stand up but Star held on to him and her body was too heavy for him to push away. He wanted to sleep.

Star's voice was breathless and he could have sworn that it trembled slightly.

"I've never been rescued before," she gasped at him.

He could see the fist now. Why couldn't he have seen it before when it mattered? He hadn't moved. Maybe it was surprise or maybe it was because if he had moved then he would have had to retaliate and it was easier to let it happen. Different scenarios of how he could have reacted played inside his head.

"I didn't do anything."

"You came. He left."

That was it. She was right. In her head the logic was simple and the events followed that pattern. It didn't matter whether he had beaten the dark-eyed man to a pulp, or stopped him with a gentle word. He had arrived to help her and he had succeeded.

His head was pounding and he could feel the blood pumping all around his face. His skin felt like it might burst open.

"What's your favourite thing in the world?" she whispered.

"What?"

Star was close up to his face and wouldn't move away. The wall was cold behind him but they were alone in the darkness. Safe. There was no need to go anywhere just yet. He let the muscles in his back relax and tried to focus on her soft face. He had never been hit like that before. He made a mental note not to let it happen again.

"Tell me your favourite thing in the world right now? It's important."

"I don't know, Star."

"I'm not Star. Not anymore."

"What?"

"Tell me your favourite thing right now?"

"Why?"

"Just do it. Tell me?"

"I don't know. I like skies."

"What else?"

"Silence. Fruit. Chocolate. TV. I don't know. It hurts to think. Stop asking me."

Star closed her eyes and considered for a moment. Then she nodded her head, as if it was somehow OK to proceed.

"OK. Fruit. What's your favourite fruit?"

"Star, I don't understand."

"Favorite fruit?" She was insistent.

"I like grapes."

Star was silent and Cat felt like he had said the wrong thing without fully understanding what the fuck was going on. This girl was fucking weird. She pursed her lips tightly together until they were white from the pressure and held her breath. When she exhaled the air hit him like a fan. It was a little stale but tasted nice, like a girl's breath.

"I'm OK with that."

"OK with what?"

Star ignored his question and carried on with whatever direction her one-track mind was travelling.

"If you had to change your name right now what would you call yourself?"

She pressed her finger into his chest for emphasis.

"I don't want to change my name." He pushed her finger away.

"Please?"

"No."

"Can I pick for you?"

"No."

"You have to change it."

"But I don't want to. My face is too sore to think right now."

"This is the only time. Now is when it matters."

Star paused and locked her eyes on his like a vice grip, her mouth almost upon his. There was nothing dividing their faces in the entire universe and they were sharing the same carbon dioxide, slowly choking each other. He found himself relenting.

"You hunted me down in the bar, found me and protected me. You were a hunter. So I'm calling you Hunter."

It did sound nice. Hunter. A man's name.

"Hunter?"

"Yes. Do you like it?"

"Kinda."

Star smiled at him, then kissed the wound on his head again. There was a little bit of blood on the side of her mouth when she sat back from him. He felt like the blood was his fault and it made her look crazy. He tried to wipe it off but his touch was clumsy. She let him try though, his sleeve wiping roughly against her pale skin. He couldn't focus properly.

"Star?"

"I'm not Star anymore."

"What?"

"I'm Grape. You're Hunter. The Hunter and the Grape."

"Oh. OK."

He felt his eyes close. He liked that name. Hunter. Hunter and the Grape. It sounded important. She held him against her chest and everything seemed to make sense for a while. Fruit and bar fights.

Ten

Changing names was a ritual for Star. For Grape.

She wouldn't tell Cat, who was now called Hunter, how often she had done it, except that for every affecting life event she would change her name to always remind her of it. She had a bad memory and life hadn't been kind to her, so when something nice happened, something important, she would change her name to reflect that. This way she could never forget. A woman whose name she couldn't remember, and whose face was only a blur, had told her to live in the moment and to search for the cataclysmic events in life. She couldn't remember how often she had changed it.

Cat, now Hunter, wasn't sure if she was lying or not. It didn't matter. He figured that this gave her a semblance of control on her own life, something that maybe she didn't have before. He wasn't sure why he knew this but he did. She was running from something but she wouldn't tell him what. Everything was cryptic, and innocent. There was a happy naiveté in ignoring the past. If you didn't remember then maybe it never happened. Maybe she knew that he hated his name and that he was too afraid to change it by himself.

In a way it made sense. He was beginning a journey and he needed a new name. Or so he convinced himself. She told him that she had been called Sky before she was named Star so she couldn't use that. Because he had inadvertently named her she had named him, although there weren't any concrete rules. He didn't think there were many concrete rules in anything she did. She wouldn't tell him where Star came from. He pretended like he didn't care.

They had spoken as they walked to a motel. There had been one blinking in the distance and Grape had slowly guided her dazed companion, then paid with her own money.

He wasn't sure what time it was but it was still dark outside. He watched her sleep beside him, chest heaving gently. She had nice breasts and he felt himself harden as he watched her. If she wasn't in the bed beside him he would have masturbated. He needed to. Maybe he could go to the bathroom. He got out of bed as quietly as possible and walked in the dark. He didn't shut the door fully so there was a slight glow from the outside street lights through the shitty curtains which gave him just enough light to aim his dick at the toilet bowl.

"Hunter?"

She was awake.

"Why are you going to the bathroom in the dark?"

"I didn't want to wake you."

He turned on the light and shut the door self-consciously. He was still hard but the toilet looked dirty in the bright halogen, the bowl stained from many previous lives. He felt like he could get a disease from the air. He put his dick away and flushed the toilet. His face was still sore.

Grape was asleep again. He lay down beside her but didn't get under the covers. He thought about starting again and reached his hand into his pants, the taboo exciting him, when Grape turned to him in her sleep and her arm flopped across his chest. His hand froze. He couldn't continue with her lying across him like that. It was wrong. He tried to push her off but she was heavy and soft and it made her curl into him with more certainty. She began to suck her thumb and her eyes flickered. She was dreaming. He removed his hand. His balls ached and he knew it would take him a long time to sleep but he couldn't do it. Grape was a gentle sleeper.

Cat. Hunter now. It felt odd to call himself by a different name, but he was sleeping in a motel with a strange girl and it did make him feel like a new person. He was changed somehow. He closed his eyes and fell asleep with a new name.

When morning came Grape was already awake and sitting fully dressed on the corner of the bed. He pulled himself onto his elbows gingerly and looked at the clock radio.

"The bus to Los Angeles leaves soon," she announced.

"I had better leave."

He clambered out of bed, feeling her eyes on him.

"Are you going to get this bus?"

"Yes. I told you. I'm going to Los Angeles."

She didn't reply, leaving the air sit heavy with expectancy.

He went to the bathroom, splashed water on his damaged

face, relieved himself and stretched a little. When he came back out the room was empty.

"Grape?"

Nothing. He peered outside, the sun frightening his eyes. She hadn't gone far, but was walking proudly away from the motel. Nose held high.

He closed the door and ambled after her. She was pointedly walking down the street but he didn't chase after her. Morning wasn't his friend and it took his muscles a while to wake up. He followed her absentmindedly across the street to the bus stop, confident that she wasn't leaving but unsure quite what was going on. Grape seemed certain though and it too early to question her. It was nice to have stayed in a motel beside the bus stop – everything seemed very grown up and civilised. He was going to Los Angeles to find Sophie Durango and make her fall in love with him, Grape could do what she wanted. He liked following women, it made him feel masculine. A romantic figure in his own story.

Sophie Durango had said she was hungry, and that she wanted to go dancing so Cat had simply followed in her slipstream. They went to a diner and both ordered cheese burgers and double fries. She ate half of his. He felt uncomfortable eating in front of her. She didn't care. She ate her fries with gusto, devouring them like a wild animal, ketchup everywhere. It was messy and it was sexy. They didn't say very much, they just ate. When she had gorged herself Sophie Durango had burped long and loud. The entire diner seemed to freeze, even though it seemed like the sort of place where one should burp after a big meal. Some people looked over covertly, pretending that they were distracted by something else. Sophie Durango looked proud of herself and Cat was proud to be with her. She was so cool. She didn't care what anybody thought. And Cat had just lost his virginity to her. He would follow her anywhere.

There were two other people at the bus stop. A perplexed-looking woman who appeared confused by the early hour. Her shirt was on inside-out, you could tell by the seams. Apart from that she seemed normal. A small compact man stood a few feet back, staring at the ground. He projected a sadness that seemed to eat him up and make him ever smaller. When he was happy perhaps he blossomed into a giant that filled a room but for now if he didn't move nobody would even notice him, or care if they did.

A bus began approaching in the distance. Grape still hadn't said anything. Hunter liked silences. He didn't have that much experience with girls so maybe they were all like this. He wasn't sure if he considered Grape to be a girl. He had got hard lying next to her but he still didn't find her attractive. Did that still make her a girl to him? She wasn't ugly, in her own way she was interesting, she was the same height as Sophie Durango and just as unfathomable, but she didn't exude anything much else. She wasn't feminine or masculine, she was simply a strange person to him. Sophie Durango automatically negated any other female.

The bus driver accepted their original tickets, not caring for Hunter's explanation about the previous bus, nor did he apologise. He was just a bus driver – why would he give a fuck?

It was a strange journey to Las Cruces. They would get off there, then get another bus to Phoenix via Tuscon and from there get the bus to Los Angeles. There were direct buses but they were more expensive and didn't go every day. It was a strange journey. They sat side by side in silence. Grape took the window seat and stared past the glass, Hunter wasn't even sure if he saw her blink. It was just beginning to unnerve him when she closed her eyes. It was a short journey to Las Cruces but having spent the better part of a day walking 18 miles Hunter appreciated every bit of road the bus ate up.

They got off at Las Cruces and Grape immediately began walking away from him. He watched her for a moment, expecting her to turn around and wave for him to follow. He wasn't sure why but he felt that she had a plan. Her ass did look good when she walked, he decided. It rolled from side to side nicely. Like a girl's ass should. She wasn't turning back. He cupped his hands to holler after her.

"*Star! I mean, Grape! Where are you going?*"

She didn't respond. Maybe she hadn't heard him. He felt that she had. He tried again – his throat hurt a little.

"*Graaaaaaaape!*"

She was walking faster now. Fuck. Should he run after her? If he had been hoping to get rid of her this was the chance. He had ignored it last time and had the bruises to prove it. Something told him that she was trouble. But he couldn't leave her without an explanation. He cursed, spat on the ground and with his bag hung uncomfortably off his shoulder ran after her. His face hurt when he ran, the motion pressing the hard blood against his tender skin.

She heard him approaching and began to run. He almost stopped in surprise.

"Grape? What the fuck?"

She ran surprisingly fast. He upped his pace. He was willowy, all sinew and bone, not strong but he could run fast and for a long time. He was perversely enjoying this chase so that when he did catch her it was almost disappointing. He grabbed her arm and spun her around.

She stopped running but kept spinning, refusing to face him. She kept her eyes closed and her arms stiffly straight down her sides. He tried to move around to look at her face but she turned and turned and turned like an eager spinning top.

He stopped moving and she continued turning until she realised that he wasn't turning with her. She stopped, back to him. He didn't say anything, just stared at the back of her head, focusing on her tender locks of hair. He began to question why he had run after her.

"Look, Grape. What's wrong?" He spoke carefully.

He moved slowly as he spoke, to cover the sound of his body's motion until he was looking at the side of her face. Her eyes were tightly closed. She had a nice chin. It was strong. Her nose was a bit odd.

"If you're not going to talk to me I'll just leave then?"

She closed her eyes even tighter. Fuck this. He slapped her. Not hard, but with enough of a sting to make her leap backwards in shock. Her cheek immediately slipped to red and she glared at him, eyes tearing up. He couldn't be sure if it was from the slap or because she was upset.

"Sorry, you were being stupid," he said.

Her little face shook with fury and her body trembled.

"What is it, Grape?"

"You never answered me." Her words were terse.

"What? When?"

She wasn't blinking now, just staring at him with venom. Venom and sadness. Was there a word for that?

"You said we would talk about it when we got to

Alamogordo. We didn't. We are in Las Cruces and you still haven't said anything, so I don't want to be around you anymore. You're not Hunter and I'm not Grape."

Hunter, now Cat again apparently, had no idea what she was talking about. His blank look told her that.

"Talk about what?"

"Los Angeles."

Shit. He had said that to her. He had forgotten.

"I asked you if I could come with you and you haven't answered yet, so you must not want me to come. You don't like me."

"I do like you."

"Then why can't I come with you? Is it because of the girl with the funny name that you keep thinking about?"

Cat didn't think that Star was in any position to cast judgement on somebody else's name but now didn't seem the appropriate time to bring that up.

"Look, Star, it's not that. It's just ..."

"What?"

He didn't really have any reason to tell her not to come with him. He was growing fond of her and it would nice to have a companion. Maybe he could take her with him to meet Sophie Durango and she might get a little jealous, which would be cool. Then he could explain how he had been helping Star and Sophie Durango would think he was kind and wonderful and fall in love with him.

"OK then," he said finally.

"What?"

"Come to Los Angeles with me."

"I don't want to." She looked away stubbornly.

"Why not?"

"Because you don't mean it. I had to beg you. You're only

76

saying that because you want somebody to look after you."

Cat hoped that he never needed Star to look after him.

"That's not it. I like you," he replied calmly.

"No, you don't."

"I do."

"You're lying."

He felt like this could go on for a long time.

"Look, I want you to come with me so just come? Please?"

His tone was a bit more exasperated than he had meant but it seemed to resonate. Her face softened and she blinked. Her eyes were dry, the tears long since evaporated – she had needed to blink.

"Fine. I'll come because you begged me."

Cat had to smile. They began to walk back slowly side by side, falling into an easy step. It was getting hot again.

"I'm still Grape of course. You're still Hunter. You can't change your name back once you've done it," she said matter of factly, as if it was the most obvious thing in the world. Her face was impassive.

"OK."

Hunter needed a drink – Grape was exhausting – but he was glad she was coming with him. It made him feel needed and he liked that.

Eleven

"I'm sorry."

"It's OK."

Sophie Durango smiled at him. He felt guilty for making her feel bad but she had been unnecessarily harsh.

"I don't think before I speak sometimes. I thought you might find it funny." Her voice was tentative.

Cat nodded. Maybe he should have found it funny. At least she had been sexy and beautiful when she had told him it was ridiculous that he was still a virgin until he had met her. He felt like less of a man. She had mocked him by giggling in his face and grabbing his balls in front of the cinema ticket agent. He had laughed with her. It was playful, but it hurt. He thought that he might be in love with her.

Sophie Durango was silent again as they sat on a wall in the car park facing the cinema. They had missed the movie by now. He didn't want his Coke and popcorn anymore, it looked pathetic in his hands. Warm flat Coke in a plastic cup and chewy stale bits of popcorn in a big box. *Ridiculous. He hopped off the wall, walked to a trash can and thought about his life. He took his time, each step heavier than the last. Was it really pathetic that he never had sex with a girl before? That he had never left the state? Did it matter? No. No. No. It did not. Fuck Sophie Durango. He was going to tell her exactly what he thought. The popcorn drizzled into the bin in small clumps.*

He approached her with a zest in his step. Before he could speak though she moved to him, grabbed his face in her hands and kissed him softly. It was warm and wet and he forgot where he was.

When she had finished kissing him it occurred to him that he hadn't moved his tongue. She leaned against him. She was smaller than he was, the perfect height to rest her head on the top of his chest.

"I think you're the only real man I've ever met," she said softly.

He wasn't going to disagree. He didn't need to. He was nineteen years old and he was a man. A man who had just fucked a woman. A woman he was going to love.

"What do you think about when you do that?"

Grape sipped her Sprite and didn't look him in the eye but spoke openly to the air. He was staring at his reflection in the store window behind the bus stop. The bouncing sunlight created a perfect mirror. Grape stood to his right. Or was it his left? It took him a while to configure where the reflection was spatially.

"I don't know. I think about lots of things."

"It's her, isn't it?"

"Yes. I guess it is."

"What will you do when we find her?"

He looked at her. 'We'. Fuck. He had begged her to come only minutes before. The thought sobered him up.

"Are you sure that you want to come to Los Angeles?"

"Yes."

"Why?"

"We're Hunter and the Grape now."

"That's not really a reason though."

Grape was silent.

He looked at his feet. He felt stupid.

"Of course I want you to come. But I don't understand why you would want to come?" he continued, to appease her.

She didn't look at him. She was crying again. She didn't make any noise but two tears, in tandem, ran down her face. Her crying made him uncomfortable. He hoped that nobody else was watching or they might think it was his fault.

"I don't have anywhere else to go."

"Can't you go home?"

She looked up. Her eyes were red and he wanted to hold her.

"No."

She was only a child then.

It didn't seem right to press her further so he turned and held her. She was limp for a moment, then exhaled and her body sagged like a limp balloon. It was as if all the problems of the world suddenly left her in one moment. She was a shell. A shell made of flesh. Soft flesh, some delicate bones and a strange idea of who she was as a person.

"I don't want to go to Los Angeles."

For some reason Hunter knew what to say. Instinctively he knew.

"I want you to come to Los Angeles. I mean it."

Grape fit against his chest in the same way that Sophie Durango did. Grape seemed slightly smaller somehow. Or maybe because she was more compact she appeared smaller. She was a round box and Sophie Durango was rectangular. Flatter.

"I need you to come with me. I've never been. I need a companion."

"OK. Only if you want me to?"

"I do."

"Like, really want me to?"

"I really want you to."

"OK. I'll come."

"Great." He felt like thanking her somehow.

The bus was coming. Grape watched it approach but didn't make any move for it. It felt nice holding her. As if he had achieved something, or knew more about life. Or less. He was content though. It was happening and it felt best to just let it happen.

They broke apart and stood behind the small line of people. A couple in their twenties and a middle-aged man who looked like he understood life had arrived. They filed onto the bus slowly.

"Ten dollars to Tucson. Twenty to Phoenix."

The bus driver indicated the price list stuck to the side of his small side door. The sticker was faded and peeling and illegible. Hunter handed him twenty dollars. There was a movement at his ear and then Grape's soft voice. It tickled a little.

"I don't have any money left."

Hunter looked at his new travelling companion. She was so scared and vulnerable. Did he have to look after her now?

He blinked and took out another twenty. He hadn't even reached Phoenix and half of his money was already gone. At this rate he would get to Los Angeles and be totally broke. He wished that he could call his mother, but that wasn't possible anymore. The thought made him sad. Then angry.

Grape must have noticed because she held his hand tightly. They sat down near the front of the bus. Grape took the window seat.

The bus began to pull off through the little town, and Hunter looked out past Grape as the streets began to move away, each as bland and similar as the others. Closing his eyes slightly gave it a moving cinema feel, the buildings blurry. He could pretend that he was in a movie theatre, watching the opening credits of an epic. The love story of Hunter and Sophie Durango. Grape was his sidekick. The thought made him smile. He wondered what his mother would think. He suddenly missed her. He had always liked her smell. It was calming, of soap and fresh bread. Or it had used to be.

Grape squeezed his hand, put her head against his shoulder and fell asleep. He forgot about his mother and watched the movie world pass by outside.

It was nice journey although Tucson didn't look like somewhere he wanted to spend any time in and he was happy when the bus continued on its way to Phoenix. They were in Arizona now. The thought both frightened and excited him. A different state was alien to him – what would he find?

Phoenix looked the same as everywhere else. The bus pulled into a depot, finding a space in the shade, flanked by lines of identical buses on either side. The door opened and everybody filed out in a hurry. Hunter was content to wait. When there was nobody else still to exit he shrugged his shoulder lightly and Grape awoke with a start. She had drooled over his shoulder again, exactly like when they had first met. Grape seemed younger to him now. More childlike. How old was she really? She didn't appear to be any age. One moment she was a woman, then a girl, then a lady, then a child. She had one of those faces.

She looked at him. Bright-eyed.

"Phoenix?"

He nodded. She smacked her dry lips, then licked them to get rid of the crust. He stood up and they got off. He almost forgot his backpack but when he turned back for it she was holding it.

They walked out into the lobby of the bus depot. Hunter needed to pee.

"I'll wait here," Grape stated.

"OK."

"I won't leave this spot."

Grape put her arms down by her sides like a toy soldier and straightened her back. She looked ridiculous and he laughed even though she hadn't meant to be funny.

The restroom was clean. He never liked using public restrooms. If he could he would pee outside, against the back of a wall or into a bush. He liked fresh air on his balls. Maybe that was why he had liked Sophie Durango when he saw her do it. It made her seem purer somehow. Natural.

His pee hurt when it came out, probably from holding it for so long on the bus. A slight sting. He examined his penis when he was finished but it looked the same. He never spent much time looking at it but now that he was no longer a virgin it didn't bother him to hold it with confidence. It had been inside a woman. The thought began to make him a little hard and he immediately felt gross. The air felt dirty even though it stank of lemon cleaning product. Like a school swimming pool. That smell definitely meant that it was filthy.

He heard people shuffling outside his cubicle but he had to wait until his hardness had left before he could put his penis back in his pants, then he exited, making sure to wash his hands twice. You could fool the germs. The first time they were expecting it.

He went back outside but Grape wasn't where he had left her. The bus depot suddenly seemed much bigger than it had been moments ago. He looked around slowly, but he couldn't see her. She was gone.

He felt a momentary panic coming on. Bile rising in his throat. He missed his mother. Where was Grape? He began to look around frantically, searching. Should he wait here? What if she had only gone to the restroom? Where the fuck was she? Fuck. Why had he left her? Why did he care?

He tried to calm himself but that made it worse. Grape was definitely gone. He was alone again. Alone. He wished he could talk to his mother. Just to tell her about Sophie Durango. She would be so proud. His eyes began to well up.

Then he saw her. Grape. She was just outside the main entrance. She was unmistakable – the shape of her ass and how she leaned sideways on one hip, jutting a cheek boldly into the world. She was talking to somebody he couldn't see, hidden behind a pillar. A man judging by the boots. He felt a pang of jealousy. And anger. Why hadn't she waited for him like she had said she would? She looked up, saw him and waved, beckoning him over. She had been waiting and watching for him all the time. He should have known that she had. He was glad he knew so that he wouldn't say anything stupid. He let the tears go back inside his face and then he walked towards her.

Twelve

"Why are you following a girl to Los Angeles?"

"Because she's the most beautiful girl in the world," Hunter replied. There was no other answer.

Grape looked away so that he couldn't see her face, feigning interest in something on the far side of the room. He wished he hadn't said that. The Biker looked at him. His bleak eyes roving over Hunter's face, searching for truth. Hunter held his gaze and picked out each individual pockmark on the man's skin. He was a biker. Or said that he was. Divorced and both fearful and tired of women. He had said this even before Hunter had told him his name. Grape had spoken to him on the street outside the depot, complimenting him on his leather jacket. She liked talking to strangers. He was immediately enamoured and invited them to join him for a drink. Hunter and Grape had an hour to wait for the next bus so they followed him across the street and accepted the free beer.

The Biker sat on the inside of the table, Hunter and

Grape flanking him in a semicircle. He stared grimly at Hunter, then flicked his eyes to his beer and pulled on it deliberately with a heavy arm.

"You're an idiot," he muttered, matter of fact.

Grape turned back into the conversation, whatever had taken her interest suddenly forgotten. She smiled at the Biker which Hunter noticed. He felt jealous again. It was odd.

The Biker took another swig and continued, as if the silence was his alone to fill. There was soft country music playing in the bar but it wasn't loud enough to be intrusive – it allowed you to think.

"There is nothing for you with that girl," the Biker continued.

Grape hung on his every word.

"Why do you say that?"

"Because she's pointless. Your pursuit is pointless. Do you love her?"

"Yes."

Hunter wasn't sure why he said that. But he had. He needed to – how else could he justify it? Besides, he was in love.

"You're an idiot."

The Biker scanned Grape as he repeated himself. He drank again, letting that settle as if reaffirming his remark made it more true and important. His hands gripped the glass of his beer like a claw. He had dirty nails.

Hunter felt the blood rising to his cheeks.

"You don't know what you're talking about," he said fiercely.

The Biker smiled darkly. Hidden depths of disregarded pain.

"Women are not complex. Books tell you that they are. Stories depict them as layered colours of divinity, graded emotions surrounded by eager soldiers protecting their secrets. The only secret, however, is that their special room is empty. They are guardians of emptiness. Women know this. They know that they mean less than you think, so they create a facade – drawing on societal blood to create a vampiric husk that belongs to somebody else, not them, only the idea of them that they want you to see."

Hunter didn't know what to say to that. Even Grape seemed perplexed. Or more perplexed than usual.

Then the Biker looked at her.

"Except for this girl. She is a real woman. A rarity."

He smiled thinly and put his hand on her leg. His dirty poetic nails scraped her thigh.

He continued bullishly. "There are no real women left in the world. This girl understands herself and all the bullshit around her means nothing. She is pure. A pure vessel."

Grape didn't push his hand away. Hunter shifted in his seat – his ass felt numb. He wished he could verbalise a response to this man but he seemed too smart. It was intimidating.

The Biker was rubbing Grape's leg now. Men just seemed attracted to her. Maybe her cow-like eyes convinced them that she was docile and that they could have their way with her. There was something about an unchallenging woman that turned men on. They weren't threatened and Grape made them feel totally in control, more like a man than they had ever felt before, and maybe ever would again.

Eventually Hunter managed to break the magic of the Biker's hands on Grape and replied: "You're an idiot."

It was either the greatest or more ridiculous thing he had

ever said. He even said it in the same tone that the Biker had. A scathing reply. The Biker looked him dead in the eye. He had long thick lashes that swept up and down like a heavy moth, scattering the air. Defensive.

"A woman who has power over you is a dangerous thing. You will not be yourself. You will believe that only you can unlock her secrets and that when you do all will be well in your world and nobody else will understand life like you do. And you'll be wrong."

"What if *you're* wrong? What if I love Sophie Durango and she's all that's left in the world?"

"Then nothing you do will mean anything to anybody. Isn't that right, Grape?"

Grape wasn't sure if she should support what the Biker was saying or side with Hunter. The Biker had split them. He rested his eyes on her gentle face, devouring her. His face seemed to challenge – if Hunter didn't want her then why shouldn't he have her?

The Biker was talking again.

"Grape. She isn't like that. But she's still a woman. Until a man has experienced the sex of a woman he can't know anything about her. But once he does he will know how empty, or full, her secrets are. But I know things. I know who Grape is."

Hunter wouldn't let this man manipulate them. He still had his hand on Grape's thigh.

"I feel sorry for you," Hunter said.

"I don't care what you think."

The Biker swallowed the rest of his beer and beckoned the waitress over. Hunter couldn't finish his in the time she took to arrive. She was too eager. It was annoying that he wasn't finished – it made him appear even more of a boy.

Her ponytail made her look younger than she was and she smiled too warmly at the Biker and ignored Hunter.

"Yes, sir?"

"Three more beers, please."

"Sure."

"And tell this young man that you have no secrets."

"Excuse me?"

"This young man is in love with a woman. He thinks that she has secrets more than the world knows. Tell him that a woman's secrets are sex and lies."

"Sex and lies, sir. Of course. I'll get your beers."

She moved away, eager to please the Biker, giving Hunter an irrelevant smile as she did. Probably felt sorry for him. She seemed secretive.

"She seems secretive." The Biker had read his thoughts. "But she's not."

Hunter wished they didn't have to drink more beer. The Biker was tiring him. Finally Grape pushed his hand off and announced that she had to go to the bathroom, saving them both. But before she did she leaned in so that they both had to lean in with her to hear what she was saying. Her voice was no more than a whisper and her eyes flickered at them both.

"A woman has secrets that a man can't know. This makes him insecure. He rages like a lion. Nowhere to go. Nobody will listen because nobody wants to admit that they feel the same, that they know less than he does. I have a secret but I will never tell either of you. Because you wouldn't listen."

When she left she deliberately shook her ass, hips popping from side to side. Hunter wasn't sure what had just happened.

The Biker began to laugh, then he clapped him on the back just as the waitress brought over their beers.

"She may be the only woman with a secret that I want to know."

Hunter nodded, tangled in his thoughts, trying to figure out what he felt and not understanding any of it. The Biker's show of camaraderie made him feel insecure.

"I don't know what to make of women. They confuse me," Hunter said.

The Biker was suddenly serious.

"And that's why you can't go to Los Angeles."

He rummaged around his pockets for far too long until he found what he was looking for. Then he passed a tattered business card to Hunter. His face was softer now, as if a challenge between them had passed and everything was fine now.

"This is my friend who runs a club in Vegas. If you want to understand, then go to Vegas and call him up. Tell him you're my friend. He will look after you."

Hunter smoothed the card out as best he could, the creases in the paper rugged under his fingers, trying not to be too friendly.

"OK," he said. And that was it.

They finished their beers in silence, like two men, and waited for Grape to come back. Minutes passed, until their beers were drained. The Biker made a face and Hunter made his excuses and went to find her, hoping to intercept her before she came back. He couldn't figure out what the Biker wanted and that was worse than hating him.

Thirteen

"I can't go."

Grape wouldn't look at him, keeping her nose pressed firmly up against the wall of the women's bathroom. The bus was leaving in less than fifteen minutes. Hunter was getting nervous. The Biker had done something.

His voice rose an octave. "We're going to miss the bus."

"You go. Leave me here."

He couldn't tell for sure but he figured that Grape was crying. Just like Sophie Durango had. It had been different then, but felt the same. All girls cried alike, he decided. They cried for the attention that crying brought to them.

Sophie Durango had hit him when he had tried to comfort her so he kept his distance from Grape. Time was running away. The bus was soon.

"I'm going to go then. If you're not coming with me then that's too bad."

He felt his lips move and say the words. He liked Grape but this was taking it too far. He was going to Los Angeles to find Sophie Durango and nothing was going to stop him, especially not Grape having a panic attack or vacillating between needing affection and respect.

He stepped backwards, opened the door without taking his eyes off her, and then was gone. He thought he saw her face turn towards him as he closed the door but it was too late then. He was going. She could talk it out with the Biker.

He ignored the chiding look of a matronly woman waiting her turn outside, walked through the bar quickly and into the sunlight. The Biker was probably still in the bar but he didn't look to see. He hoped that Grape would be OK. He figured that she would be – she had been before he had met her. Besides, she wasn't his responsibility. She had made her own decision and would have to live with that. He pretended peace with himself and kept walking.

He still had ten minutes. His feet moved in front of him like aged gas pedals, with great effort, but definite. Sophie Durango. He was going to find her. He felt vaguely naked without Grape. Even though she was openly critical of his quest, it felt nice to have a companion. He was thinking of Sophie Durango's taste on his tongue, her skin soft and smelling of honey when the first punch hit him.

When Hunter, or Cat, was younger he was regularly involved in fights at school. It became an almost daily ritual, that constant struggle for supremacy. It was futile now in hindsight, but when he was younger it was all that mattered. Cat wasn't a particularly good fighter but having an older brother whom he hated and who frequently attacked him had toughened him up a little. He still lost more than he won. He didn't dare imagine how often he would have lost if he didn't have a bullying sibling. He hadn't been in a proper fight in quite some time though and was completely blindsided when the first punch came. He didn't even know what had happened.

The second punch was much harder than the first which loosely grazed the side of his skull. The second was straight down the bridge of his nose. He swung away from his attacker on instinct but turned into a new tormentor on the other side. There were two of them. Blows rained down in quick succession and his head bounced from side to side like that tennis-ball game on a string he had played as a kid. It was strange to remember that while his face was being pummelled. He tried to swing back but the two boys were fast. Younger than him but stronger. He was aware of blood streaming down his face and spraying through the air, coating the oxygen in a layer of crimson haemoglobin. Then he lost his balance and went crashing to the ground for the second time since he had left Albuquerque.

He hardly moved as they took his jacket off him. Most of his money was in his shoe. Or he hoped it was. Maybe he had split it. He couldn't think clearly. He just wanted to be left alone. The bus. Could he still make it? How many buses would it take to get all across the world? He should travel the world, travelling was easy. Maybe fly. He would like to fly. Then one of the boys kicked him in the head and he saw black.

Nothing. Peace.

Absolute serenity.

When he came to, the matronly woman from the bar was fretting over him as if he was her own offspring. He pushed her away roughly and sat up, retching as hot acid spilled into his throat. His nose felt full and wet.

"Careful," she whined.

He didn't like her. His shirt was covered in blood. They

had taken his jacket and his shoes. Why would they take his shoes? He panicked. Struggling to his feet he looked around but there was no sight of them. He hadn't even seen their faces in any case. It could be anybody. He felt his belly squirm and then he vomited violently onto the matronly woman's feet. She squealed in disgust and he giggled. It was funny. He was fucked and in a way that was amusing.

Grape was still in the bathroom when he went back inside. He didn't notice the Biker anywhere. He had found his backpack on the walk back, his clothes and spare sneakers strewn across the ground like a marker of shame.

He knocked for what seemed like an age before she opened the door. Her eyes were puffy and she scowled at him, but when she saw the blood on him like a bad Halloween mask she ushered him inside and began fussing over him. He liked her attention and sat down on the toilet bowl to let her worries spill over him and make it all better. He didn't know why he had thought Grape would help but he had nothing else. She reminded him of his mother in a way. Maybe it was how she wiped his face, using her own spittle to get at particularly heavy clots of dried blood. He missed his mother again. He had no money. He didn't know how to find Sophie Durango and his mother was dead. It was too much.

Tears flowed and he buried his wet bloody face against Grape's chest. She had large breasts. It seemed like she had a bosom and not breasts. He forgot about everything and let his face press against her skin. She smelled like sweat and candy. He pressed harder until her nipple protruded from the top of her shirt. She didn't seem to notice until his mouth touched it. She noticed it harden and so did he. His mother was dead. He had forgotten that in a way. Never let it become a reality. The money he had found in her drawer kept her alive. Now that was gone. Grape's nipple brushed his lips. Suddenly he was embarrassed and he pulled back. She stared back at him, eyes wide and bewildered. Her breasts were smeared with his blood, left nipple protruding lewdly. He stared at it, transfixed by its curves. Then he averted his eyes, suddenly ashamed. Grape stuffed her bosom back inside her shirt and Hunter handed her some tissues to clean up. Her shirt was ruined. His face hurt and one of his front teeth wobbled under his tongue. He had no money anymore and his mother was dead and nobody knew. He was fucked.

"You left me." She spoke just for something to say.

She said it simply, without recrimination. A statement.

"I was going to come back for you."

"No, you weren't."

"No."

He hung his head. If he hadn't left her maybe he wouldn't have been attacked. If he'd left her sooner maybe he would have been on the bus before they saw him. If he hadn't been thinking about Sophie Durango maybe he would have noticed them in time. So many variables, so many little things that could change an event.

"Fate." She spoke to the tiles on the floor.

"What?"

"It was fate. You're not supposed to leave me just yet."

He smiled even though it hurt like fuck. She was smiling too. She had a way of simplifying things. He liked that. She kept looking at the floor, wiggling her feet up and down. Sophie Durango had done that. It was endearing. Feminine.

"They took all my money," he said finally.

"It's alright."

"Do you have any money?"

"No."

"Then why are you so sure it's alright?"

"I'm not."

She began unbuttoning her shirt and then removed it and her bra. Her breasts spilled out into the air of the dirty bathroom and lay on her chest. His mouth was open a little and he bit his lip. She moved to the basin and began to wash the blood off slowly, lathering the top of her breasts with soapy water. He stood up, turned away and faced the wall, trying to focus on something else. She oozed sexuality.

When she had finished she dried herself off and dressed. Then she looked at him. He had his face close to the wall but he could feel her gaze.

"Why did you stop looking at me?" She sounded perplexed.

"You were topless."

"I wouldn't have minded if you looked."

"Oh."

"I like my breasts."

He mumbled something that even he didn't understand and shifted from his left foot onto his right. He always naturally leaned to his left and it wasn't as comfortable on his right.

"I need to pee," she said.

Hunter took this as his cue to leave. He exited the bathroom and went to the bar. He still hadn't cleaned his face. The barman smirked at him then placed a bottle of beer in front of him. The waitress beside him seemed confused. The Biker was long gone. The barman examined his cuts like a map.

"On the house, buddy. You look like you need it."

"Yeah. Thanks."

He was thirsty and the cold alcohol slipped down his throat like sliding frozen honey. He had no idea what to do. He was fucked. He had no money. He had no idea how to find Sophie Durango and he still hadn't told anybody that his mother was dead.

Fourteen

His mother.

Her eyes were open when he had walked into her room. He thought that was strange. She was never still like that, she was always fidgeting, moving, making the air around her uncomfortable.

He walked forward slowly, each step gravely significant. Her skin was drawn around the skull tightly, like how the bed sheets on the laundry line would wrap around the bushes when the wind blew hard in the wrong direction. He could see where her cheekbone had been broken when she younger, it was sunken near her nose but protruded sharply at her temple. Her lips were cracked and there was dried blood on her chin. He didn't immediately know what had killed her. Maybe she wasn't dead?

"Mom?"

His voice sounded alien to him. Confused. He felt too young to be in this room.

"Mom? You OK?"

She didn't respond. He became aware of a smell. Once he noticed that it was there it grew in intensity until it was overwhelming. The room stank. His mother stank. Not of dead flesh yet, although she had been dead some time, but her bowels had released their contents. It was putrid.

He ran out of the room and shut the door.

Whenever he envisioned her face now his nose would wrinkle from that smell.

He hadn't told anybody before he had left. He had simply got dressed and made a decision. He wasn't close to his mother. She was distant, preferring to lose herself in the atmosphere of drugs and booze. He liked her though. She had been nice to him when she had cared to be. He was going to tell her about Sophie Durango. He had wanted her advice, he wasn't sure why but he felt that she might know about these things, about women and sex. Now when he had finally needed to talk to her she was dead. What a bitch.

He didn't care to understand why she was dead. The why didn't matter. She was dead and that was it.

He could have called somebody: the uncle he hated, the cops, his aunt, a neighbour. He could have done a lot of things, but instead he had taken the money from his meagre secret stash in his room and decided to find Sophie Durango. He wondered if she would remember him.

Sophie Durango.

There was something in her eyes. A darkness that both scared and excited him. When she spoke it was only to him and he knew that the world was jealous, but something told him that she liked the world being jealous and that was a dangerous thing.

She had cupped his balls when she had kissed him. He

had never experienced anything like it before and she revelled in knowing that. He wouldn't have told his mother that part. He was going to tell her about how Sophie Durango had kissed him and whispered in his ear that he was the most amazing person in the world. Then she had danced for him. He never asked her to dance, she did it anyway. Her eyes on him and the stars above. It made him feel special. The stars weren't going to share her.

"I have to leave tomorrow." Her voice cossetted the words.

"Why?"

She smiled at him, a gentle smile that intelligent people bestow on those less fortunate than they are.

"I have to go home."

"Why not stay here?" He let alarm fill his voice.

"I can't."

That was it. Nothing more. He had a fleeting thought that she might be fucking with him, but she was so beautiful that there was no world where anything Sophie Durango did had any kind of malice to it.

"Where is home?"

"Los Angeles. Have you ever been?"

She knew that he hadn't. He shook his head and looked away. It was almost dawn. It wasn't cold, the summer in the desert was still warm enough. She grabbed him and pulled him out onto the dust, into the vast open expanse of the world, stretching his arms out with her. Breathless.

"What's your greatest fantasy?"

"I don't know."

"Then make something up."

He tried to consider something but she was dancing with him, swaying her hips into his and he couldn't focus on anything except the smell of her sweat and the lightness in her eyes. He couldn't say what he wanted to say. She was waiting.

"I want to stay here with you forever."

She hadn't been expecting that. A tight smile.

"I like that." Her voice was distant.

"Cool."

They danced a little, slowly and out of sync, and she leant into his chest. He didn't know where to put his hands and so he held her back. They were having a moment and he didn't want to ruin it. He had to try and figure out what the moment was about. The sky was brightening. Sophie Durango closed her eyes and let him lead her around in a rudimentary circle. It was going to be a nice day.

Fifteen

Grape removed the bag of weed from her underwear and held it out to a wide-eyed Hunter. The shadows in the alleyway from the encroaching dusk made it even more illicit, like something from a movie. Hunter's belly turned in on itself.

"Smell it. It's strong. Skunk."

He opened the bag and reeled back from the heady stink.

"Fuck. I feel high just from smelling that."

"That won't make you high, silly." She giggled.

"I know. I just meant ..."

Grape took the bag back from him and pushed it back into her underwear. She was wearing large panties that devoured her body. This was why – to hide her bag of weed. She was a weed dealer. Or a courier for her uncle apparently. Hunter was still processing.

There was the sound of footsteps approaching and Grape quickly turned away until the weed was safely hidden again. It was the Biker. His face visibly lit up as if he had been searching for them. Satisfied that there wasn't anybody else around he stepped into the alley. He was a little unsteady on his feet and his mouth hung open in that intoxicated manner that older men have. His gums were raw and his teeth more yellow than they should have been. He leered at Grape.

"I was looking for you."

Hunter tensed up, waiting for what he felt sure was about to happen. This was a really shit day. His fists hurt to bunch but he did it anyway. Grape smacked her lips together.

"I'm sorry. I promised you some weed," she apologised.

"Yeah. You just disappeared." His voice was plaintive and he wrung his hands in front of his body like an unhappy spoilt child. "You promised me some good stuff. I need to get high."

"Sure, honey."

Hunter watched the transaction from a place far above his body. He didn't even exist. It was over so quickly. Grape took out the bag, quickly measured a little into some toilet paper, the Biker handed her a few twenties, inhaled the skunk deeply, exhaled with contentment, tipped his head to her, and disappeared into the gloom. Grape turned to Hunter and he existed again.

"You OK?" She was suddenly self-conscious. "You don't hate me for selling skunk, do you?"

Hunter shook his head. There was still some dried blood on her shirt. His mouth was swollen and his left eye hurt to keep open. He just wanted to sleep.

"My uncle ..." Grape began but Hunter shook his head.

"Tell me later. I need to lie down."

Grape held up the money and waved it around a little proudly.

"Will we get another motel?"

"Sure."

He moved back towards the street and she immediately fell into step close behind him, following the strange proximity pattern she seemed to like. He suddenly stopped and she bumped into him. She reminded him of a cow when she did that and he forgot about her nipple.

"Why didn't you tell me that you had money?"

"I didn't have any money. I had to sell some weed first."

"But why didn't you tell me that?"

"You didn't ask."

He stared back into her slightly glazed eyes and let out an audible sigh which Grape took as happiness. She locked her arm into his and took the lead, pulling him forward along the street. His legs were moving through transparent treacle. She began speaking but he wasn't listening.

"My uncle grows it. Up in Utah. He has a pig farm. The pigs eat the plants when they die. They smell so bad that they cover the smell of the weed. It's very clever."

Hunter nodded. Then a thought prodded his mushy brain.

"What does your uncle call you?"

Grape looked at him and smiled.

"Whatever my name is when I come back to him."

Sixteen

This time when Grape took off her clothes he wanted to see everything. His breath was tight in his chest when she stripped to her underwear. He had deliberately slipped under the sheets first so that he could watch her get undressed. He hoped that she would remove her bra first so that her breasts would swing out and roll against her when she bent down to remove her pants.

She didn't though. Once she was in her underwear she got into the bed and self-consciously pulled the sheets up to her neck, then turned onto her side facing away from him. Their breath seemed to hover in the air above their lungs until Grape let out a little sigh and appeared to go to sleep. He lay there for what seemed like forever until he worked up the courage to lift his hand up into the stale air and towards her shoulder. He wanted to touch those breasts.

His hand hovered above the naked skin on her neck but didn't drop. She was snoring. Not loudly, but enough to put him off. It had a deep grunting quality to it. He pulled his hand back carefully. Then he thought of Sophie Durango.

"*What do you think about when you dream?*"

Sophie Durango was looking at him earnestly, as if this was the most important question in the world. Sophie Durango asked a lot of strange questions.

"*I dunno. Whatever I want.*"

"*You can decide what you dream about?*"

"*Yeah, mostly.*"

"*That's cool. I find it hard to dream. What do you like to dream about most?*"

She was very serious, which made her seem younger. Hunter considered it, trying to make his thoughts appear important.

"*People. I like to imagine I'm a different person. I'll walk through the street and meet a person, then follow them and merge into their body, feeling all their thoughts, how happy or sad they are, and I'll experience it all. How big or small they are, the taste of their breath, the itchiness of their scalp, if they have a cough, or a lightness in their legs. Everything.*"

He had said too much. Although it was true. He liked pretending to be other people. He wasn't sure if he dreamt about it specifically or if it was when he was in that limbo state of pre-sleep where he would create stories. He wasn't lying though. Sophie Durango's deep slitted eyes travelled over him.

"*That's so cool,*" *was all she said.*

She sipped her orange juice thoughtfully. His coffee was getting cold – the steam wasn't rising off it very much now. He picked it up and drank it to check. It was still warm.

A different waitress to the pretty girl who taken their order brought their pancakes. He was hungry. They both were. It was exciting staying up all night in the desert, having sex and falling in love but it was exhausting. He wanted to eat and sleep for a while. Maybe he could dream of being inside Sophie Durango's skin. The thought made him chuckle – he should fantasise about being inside her sexually, not in the other way. She hadn't noticed his giggle.

When she looked at him there was a sadness in her voice. "I always want to dream about flying. But I never can." "Oh."

That didn't sound so bad. He was going to press her further but the pancakes looked good and he took a bite first. Once he had eaten something then he would ask her. Then she noticed the pancakes and her face lit up. She dived into the soft food with her hands, taking pleasure in the texture and stuffing it into her mouth like an animal. It was strange and sexy. Sophie Durango. Strange and sexy. She ate vigorously. Noise.

Grape's body heaved up and down like a compression jack on every breath. Her snores were methodical and annoying. He sat up, the cover falling down his chest. He wished that he had chest hair.

Walking to the bathroom, the tepid air-con nice against his skin, he wondered if Sophie Durango was in love with him. If she thought of him the way that he thought of her. He felt chastened for having sexual urges towards Grape – he had no reason to be monogamous towards Sophie Durango, but he still felt as if he was being unfair. The thought of sex with Grape being illicit shamed him but made her even more attractive.

He sat on the toilet bowl and looked at his face in the mirror. An image of himself reflected back at him. He never thought much about his face. He didn't like nor dislike it –

it was his face and he couldn't change it so why worry about it – but now he considered it. The left eye was puffy and purple. His cheek was risen up above the bone with a thick layer of clotted blood underneath that hurt to touch. His lip was still swollen and his eyebrow was a bit of a mess.

He pulled at his skin absently, stretching the soft tissue below his eyes. It was aggressive but didn't hurt much. Then suddenly it hurt a lot but he didn't let go, fascinated by the white colour that seeped into the dark red of the battered flesh.

His teeth were straight, he was proud of that. His front incisor had been loosened when he was younger in a fight, he couldn't remember who with, but then they were solid. He rubbed his left incisor with his tongue, it moved, knocked a little loose, but not enough to fall out. They may have robbed his money and his dignity but he still had his teeth. What was the phrase? As long as you have your health. He felt that right now. He was a man who had fucked a woman, been in two fights and he wasn't going to let anything stop him.

He still had no money though.

He toyed with the idea of going home. He should call his aunt to let her know that her sister was dead but he reasoned that eventually somebody would find his mother and inform the relevant people. What would he do at home? Wait for somebody to organise a shitty funeral, shake hands with some dead-eyed people who didn't give a fuck and then go back to an empty house? He might not even be able to go back. His mother had rented and he doubted that she had paid any rent in advance. She received some random unexplained monies every now and again, and a regular cheque from the state, but he wouldn't get those. He was technically an adult now and would be expected to look after himself.

No. Going back was fruitless. There was only forward.

Seventeen

The sky was dirty and unhappy. It made Hunter feel uncomfortable. The streets were empty and reminded him of a cheap horror movie. It had been a long time since he had taken in a film at the cinema. He liked the re-runs of old films with Paul Newman and Marlon Brando. The films weren't great to look at but the inherent masculinity appealed to him.

Grape was still wearing the same clothes. It had been three nights now. She didn't seem to notice, or care. She was fastidious about cleaning her body, showering for twenty minutes before they left the motel, but what covered her body apparently wasn't important to her. He admired that. He was thankful he had put on fresh clothes though. The bastards who robbed him hadn't stolen his clothes and it felt like a 'fuck you' to wear them because he could. It also made him feel important when his clothes were clean. That was one of the few nuggets that his late mother had left him with. Maybe the only one. Even when she was high as fuck she always made sure that she wore fresh clothes, something about not being caught unawares in hospital with dirty underwear on, or smelling bad. That's how he knew when she was planning on getting high and why he could never forgive her protestations about it being spur of the moment, because she would always get into clean clothes. It was always premeditated. He wished that she was still around. He had so much to ask her now.

Grape watched the sky with those gentle round eyes of hers then languidly swung her gaze over onto him.

"Well?"

"Well, what?"

"Well, what do we do?"

He sighed. He had to put up with this now even if he didn't want to. She knew and he knew. He could have sworn she had changed since he had lost his money, like she now had the power and wasn't half as dumb as she seemed.

"Look, Grape, I can't get to Los Angeles without some money. You have weed, which you can sell to make money. But not enough. So ..."

"So?" she prompted.

"So we get some more. From your uncle."

Hunter had decided that the best thing to do was to not give Grape any option to say no. He had thought about it whilst she was showering.

Her big eyes examined him.

"Why do you think he will give it to us?" she said softly.

"Will he not?"

"I'm not sure. He may not want to. Why should he?"

He waited. She seemed to be confusing herself. Maybe on purpose.

"He might not give it to me just to help you. He's not

like that," she continued doubtfully.

"What's he like, your uncle?"

"Mean."

"So don't tell him it's for me?"

Grape didn't say anything for a few minutes and looked up at the sky. She began to turn her body in a slow circle, staring up at the sky. Hunter sat down on the concrete and waited for her to decide on whatever she needed to decide on. She turned in a continuous circle a few times and then stopped. Her breathing was getting laboured.

"You want me to just give you the money that I make from selling illegal substances? Why should I do that?"

He was genuinely surprised. He hadn't thought of it like that. He had helped her. She had insisted on changing their names together, and he had been willing to allow her to accompany him to LA, even paying for her ticket. Why wouldn't she help him? How else would she get to LA, or would she go without him?

He said all this to her, his words coming out without pauses or full stops.

Her eyes narrowed, her face tightening. He had never seen Grape angry.

"You left me. It's your own fault what happened – you should never have left me," she chided. Her body was rigid.

He was silent. In a way she was right. But then again ...

"You don't care about me, so why should I help you?" she continued, her face heating up.

When Cat was younger he recalled being asked the same question. It had been different. He was only asking for help with his school work.

"So why should I help you?" the boy had openly mocked him in front of his classmates. Despite not caring about the outcome they had all enjoyed the moment and joined as one. A multi-headed snake living vicariously through the main insurgent. The boy's name was Dean. Dean. What a fucking asshole name. Dean was one of the smarter kids in the school, and he understood the math homework. Hunter was having trouble with it. Dean's mother was a teacher. Hunter's mother smoked weed. None of that mattered though except that he hadn't been able to complete his homework. So he had asked Dean for some help before class began. He had thought that Dean liked him for some reason, maybe because they both liked baseball. He was very wrong. That was his first fight in school. He had drawn blood, his fist cracking Dean's nose so hard that it opened up into a beautiful red mess. That was the only victory he had gained – the rest of the fight Dean beat the hell out of him. He could still never remember how it actually started, how it had come to blows, maybe he had thrown first, maybe he hadn't. But the fight itself he remembered like a crystalline celluloid dream. It all started from that mocking phrase: why should I help you?

Grape's eyes were a tempest of fire and hurt. Hunter wished that she understood. Finding Sophie Durango was about so much more than she could comprehend. Her brain wasn't wired that way and he couldn't possibly make her understand. She glared down at him. He felt the urge to stand up but he was taller than her and felt that he should give her the momentary height advantage to not threaten her further.

"Because you're a nice person and I think you want to help me. I like you and I think that you like me," he said.

Grape paused. Her entire being was stretched out against the air like a straining arrowhead, eager to loose itself into the surrounding ether. Her lower lip moved, trembled and was engulfed by her teeth. Chewing against her will, she slumped into herself. Her head nodded.

"OK then."

It was over. Grape became Grape again – meek, confused, malleable, with more depth than she could comprehend. Her thighs pressed together like she needed to piss, then loosened and she sat down next to him. The concrete felt warmer with her atop it. It felt like something had been achieved between them. It was still early and it felt as if they owned the world. The empty street beckoned to them, feeding them with the possibility of yearning. What was at the end of that street? Another street, an adventure, the road to Sophie Durango?

The sky was warming up nicely. Grape had insisted on leaving the motel early. Earlier than was necessary. Hunter had no choice but to go with her. How strange it was, now he needed her. His chest tightened. He had nothing. Nothing at all. He thought about calling his mother, then remembered again that she was dead. It seemed surreal. He would remember and then immediately forget again. Each time was a jolt to the system. She wouldn't have done anything anyway. Who else could he call?

He never finished the thought. Grape was searching his face for something important. Her eyes were big pools that never revealed any of her thoughts.

"Do you think I'm stupid?"

"No."

"I am."

"I don't think so."

She wasn't convinced. He smiled at her and she smiled back shyly. Her face softened and her body seemed to compose itself, free of its internal distractions. It must be hard to be Grape. Then her face creased into a smile. The smile became a giggle, and then she was laughing so hard the capillaries on her face stuck out like cheerful little roads on a map.

"What's so funny?" he asked.

He found himself smiling with her. Grape had an infectious laugh.

"You're going to meet my uncle. Nobody has ever met my uncle." The thought delighted her.

"Ever?"

"Nope. He thinks I don't have any friends. I can't wait to see his face when he meets you."

The thought filled her up and she rocked on her ass, clutching her knees to her chest and squeezing herself.

"You have a nice laugh. Like Sophie Durango."

He hadn't meant to say it. He hated himself for it. Grape stopped rocking, as if the motion hurt her. Her fingers whitened where she gripped them too tightly. Her face was stone. But he had to mention Sophie Durango. He knew he had to. Not to would be trouble, even he knew that.

Eighteen

People would be looking for him by now, but there would be no trace of him. Even if somebody had seen him get on the first bus, and then found out it had broken down, there would no way that they could trace him now. He imagined himself as the lead character in an exotic spy novel that he would see adorning the cashier desks in K-Mart. Sometimes he would pick one up and flick through its pages, pretending that he was looking for a specific chapter that he had read before. Then he would smile to himself smugly, titillated because the words that he had expected were still on the page. Now he was the lone wolf. He was the picture on the front cover.

Grape walked over to him from the motel where she had gone to find out when the bus was coming. She had the determined gait of achievement in her movements.

"The bus isn't for another two hours."

"OK."

"I know where we have to go, and how long it's going to take. I know it all."

Hunter enjoyed ceding responsibility to Grape. It was easy to let go. If things went wrong then he could blame her. His body filled with the hot air of subservience, releasing him from the responsibility of the last few days. Grape had physically grown before his eyes when she had taken charge of their plans in any case.

He lay back on the ground, closed his eyes and dragged up memories of places that he had never been to, moving pictures from television and movies. New York. That was the first place his character would go. He could smell the Hudson river as it stretched out in front of him, deep, rich and mysterious, filled with the secrets of all the immigrants who had sunk to its murky depths over the years. It was strange how homely New York City felt despite the fact he had never visited it. He wanted to go there. His belly pecked at him, tugging him back to reality. He hadn't eaten in a while.

Grape began stretching silkily in the morning light. It was a strange ritual that he had noticed her do before on a few occasions but hadn't commented on. In the motel this morning it wasn't as intrusive – there was a shyness to it that made it acceptable. But outside on the street it seemed unnecessary, grandiose even. Very un-Grape like. He didn't really know this girl at all.

"What are you doing that for?"

She twisted her head like a slightly unhappy owl and grunted. He had no idea what she was trying to say.

"Varicose ... varicose veins ... and cellulite," she mumbled.

He didn't know what a varicose vein was but he had seen adverts for cellulite on the television on those many days that he had lain there staring at the images like a peripheral person.

"You don't have any cellulite," he said casually.

Grape began undoing the buttons of her shorts.

"What are you doing –" Hunter began.

She ignored him and pulled the shorts down over her hips. Her dark panties winked at him and he was uncomfortable at how much it excited him.

Grape pointed at some flesh on the back of her inner thigh, which was indistinguishable from the rest of her leg. She didn't seem awkward about it, focused on proving what imperfections she had. It was one soft blur of creamy white muscle to him. Satisfied that she had shown him her most private defect, and proud of it, Grape pulled up her shorts and went back to her stretching routine which seemed to him like an oversexed pre-athletic routine.

Hunter waited for her to finish. Trying to get the image of her panties out of his head and resisting staring at her ass. He looked back up at the clouds, counting how many there were to distract himself.

When she was finished Grape let out a long whistle of contentment and stood over him powerfully, the looseness of her muscles lending her a momentary air of importance.

"We need some breakfast," she challenged.

This was one of the times when Grape was almost dominant and certain. Then without warning, as if aware of what she was in danger of becoming, she would lapse back to her usual meek self. This happened now, as if the pressure of being commanding was almost a slight upon the world.

"If you want some. Do you want breakfast?" she asked.

Hunter lifted himself to his feet, the palm of his left hand scraping on an exposed edge of mislaid concrete. There was a mournful little café on the far side of the street and the smell of baking, or reheated dough, was drifting over to them. The neon sign wasn't yet advertising it to the world, but it could be that it simply didn't work anymore. Grape followed his gaze. He wondered how much money she had. As if reading his mind, she nodded.

"I have enough for breakfast."

"Maybe I can trade with them. Save our money."

He wasn't sure what he would trade, but he had a sudden romantic urge to look after her, to be the man like in a Paul Newman movie. He could offer his services as a dish-washer for an hour to pay for their sustenance today. It was appropriate for that to happen, he decided. It would happen in the novel in K-Mart.

"That won't work."

"Why not?"

Grape shrugged and didn't say anything further.

"It will work." Hunter's pride demanded it.

Grape nodded at him gently which stoked the fires of his ego further and he marched with distinction towards the café.

The owner stepped out of the door of the café, pulling roughly on some plastic chairs. He took in Hunter's dishevelled state. His face was still swollen with the indignities of the day before and he oozed delinquent lost soul.

"Yeah?"

He didn't offer even the vaguest pretence of courtesy. Hunter stopped inches in front of him, a ball of tense teenage sinew and determined facial wrinkles.

"We would like some breakfast."

"Course ya would."

"But we are having a tough time. So. I was thinking that you and I, as two men of the world, could work out a deal?"

The café owner remained silent but glanced over

Hunter's shoulder to where Grape shrank back into the air. He didn't respond, which encouraged Hunter.

"So, could we make a deal?" He felt good saying that.

"Maybe."

"I'll wash and clean, or do some heavy lifting for an hour."

"In exchange for breakfast for both of you?"

"Sure."

Hunter stood up straight as if to emphasise his strength and power. He knew that Grape was watching his every move. He wondered what Sophie Durango would think of him right now.

She had never had a job, he recalled her saying – something about the economy, although her expensive clothes suggested rich parents. Hunter had been a little envious, but not jealous – you couldn't be jealous of the girl that you were in love with, he reasoned.

The café owner abruptly began laughing at him. It was a belly-laugh replete with a nasal struggle for breath. He almost choked on his own mucous, then spat it out to the ground beside Hunter's feet and continued laughing. Hunter's cheeks were hot and his tongue heavy in his throat. He was suffocating. Grape saw his discomfort from the slump in his shoulders and quickly ambled over.

"I thought – I thought that you were gonna offer me the girl. But no, you want to do 'some heavy lifting'? What the fuck do you think needs lifting in a café? I make coffee and croissants, you little weasel."

The café owner continued laughing as he moved back inside his café, pausing only to give Grape a lascivious wink. Grape stood beside Hunter in a show of painful solidarity.

Hunter felt ashamed. Ashamed of his actions, ashamed of leaving his mother dead in her bed, ashamed of letting Sophie Durango leave, ashamed of not being man enough to make the simple journey to Los Angeles to find her without completely fucking up.

Somebody spoke behind them. "I know a place."

They turned to the voice. A young man, early twenties, with a kind youthful face hidden beneath an overgrown bush of dirty brown hairs, stared intently at Hunter from the alley to his right.

Grape smiled. "You do?"

"Sure."

"Will you show us?" she asked the complete stranger.

Hunter wished for all the world that Grape would shut up and ignore this bum. He was becoming more and more wary of strangers. She didn't hear his thoughts and walked towards the new man in her life. Hunter legs disobeyed his rational instincts and dragged him in her slipstream into the alleyway which stank of beer, piss and fresh bread.

Nineteen

The tramp kissed Grape's hand in mock servitude as they exchanged pleasantries.

"Nice to meet you, Princess Grape. I am the errant Sir Will."

Fucking stupid name. Hunter stared at him with visible contempt. Then 'Sir Will' turned to him and gave him a disarming smile.

"Do you like dogs?"

Hunter was caught off guard by the obscure question.

"What?"

"Dogs?"

"Sure."

Sir Will looked thrilled and clapped his hands. On cue a half-grown German Shepherd bounded out of the shadows behind a dumpster and leapt into its owner's welcoming arms. Under a flood of dog slobber Sir Will giggled at Hunter.

"This is Delilah."

"Nice dog," Hunter grudgingly admitted.

Grape crowed and clapped her hands, then dived in to join the mutual affection club, a mess of fur, wet tongues and eager hands. Hunter stood apart as the trio revelled in the joy of company. He hated himself for it but couldn't cajole his body forward. He waited until they had worn themselves out and then, in a tone that he hoped was sufficiently commanding, asked where this place of food was located.

Sir Will stood to attention like a toy soldier, his playful gestures pleasing Grape no end.

"Hold Delilah, please, my little Grapefruit?"

"OK."

Grape held onto the pretty dog's collar as Sir Will dramatically crept down the alleyway to where a back door to the café was slightly ajar, a rock propping it open. With the unnecessary flourish goodbye of an over-eager circus performer, he disappeared through it.

Hunter waited grimly for the inevitable retaliation from the café owner that was sure to happen. Grape beamed from ear to ear.

"I like being called Grapefruit," she confided excitedly.

"Of course you do."

Moments passed, then more moments, then as if he had never left them Sir Will burst out of the door like an explosion from a sealed tin can in a fire, waving one arm wildly in the air, the other clutching a heavy brown bag to his chest like the Crown Jewels.

"*Ruuuuuuuuun! G-get g-going!*"

His voice was garbled in panic, the syllables caught upside-down in his throat. Hunter was smiling at this discomfort when the café owner burst out behind in a human ball of rage.

Sir Will burst past them, and as one Hunter and the Grape turned to follow, Delilah leaping out of Grape's soft grasp and sprinting after her incongruous master. She was well trained. The motely group raced away in one ungainly display of incompetence, stumbling into each other. The overweight café owner faded into the hazy past before they had even turned the corner of the next street and they were free. Hunter and Grape kept running, trying desperately to keep pace with the skinny tramp, elation taking over and reducing them all to tears of uncontrollable laughter in between pants for air.

Finally Sir Will decided that they had run enough, and finding a grassy knoll behind an old disused building, collapsed on the grass in victory. Delilah was atop him instantly, an eager lover to his errant soldiering.

Grape fell to her knees, exhausted and flushed. Sir Will managed to push the dog off and stared at her. Hunter noticed a swelling of jealousy beginning in his chest. Then Sir Will threw open his bag of stolen treats.

"We can eat like kings!" he declared to his court.

Everything they could possibly desire was in the bag – croissants, juice, bread, cheese, yoghurts, fruit. Whatever else Hunter may have felt for Sir Will was immediately distracted by a grudging respect. The man was an excellent thief.

Hunter felt as if he had never eaten food before. He was reborn in a panic of croissants and orange juice. His belly ached from eating too fast so he lay back against the dry grass and stared up at the clouds that circled lazily above. What would it be like to be a cloud? It suddenly seemed unfair that he could never experience that.

Sir Will was touching Grape's nose with his finger

playfully, entertaining her with a game that didn't exist until now. What a prick, immediately ingratiating himself within Hunter's coterie without requesting permission first. Hunter sat up and made a huge deal of stretching, until Grape finally noticed him.

"That was one of the best meals I've ever had!"

Hunter nodded at Grape's simple declaration, which made him hate her for a moment.

"Yeah, it was fine. We should be on our way soon, Grape."

She gave him a painfully bland look, then turned back to Will, eyes eager and wide. Sophie Durango had looked that way at Hunter. He felt a pang of yearning for her.

"Tell me what you did?" Sophie Durango had asked.

Sophie Durango pulled his nose playfully as she spoke, her hair askew across her face like something from the sex magazines he used to steal from the gas station when he thought nobody was watching. People were always watching.

"I ran. I ran as fast as I could," he replied.

"Going where?"

"I didn't know, but my legs wouldn't stop. I kept going until I couldn't hear them behind me anymore."

Sophie Durango stared at him, her eyes silently judging him.

"No, you didn't," she decided.

"I did," he replied, a little hurt in his voice. "Why would I make that up?"

She sat back on her haunches, her legs spreading a little so that he could see the outline of her sex in her tight pants. He averted his eyes, but she had noticed, and she rocked back and forth, gently thrusting her crotch at him like a challenge. He wanted to touch her so badly. What if she never let him feel her against his palm again?

"It doesn't seem like you?"

He looked at her, a wry smile across her face. A game.

"Why wouldn't I do that?"

"Running from the cops is a delinquent idea."

"They were running too."

"Sure. But still ..."

He was finding it hard to concentrate. Sophie Durango knew it. She leaned back, ass pressing into the dirt, knees open, face level to the eyeline of her softly swaying groin. Her sex was so close to him. Her eyes were wicked then. It didn't matter that he had walked out of the gas station and seen the two cops standing there irrelevantly. It didn't matter that they probably hadn't seen anything, or cared. It didn't matter that when he had run they had never followed. It didn't matter what he said. It only mattered if she thought that he was cool and he could touch her again.

He moved to her and she lifted her legs around his waist. Her lips pressed against his. They were dry and cracked from the heat, but when she parted them her saliva filled his mouth and it was wonderful.

Grape was kissing Sir Will. He was almost certain that she hadn't initiated it from the taut way her frame jutted forward, but he was gentle and sweet and she didn't seem to dislike it. He sat on his haunches, body arched towards hers. Feeling Hunter's sharp eyes upon them they stopped, Sir Will coughing gently in that way people do to gather their voice again from its hiding place.

"Where are you going then?" he asked her politely, as if nothing had happened.

"To see my uncle." Grape's voice was soft.

Hunter wanted her to stop talking. They needed to get away from this man. He didn't seem like a bad person, but Hunter despised him. He was a homeless tramp and his dog's skin was matted and torn, the flesh thin on the bones. A derelict animal and a struggling pauper. There was nothing to be gained from this union. The thought occurred that he himself might also be homeless and poor. Maybe their similarity was what made him uncomfortable. That made him hate Sir Will even more. When the hate came he felt aggression towards the entire world. This world that had the callousness to put him in such a situation with a deceased mother, no money, nor a home to go to. At least he had Sophie Durango. Sir Will represented everything that had wronged him.

"Can I come?" Sir Will had the temerity to ask Hunter.

"No."

Hunter spoke as he rose to his feet, enjoying the power of towering over them both. He was in charge when they sat on the earth below him. Then Sir Will stood up. He was a full two inches taller than Hunter who didn't feel in control anymore. Sir Will stared into his eyes.

"Why don't you like me?"

"I just don't."

"Why? What is it? I got you breakfast."

"Yeah, thanks."

"You're welcome."

"Cool."

"Now why don't you like me?"

"I don't need a reason."

Sir Will stared at him, considering what to say next. Then he sighed, his shoulders slumping in upon themselves, and took a step back. He looked at his feet sadly. Hunter felt ashamed, but if Sir Will was going to act so pathetic then it was best if he didn't accompany them in any case.

"Come on, Grape." Hunter nodded to her.

Grape followed him as he knew, or had hoped, she would. They walked away from the slight figure of Sir Will who sat back on the grass, and his mourning dog, who despite a wagging tail seemed aware of what had just happened. Life was hard for everybody, man and dog, and an awareness of a shit situation was a basic tenet of survival.

Grape matched Hunter's stride for a while, head hung low against her clavicle, which seemed harder to do than not. She was making a point but he declined to notice. The streets were still devoid of much life. The telephone poles running alongside the road seemed cast from a museum. A barren place. Not a fruitful arena to be poor and homeless.

Grape began mumbling to herself, her voice low and mournful, muffled against her thick mouth.

"I don't understand what you're saying," he said.

"I liked him. We should have let him come."

"No. He was bad news."

"I don't think so."

"Trust me."

"Where are we going then?"

"To find somebody to buy some weed from you so that we can get the bus to your uncle's."

Grape clamped her mouth shut and they marched in silence, two disconsolate figures both quietly angry at themselves and each other.

The sun was in the sky now and it was getting hot, which meant a long day ahead.

Twenty

They were waiting outside the depot for the bus to arrive when they spotted him again. Sir Will was watching from a corner across the street, eyes fixated on them like the sights of a gun. It felt like Sir Will threatened everything. Why was it that the companionship of Grape which Hunter had disregarded the day before, now took on an importance when coveted by another? Was it because he needed Grape and didn't want to disrupt that, or something more primitive? Hunter stared directly at Sir Will with a confrontational twist of his head and he immediately slunk back into the shadows.

"Why don't you like Sir Will?" Grape was looking at him.

"I don't trust him."

"A hunter shouldn't feel threatened like that."

"I'm not a hunter – that's a name that you gave me."

"Which you have accepted and kept. You are your name. Or else give it back."

"Give it back to whom?"

"To the universe. It belongs to the universe. You're just borrowing it and if you're too afraid to be your name then be something else."

Hunter shook his head. He was getting attached to this name now, but he wasn't in the mood to engage with Grape.

"Fine, Star, I'll be called Cat again."

"You're an asshole."

Grape seemed as shocked as he was that she had cussed him out but she held his eye contact unwaveringly until finally he dropped his gaze.

"Do you want to talk to Will?" he said.

"Sir Will."

"He's just Will."

"He called himself Sir Will, so that's his name."

"It's a stupid name."

"No name is stupid if you choose it yourself."

There was no arguing with her logic. Grape beckoned with a loose wrist for Sir Will to come over, but he acted as if he hadn't seen them.

"Sir Will? Hey, come here!" Grape shouted across the road.

Some people turned and stared at her, but she ignored them. Sir Will kept his face turned the other way in that childish manner that people do when they are being stubborn.

"Fuck, man!"

Hunter threw his hands up in the air dramatically and headed across the street, muttering to Grape under his breath as she followed dutifully.

"I hope you know what you're doing."

"I'm getting him to come with us because I like him."

"Of course you do." Hunter knew he was acting like a child but equally he couldn't win here and that frustrated him. To not accept Sir Will would aggravate Grape, and he needed her now. To accept this guy was trouble. He could feel Sophie Durango's face melting away into the dry air. This was not what was supposed to happen, by now they were supposed to be walking hand in hand through the gold-paved streets of Los Angeles, madly in love. Maybe she would become an actress and he would do something cool. He just needed to find her and declare his love for her and everything else would work itself out. Now he needed to make sure that Sir Will didn't ruin all his plans.

They stood in front of the homeless young man, waiting patiently until Sir Will finally turned blankly to them, as if he had never met them before. Delilah traitorously strained to greet her old friends but he held her collar tightly.

"Hey, Will," Hunter sighed.

"Do I know you?" Sir Will countered.

"Unfortunately."

"I don't think that I do."

"I don't really care if you do."

"Hey, Sir Will," Grape sighed shyly, leaning on one hip. Hunter was disgusted at her.

"Oh hey, Grapefruit! Who's your dick friend?"

Grape giggled at Sir Will's joke and Hunter shifted uncomfortably. Grape moved on, touching Hunter's shoulder in a gesture of solidarity. Then she took Sir Will's hand in hers and lifted it towards Hunter. She wanted them to shake and it was pretty clear that she was going to get her own way. They duly shook hands, breaking the contact as quickly as they could.

"You gonna come with us?" Hunter finally asked,

speaking to the space beyond Sir Will's head.

Sir Will made a face and rubbed Delilah behind her ears protectively.

"Delilah doesn't like buses."

"I'm sure she can handle being on a bus."

Sir Will gave Hunter a fuck-you look and rubbed his dog more aggressively.

"No, she can't, she's sensitive."

"Well, that's too bad then. Sorry, Grape, he obviously can't come with us then."

Hunter turned to go but Sir Will's high-pitched voice held him back.

"I know a better way to travel anyway."

Hunter hesitated, not wanting to ask what it was. Sir Will's eyes bored into him, waiting for the triumphant moment of victory. Hunter drew out the moment for as long as he could.

"You do?" he ceded finally.

"Yeah, I've got a plan."

Grape clapped her hands with glee. She adored plans. Obviously.

Twenty-One

Sir Will had long hair that covered most of his thin neck. His skin was pockmarked with violent remnants of childhood acne. His nose was too long, his eyes too deep set and his chin too wide for his thin face, but he had a beguiling smile. The kind of smile that would melt mothers and make them hand over their daughters in a whirlwind of trusting enthusiasm. He was too tall for his feet and his build irritatingly slight, but there was a gentle power to his movements. There was no excess fat on Sir Will, just important bone and sinew. His dog was similar – she moved like a puppyish ex-ballerina who had forgotten which foot came first, but still managed to look elegant even when she fell over herself. They were a strange combination.

Grape kept watch as Sir Will slid the coat-hanger inside the window of an old blue four-door Ford. There was more rust on it than paint.

"Have you done this before?" Hunter asked.

"Yeah."

"When?"

"OK – no."

"Jesus."

"It's fine, nobody is going to miss a car this fucked up."

"I'm not in the mood to go to jail just cos your dog is weird."

"You can't go to jail for stealing a car if it's worth less than $500."

"Really?"

"Yeah. I'm pretty sure."

Hunter scowled and looked accusingly at Grape, mouthing 'this is all your fault', but she fixed her mournful eyes upon him and he relented.

Despite his cocky swagger Sir Will had no idea what he was doing, so Hunter had to help him jimmy the coat-hanger around, pressing the window pane in and against the rubber of the frame until finally the lock popped. Hunter didn't hear it pop but Sir Will declared it with the flourish of a champion prizefighter, lifting Delilah into the air in celebration. The door was probably never locked. Grape gave Sir Will a kiss on the cheek for his achievement and Hunter wanted to hit him.

They piled into the car. Grape held court in the front passenger seat, her bubbling enthusiasm infectious, and Sir Will took the wheel. Delilah crawled over Hunter like he was a lump of bedding and he had to withhold the urge to punch the cute fucking animal.

"*Utah, here we fucking come!*" Sir Will hollered.

He turned the ignition. Nothing happened. The mood was still high and he hollered again, then turned it a second time. Still nothing.

They all held their breath, and even Sir Will faltered. Were their efforts in vain, had they stolen a dud vehicle? He whooped again half-heartedly, giving Grape a covert glance. She bent her head in prayer to some God that she clearly knew nothing about, and Sir Will turned the key again.

There was a moment when the air lay around them like a suffocating cloak ready to extinguish their little dreams. Then the engine flared into life, an old beast rearing its head back into the land of the living from an unloved stupor.

Grape and Sir Will eagerly high-fived and Delilah licked Hunter's face with grubby delirium. Revving the engine dramatically, Sir Will then pulled out slowly, almost confused when the car turned in the direction that he pulled on the steering wheel.

Then they were off, a dirty rusted old blue Ford and four idle companions that life was happy to leave behind, embarking on a journey to only God knew where. Hunter wondered what Sophie Durango was doing at that very moment and then forgot about her as the world sped by. It looked beautiful from the inside window of a car. Their car.

Twenty-Two

Sir Will's real name was William. He said it to them with some aplomb, as if it was a great secret that nobody should know. Hunter rolled his eyes and pushed Delilah's hot breath away from his cheek. She half-fell onto the floor between the seats but still persisted in trying to lick him in mid-air.

"So you gave yourself a new name?" Grape asked.

She stared at Sir Will with her big wide eyes and when he nodded sincerely at her she audibly gasped. Grape was easy to please.

"Where are you from then, William?" Hunter challenged.

Hunter put the emphasis on Sir Will's full name but the young tramp appeared not to notice. His hands were chapped and brown, ingrained with nicotine and dirt that had long since lost any pretensions of being cleansed. He clutched the steering wheel with intensity, as if he was waiting at any moment for the car to buck and disobey underneath him. Sir Will flicked his eyes back to Hunter, but there was no malevolence. He was similar to Grape: fearful of being disliked, not yet battered enough by life to hate it, but dangling on the cusp self-consciously.

"From all over. I travel a lot. Moving around is the only thing to do when you have nowhere to go."

"Originally?" Hunter persisted.

"Upstate New York. My parents were both artists. Hippies. Did a lot of drugs."

"That what happened to you? You do too many drugs?"

Sir William looked hurt that Hunter had the temerity to ask such a question, nevertheless he replied evenly.

"Yeah. I did. I thought I could do what they did. I just did it wrong. It's hard work getting kicked out for doing too many drugs by two drug addicts. I like to think that they were just soft. I'm clean now though. Sort of. None of the bad shit anymore."

"That's terrible. I'm so sorry, Sir Will," said Grape.

She touched his arm and Sir Will nodded with stoicism. It seemed like a bullshit story to Hunter. He had seen enough through watching his mom, so he had no sympathy for dickheads who did too many drugs. He wondered if he hated his mom without even realising it. She did have such beautiful hair. She would let him twirl it when she was in a good mood. They would lie on the sofa together and watch television, his hands twirling her hair into every tighter circles until it got too taut. Then he would let it go and start again. It was soft in his fingers. He absentmindedly began to twirl the hairs on the top of Delilah's head. She didn't seem to like it much but he was touching her so she bore it.

They drove in silence for a while, Sir Will's sad story hanging in the air. Sir Will's face twitched and he shifted in his seat. Then he abruptly shook his head angrily.

"They didn't actually kick me out for that. I lied."

Hunter looked at him with interest. Sir Will kept his eyes trained on the road, then his voice went very quiet.

"I'm gay. They hated that I was gay. So they kicked me out."

"For being gay?" Grape looked aghast.

"Yeah. Threw me out on the street."

Grape looked like she was about to cry.

"They did that? How awful." Her little voice shook.

"Yeah. It sucked."

Sir Will was on a roll now. He took a deep breath, holding back tears that had suddenly appeared, ready to launch alongside his sob story.

Hunter wished he had never asked but even so he felt bad for the guy. He had terrible skin – it was flaky in places where it should be smooth, and smooth where it should be creased. A single dramatic tear rolled down Sir Will's cheek. Hunter hated him again.

"I never wanted to leave, but they gave me no choice. Delilah was our pet dog. My dad gave her to me as a puppy, he got her for my birthday. We went for our first walk together, just the three of us. She's almost two now. I trained her myself and I would show my dad the tricks that I taught her. When he found out I was gay, I was in bed with my best friend. It was the first time either of us had really done anything, but it was pretty great. He walked into the room, stared at us without moving for what seemed like a lifetime, then grabbed Joe by the neck and threw him down the stairs. He locked Delilah up and told me I would never see her again. I didn't understand – he was always the one encouraging me to listen to rock 'n' roll, to make love not war. We always had Jimi Hendrix,

Abba and Bryan Ferry vinyls playing. I don't even know what my mum thought. She was gone to her sister's house for a week. He told me to leave before she came back. I had never seen him so angry. I tried to apologise. He hit me when I tried to talk with him, only once but so hard that I thought my head was going to shatter into tiny pieces. My cheekbone broke, but I didn't even care. I couldn't believe that he had raised his hand to me. So I left that day. He threw all my stuff out on the street and I had to pick it up alone while he watched. He was so quiet and calm about it. I was leaving and that was it, no discussion. I came back that night for Delilah. I picked the lock, stole her away, got on a bus and left. I never saw him again. Or my mom. I still don't know if she hates me or not. But I don't wanna take the chance that she does – at least this way I'll never know, and that's better."

Sir Will was openly crying now, tears covering his face in a river of cleansing pain. Hunter wondered if it would clean up his skin a bit, then felt bad. Grape was crying too, her hand on his leg. That didn't bother Hunter now that Sir Will was gay. In fact, he was glad. Sir Will blinked some tears out of his eyes and the car swerved across the road violently.

He abruptly pulled over into the dirt on the side of the road, going a little too far right so that one side of the car was unbalanced on a little dip. It seemed appropriate. Sir Will's body began to tremble. It began slowly then swelled into a heavy full-bodied shaking. He shook so violently that Hunter thought his bones might break. Grape instinctively opened her arms to him, her heavy breasts offering him sanctuary. Sir Will leaned into her warm embrace and his wet face stained her blouse. Delilah moved onto Hunter's lap, her foot stomping on his groin so hard that he yelped but nobody noticed. Hunter's problems were his own again. He squirmed to push the dog away and got out of the car into the searing sunshine.

The air was dry and comforting. He hoped that it would dry Sir Will's tears, even if he did feel a little sorry for him. He looked back over his shoulder into the car. Sir Will had his hand on one of Grape's breasts now, kneading it gently, like a stress ball. Hunter turned away and scuffed his feet against the roadway. A car sped past, in a rush to get somewhere else. The noise was incredible. The air building up, then whipping past within an aggressive vacuum. He wished that he was a rally driver, always going somewhere without needing a final destination.

Sophie Durango. Sophie Durango. His mother. Grape. His mother. Grape. Sophie Durango.

He wished that he had some cigarettes because it would give him something to do. Picking up some loose stones on the side of the road he fondled them with his eyes closed, until he decided on the one he disliked the most, then threw it as far as he could into the desert. It didn't go as far as he would have liked. In his head he could hit the electricity wires in the distance, but the reality was different. The second and third stones went no further than the first so he let the remainder trickle out of his fingers like hard water onto the ground. He looked back at the car again. Sir Will was still embedded in Grape's chest. It looked like they were kissing. Or that could just be the distortion of the shapes and the sunlight. It didn't matter either way. He hoped that Sophie Durango hadn't kissed anybody else. He didn't even know if she had a boyfriend, he just assumed that she didn't. The thought made him queasy. She had asked him but he had been too afraid of the answer to ask her.

"Have you ever had a girlfriend?" she had asked playfully.

"No."

Sophie Durango kissed him gently, her lips soft against his. It wasn't sexual like before, it was almost motherly, but he didn't mind. Her lips were intoxicating and tasted of sugar and lime juice. She pulled away and he was left with his eyes closed and his mouth pulling at the air like a juvenile fish. She giggled, then kissed him again before he opened his eyes. He watched her kiss him, gently and a little too softly. She looked beautiful. Her cheekbones were a little too high and her forehead was a little too big, in fact up close Sophie Durango's face was strangely askew, but when she pulled back everything fell into place perfectly, like a jigsaw.

He knew that he was in love.

"Why haven't you had a girlfriend?" she prodded.

He wanted to say something witty in response, maybe be super-cool like a New Mexican James Dean but nothing came so he just shrugged his shoulders gamely.

"I've had a girlfriend before," she said. *"It's fun, you should try it."*

"OK." He tried to act unaffected by that exciting statement.

"You want me to tell you about it?"

Of course he did, but he didn't want to get too excited. Why was it that he couldn't get jealous of her having a girlfriend? Maybe he could if he tried.

"Did you love her?" he finally mustered.

"That's a strange question."

"Why?"

"Usually guys will ask how often we fucked first, and how we fucked, and then ask for details."

"Yeah, well, I want to know all that too. Obviously."

"You're sweet."

"You too." He didn't know what else to say.

They walked down Central, the diner behind them receding into the distance. He needed to get some sleep. His legs felt heavy.

"Sir Will is feeling better now."

Grape was standing over him awkwardly. He didn't even remember sitting down. His eyes felt sore. A small sand pile lay awkwardly at his feet where he had dug them in. The dirt felt old, not like the nice clean dirt you would get deep in the desert that you wanted to run your hands through.

"That's good. Is he OK?"

"I don't know if he will ever be OK," she said dramatically.

"Right."

"But he's fine for now. We kissed a little bit. That seemed to calm him down."

"Sure."

Grape shifted uncomfortably and he smoothed the old dirt out flat against the world. She seemed to be waiting for him to say something then she took a breath and began rambling.

"It's not a big deal. He was just sad, and it seemed to make him feel better. But that's all. He smells a little. I didn't like kissing him. Not really."

He looked up at her and forced a smile which was almost genuine. She smiled back. Lifting himself to his feet, he took her arm for support but she wasn't expecting his weight. Her knee buckled and she stumbled a little. He fell into her, his shoulder hitting her hip, and pushed her to the ground with a little exhalation of air. He landed on top of her and she immediately began laughing. Her laughter was intoxicating and quivered with such unbridled enthusiasm that he began giggling with her. Her hands squeezed his shoulders and his hands grasped her waist firmly. Rolling around a little before they clambered to their feet felt nice, her warm body squashed against his. He didn't want to get up.

Sir Will watched them through the wing mirror in the car and wiped the tears from his face with dirty hands. His eyes were red and hurt a little. He missed Joey. Joey hadn't spoken to him again. He had even told him to fuck off when he had looked for a place to crash. Joey had said that his dad was one of the worst kind of people, and that the apple never fell far from the tree so that he must be just as bad.

Delilah sat in the back seat and panted hard, totally unaware. Sir Will loved that dog more than anything in the world.

Twenty-Three

One of Hunter's earliest memories was sitting in the desert with his father watching coyotes stride out of the encroaching dusk. His father alternated between drinking from a whiskey flask and smoking a thick roll-up, and shook his head when Hunter tensed up to move back into the car. He trusted his father more than anything so he sat still, despite his entire body screaming at him to run.

The beasts fanned out carefully, then came together as one, their watchful eyes examining their every movement. But they were fearful little creatures and when his father gracefully rose to his feet and stepped towards them they melted away into the darkness. One moment there, then wilting shapes, then nothing.

"Are they gone?" Hunter timidly whispered.

Hunter was called Thomas then. This was a few years before his father had died. His uncle would never have had the temerity to nickname his brother's son 'Catherine' otherwise.

His father was a broad man, small in stature, but heavy on presence. Without turning he beckoned Thomas forward. The young boy had stumbled in his wake, muscles still taut with tension. When they were side by side his father looked down at him. Hunter would never forget the way his face looked, weathered, stern, proud and almost smiling. A man.

"Most of life is a bluff. Remember that," he said.

Hunter had never forgotten that. It was the entire point of that excursion into the petroglyph area in search of a band of coyotes, and it was time well spent. It was a lesson that had served him well throughout his years in school, and when he had confronted Grape's overeager suitor in the bar.

They drove for what seemed like an eternity, each moment becoming a hundred moments, passing small towns in silence, Delilah's panting the only soundtrack. Sir Will's exposé had tired them all out, and nobody seemed to know what to say.

Finally Grape broke the monotony.

"I'm hungry and I need to pee."

"Me too. Let's stop," Sir Will agreed.

"Fuck, yes." Hunter needed to get out of the car.

Like a gentle marching-band triumvirate they spoke delicately in turn, then they pulled over in the next little town they passed beside a Taco Bell.

They stopped in the parking lot and both Hunter and Sir Will looked at Grape expectantly. She nodded, reached into her bra and released a bunch of filthy notes. It wasn't much, and would just barely get them all food and half a tank of gas. She seemed disappointed in herself.

"I guess I should try sell some weed."

Hunter felt like a pimp. He hoped that Sir Will felt a little shame at the idea of getting Grape to break the law for them, but he sat there passively, a yawning smile on his face.

"Melted chicken tacos, I can smell them!" he declared.

Delilah leapt out as if released from a sabbatical in jail when Hunter opened the door. The evening sun was warm upon their faces. Spinning around, wafting her tail in confusion, Delilah couldn't fail to lift the mood.

The aroma of cheaply cooked food filtering through the vents was overpowering and Hunter's mouth watered. Nine tacos later, two each and then three for Delilah who ate like food was a foreign delight, they leaned variously against the car as if afraid to leave it for too long in case it disappeared. They were driving a stolen vehicle but nobody mentioned it – ignoring it meant that it had never happened.

Dusk was beginning to settle and Hunter was just about to suggest that they move on when there was movement at the far end of the car park. Delilah went rigid.

The moment that Hunter saw them he knew that they were trouble. He hoped that his father's advice would work again, but something in the pit of his stomach told him that they were fucked.

Darkness.

There is always a momentary darkness on everything in the moments that precede a clash of violence. Hunter had experienced it before. He hated it but knew what this blackness meant.

There were two of them. Heavily built muscular men with mottled gnarled faces and greasy hair. Their accents were heavy with poor education. English seemed difficult for them. The taller man spoke initially in Spanish, then segued into guttural English.

"Ustedes tres son lindos. Nice dog," he grunted powerfully.

They towered over the trio with thinly veiled menace. Delilah shrank back slightly behind Sir Will but leaned into her haunches, ready to spring into attack. The taller man took control, his neck sinking into his shoulders, and announced casually, "We want the car. And the dog."

They would happily have handed over the stolen car for obvious reasons, and maybe then called it in as stolen. But not the dog. Delilah was one of them. Sir Will stepped forward, fists clenched, belly pumping in and out like a stressed gerbil. His slender frame was ridiculous in front of these two giants who sneered down at him.

"She's my dog."

"I know. That's why we want her."

"Fuck. You."

Hunter had to admire Sir Will's bravery. He really cared for this dog and was going to get his head smashed in for her. Hunter could tell that these guys didn't want the dog – it was all a game to them. Grape didn't move. It was happening too often for her – the violence and confrontation. Her face was white, drained of blood and any presence of mind. Hunter could feel her fluttering beside him, moments from falling dramatically to the earth.

There was a slight breath of wind as the taller man smiled grimly, then languidly cocked back his right hand. Hunter could have let him take the punch, but he admired Sir Will too much in that moment. Delilah's growl grew so bass that it was almost silent, and her teeth stood out like nervous daggers. She was moments from pouncing. They were all moments from hell. Something had to give.

"*Ga, gaga, ga, haha, gaaaaaaaa ... gaaaaa ... jaaaa ...*"

Hunter threw himself to the ground, arms and legs flapping about maniacally. Spittle flew from his mouth and a confabulation of animalistic sounds emanated from his mouth in a flurry. He flopped and rolled, mouth gasping for air in the dirt, arms flailing and grasping at the universe, eyes rolling, screaming violently.

"*AAAAAAGAGGAGAGAHAHAGAGAHHAGAHA GAHAGAHAGGGGAGAGRRRRRRRRAG!*"

Even Delilah stepped back in confusion. The men stared at him for a moment, uncertain whether they should feel threatened by this act of madness or if they should ignore it. Then Sir Will took the initiative and grabbed Hunter's flailing hands in fear.

"Shit shit, he's going to spazz out. It must be that allergic-reaction thing he has. He's gonna DIE. Fuck!"

He looked up at their would-be assailants with pleading eyes.

"Get help please or he'll die. Call somebody! *Help! HELP!*"

Grape began to scream, unaware that Hunter was faking. Then she fainted, the entire event overpowering her. The momentum left the men, and wary of people beginning to stare from across the street at the commotion, they visibly deflated and began to slink away backwards, one step at a time. Then swiftly spinning, shoving their hands in their pockets, they left promptly.

When they had disappeared around the corner Sir Will shook Hunter's hand and he stopped spazzing out. Dripping with sweat, he sat up on his ass. He felt dizzy and his eyes and throat hurt – acting crazy was a lot of hard work. Sir Will grabbed his shoulders for support, then hugged him tightly. Hunter let him do it.

Delilah, now aware that everything was back to normal but not understanding what had happened, snuck over and nuzzled Hunter's hand, gently at first then with more vehemence, as if to chastise him for frightening her. Grape sat up slowly, shaking her head loose of the pain where she had hit her head against the concrete on the way down. Sir Will let go of Hunter and moved to help Grape to her feet.

"You OK?"

"Yeah, I think so. What happened?"

"Hunter just saved us."

"Really? From the men? Where did they go? How?"

Sir Will indicated Hunter with a tilt of his head.

"Hunter. He's got skills."

Grape looked over at Hunter with those wide hopeful eyes of hers. Hunter caught her eye and blushed. It felt good to be adored. He looked away, shrugging her admiration off like a man should. Then Sir Will put his hand on his, squeezed and grinned covertly. He didn't mind him being affectionate though. Sir Will had stood up strong and that was worth something. It was also nice to be seen as the saviour, to be commended. Maybe he wasn't so bad after all.

Sir Will and Grape embraced and Hunter stepped back to let them do it, confident of his place in the hierarchy now. Then his smile cut short as his belly abruptly began whirling around like an offbeat washing machine – cheap food wasn't a good idea before a giant fake spazz attack. He remembered his father again. "Most of life is a bluff. Remember that." He felt uncomfortable.

He wished that his mother was still alive. He wished that

he had never let Sophie Durango leave. He should have never been late. Why was he fucking late for her? He didn't even have her number, or her address. What was he doing? Why the fuck was he going to Los Angeles without knowing where to go? Did he think that he would just meet somebody on the street who knew her? What the fuck was wrong with him? He liked Grape and Sir Will. They were the closest he had to friends. Why did he have to leave them? Did they even like him? Now wasn't the time to think about it. Why was the world spinning so hard?

His belly twisted like a tortured slinky. His throat was raw. His head hurt. He bent parallel to the ground and it got worse. Then he got sick.

Twenty-Four

They drove through the night, taking turns to sleep in the back seat with Delilah as a pillow, rug and generally all-purpose heated sleeping companion. They had no money for a motel and there was something romantic about travelling in the car.

It wasn't a long drive to Brigham City if they didn't stop, and although none of them had a map or a working cell phone they reckoned that they would get there some time the following day. Hunter was the only one with any specific purpose and even a vague time frame. Hunter had never been to Utah. He knew it had a lot of Mormons but that was about it.

Grape began regaling them excitedly with stories about her uncle. He kept a small pig farm on the outskirts of the city, which was where he grew his weed. Grape and her two cousins were 'pony dealers' as he liked to call them, a bastardised tribute to the famous Pony Express mail service in the 1800's. She had been working for him since she first hit her teens and took pride in her experience of it. She liked being good at it. Sir Will was driving, sticking rigidly to the speed limits. Hunter was spread out like jam on the back seat, trying to pay attention as Grape gushed about dealing drugs.

"The first time I was so scared. What would happen? What if they wouldn't give me the money, or if I lost it, or if they didn't want any and they rejected me? But everybody secretly wants weed – what you have to do is offer it to them at the right time. I've never been told no. Never."

She said the last part proudly, and sat up straighter in the seat, jutting out her chin and breasts for emphasis.

"My cousins though, they're not like me, they get refused often. Anabella May is a little quiet and people don't trust her. I don't trust her. She has these dark eyes that never blink and it's uncomfortable. Cherie is better than her, and I like Cherie but she always seems to have sex with her clients, so I don't know if they buy the weed cos they want it or if they want to sleep with her. She's odd."

And so on and so on. Apparently Grape was a talker when she got her sails up. Hunter bit his lip, and Sir Will gave him a covert glance that was a little too private for Hunter's taste. He might have to let Sir Will know that he definitely wasn't gay. He didn't know many homosexuals, but on television they always seemed to be convinced that they could seduce any man. Maybe he should tell him about Sophie Durango. Sir Will had never questioned why Hunter wanted to go to Los Angeles. In fact, it seemed like he now wanted to go there himself, mentioning something to do with the weather by the beach or something, or maybe it was just because Hunter was going. Fuck. He had better mention Sophie Durango.

Dawn was unfurling and the world was beginning to show its beauty. Nothing bad could happen in a world like this.

Sophie Durango had waited for him on a day just like this, when it seemed like nothing bad could happen. He knew that she had waited. He just knew.

She hadn't told him anything about herself, or where she was going, or why she was in Albuquerque. None of that mattered to Hunter. He was in a cocoon that the outside world couldn't penetrate. But when she said that she needed to get some sleep and had raised those sparkling eyes at him he froze. He couldn't bring her home. He wanted to, more than anything, but his mother made him hesitate. He wasn't embarrassed, but he was afraid. He had never brought a girl home, and he didn't know what could happen. Sophie Durango might judge him. Or worse she might judge his mom.

Sophie Durango convinced him that it was a good idea for her to sleep at his house though and of course he had eventually agreed that it was. For Sophie Durango he would agree that day was night and lie about all the secrets in the world. But he needed to go home first, to make sure he could plan it out, so he told her to wait for him at the corner of the street by the Sante Fe coffee shop. And as he kissed her goodbye, his belly lifting out of his pants, he promised her that he wouldn't be late back to meet her. He promised himself that he wouldn't be late.

Life had changed that promise and he had been late.

When he quietly entered home through the back door, the rusty frame hanging off its hinges and creaking as he pulled it aside, he heard her voice. So much for stealth.

"Honey, is that you?"

His mom's voice was still sweet and youthful. She had been fifteen when he was born and she still acted that way. No matter what shit life threw at her she responded in the same juvenile manner, never learning or changing her habits. She was convinced that everything would still be alright if she simply ignored it.

"Yeah, Mom, it's me."

He reluctantly crossed the threshold into the house even though the little man in his belly screamed at him to turn back and go to Sophie Durango. Life was easy and pure with her. He should never have left her. He smothered the call of reason and followed the sound of his mom's little voice to her room.

The door was open and she lay on the floor beside her bed, sheets askew, clothes everywhere, vomit at her feet. It was carnage. The stink of stale whiskey, beer, bile and weed filled the air. At least she wasn't doing meth because she was still relatively lucid. Then she looked up at him and he blanched. Her eyes were almost pure red, the veins expanding their dirty territory from the red pupils onto the wrinkled skin that flanked them.

"Hey, baby. I don't feel well," she croaked up at him.

"You look fine," he lied.

He stood his ground in the doorway, refusing to enter her hell. He had been there too many times and now Sophie Durango was in his life and she was more important.

"I need my shit," she whined.

Fuck. He knew that she did. She began to dry-retch and he moved to her. He had no choice. He could feel Sophie Durango slipping through his fingers like the sanity of his mother.

He rifled through her drawers by the bed searching for

the packets of Adderall that she kept for when she was too high and in danger of passing out. He was glad that he hadn't brought Sophie Durango here first.

The drawers were devoid of anything useful. Old receipts, balls of tissue paper, stale panties which made him want to retch, some coins, weed, lighters, a syringe and various bits of broken plastic. But no Adderall. The drug was necessary to calm her down, it helped her focus and stopped her going too crazy. Then she would lie down in front of the television and he might sit with her until she was safe again. Once she had almost died from vomiting when she was passed out. That experience had never left him. Watching your mom almost die never did. He had found her gurgling in her own waste on the floor in the kitchen, panic overtaking him so that he froze for what seemed like an age, watching her body convulse in slow motion, chest lifting up and down like a dying animal. Then he had remembered some shit that he had seen on the television and grabbed her in his arms, lifted her head to the side and scooped out the vomit with trembling fingers. Her airway had opened and he cradled her, keeping her head down and hoping. She had spluttered, gasped for air, hit him wildly with her head and fists, then collapsed in a deep sleep.

He had lain there on the linoleum, the stench of piss and vomit numbing his senses until eventually he managed to carry her to her bed. He had been too nervous to leave so sat on the edge of the bed watching over her all evening and through the night, shirt damp from her spittle and his sweat.

She eventually awoke and smiled at him sweetly.

"Hey, baby. Why are you watching me sleep?"

He was silent but she didn't notice.

"I'm hungry. Will I do us both some eggs?"

She stood up, shaking a little from vertigo, and went to the bathroom where she washed the vomit from her mouth. She pretended like nothing had happened. Or else she just didn't remember. She wasn't his mother anymore after that, she was something less, something more dangerous. He was afraid then, not of her, but of what she could do to both of them.

She had mentioned once how she had struggled with the rent, how she struggled with everything, but she was stoned at the time. When he had pushed her about it more she clammed up, then chastised him for asking questions. He was too afraid of the truth to ask her when she was sober. But it was always there, hanging over his head. Once he could leave school and get a job he had done so immediately. Walgreens was the closest store that gave him a job – he could walk or cycle there. His mother never asked him for money but he would leave some lying around in different places, twenty-dollar bills on the counter, under the sofa, or beside her bed. They would always be gobbled up and they both knew that she took them. They also both knew that she bought her shit with them. But it was easier to pretend otherwise.

When he knew that Adderall calmed her down he painstakingly stocked up on some from the pharmacy. He would swap some packets with Ibuprofen, then reseal them so nobody would ever know. She took more than he could ever collect and once she was aware that he was replacing her supply she stopped buying her own and he had no choice but to continue stealing it. It was exhausting.

When she died he didn't even want to know what had

happened. He just left. It felt like a release, almost a motivation to find Sophie Durango. His mother had prevented him from meeting Sophie Durango that day. She had lost Sophie to him, so now that she was gone it seemed appropriate to find her. Which he would.

He should still never have been late to meet her, but when there was no Adderall in the drawer that day his mom freaked out, a minor panic attack developing. When she got that way it was more frustrating than anything else. Once she had ripped off all her clothes and ran onto the street. He had to chase her and drag her back inside, his hands clutching at her skinny naked frame. He had hated every second of it. Her skin was clammy and smelled funny and he wished he never had to feel her naked flesh again. She had scolded him, then laughed about it later.

So this time he had stayed in the room with her, sitting her down whenever she stood up, the sun going through its full cycle through the window until eventually she had calmed down and fallen asleep. Then he had run out of the room to try and explain it all to Sophie Durango.

Why had he even gone back alone? He wished that he hadn't – he could have just brought Sophie Durango in through his window and his mom would never have known. But he was afraid. Afraid of everything to do with his mom and girls.

Sophie Durango wasn't at the coffee shop anymore. It was nearly 7.45 and they closed at 8. The guy behind the counter didn't give a fuck and when Hunter asked him about Sophie simply scoffed and told him to buy a coffee or fuck off so he could close. A young woman in the corner overheard him though, maybe sympathising with his frantic desperation. Her words didn't help.

"The pretty girl with the crazy eyes?"

Sophie Durango did have crazy eyes. He loved that about her.

"Yeah, that's her. Where did she go?"

The young woman hesitated, as if uncomfortable with the significance of what she knew. Cat bounced on his toes edgily.

"She was sitting on her own by the window a long while. Then a man spoke to her, they chatted a bit and they left together. About an hour ago now, I guess."

He froze. That didn't make sense. It couldn't be true. He shook his head at her, as if that action would change her words.

"No. You're wrong."

"Maybe I am. Sorry. I have a bad memory."

The young woman gave him that look that superior people hold for the less fortunate. That look that they secretly enjoy because it means that they aren't suffering like you are.

"Are you sure? Did it look like she knew him, or maybe they were friends? It wasn't like, you know?"

She shook her head at him. They both knew the answer. The barista laughed behind him, the irritating cocky stupid laugh of the uneducated asshole. His mouth was fleshy as he spoke.

"Yeah, man, I remember her now. Super ass. She was looking to get some, man – fuck yeah, I thought about it."

Cat picked up a chair and flung it across the room, so that it clattered into the barista's legs. He fell to his knees awkwardly with a yelp of surprised pain. Then Cat walked out before any recriminations could begin.

Her car wasn't outside where she had parked it so he

walked around all night, searching the street corners, the diners and the bars when he could sneak in, searching for any sign of her. She was nowhere to be found. She had disappeared. The girl he had just fallen in love with had vanished. He hadn't even known her for a full 24 hours. The worst part was that he had nobody to blame but himself. Or his mother.

The days that followed were painful. He would walk to work and hope to see her again, staring at every car that approached in the vain hope that she would appear and mock him for doubting her return. That never happened. The pain of self-doubt and blame hurts more than anything else, he decided. He couldn't lash out in anger because he was the protagonist in his own demise. He didn't want to openly blame his mom. Maybe that was when he had begun to hate her a little bit. He gradually conveniently forgot that Sophie Durango had been the one to not wait for him. But who could blame her anyway? He wasn't much to begin with and maybe she thought that he had abandoned her. Young and fearful and immature. The young woman was surely wrong in any case.

Sophie Durango. He had lost her. And now he was in Utah trying to sell weed. Or getting a girl to sell weed for him, so that he could find the original girl. He wondered what his mom would think. Would she be proud? She probably wouldn't care, he decided.

Twenty-Five

Brigham City was a peaceful place, overflowing with a tangible taste of optimism and cheer. Hunter hated it immediately.

Delilah pushed her head out the window and barked a constant challenge to the world. Grape's energy levels reached boiling point and her eyes rolled in her head as she consumed the sights around her, chattering excitedly.

"That shop does the best cupcakes in the world – that place is run by a woman with the smallest dog – that place is where I went to school – that corner is where I broke my ankle being chased by boys when I was eleven."

And so on and so on. The town was too clean for Sir Will and his veiled eyes darted around furtively.

"I think we should pull over somewhere or get to your uncle's quickly. We are driving a hot car and this feels, well, you know, strange," he said cautiously.

Hunter knew what he meant. The air tasted of ill-conceived perfection, which worried them both. Tramps, vagabonds, runaways, stray dogs, drugs and stolen cars had no place in such a well-maintained world. They needed to be careful. They would have been safer in downtown Albuquerque – nobody gave a shit how you dressed down there.

Grape took umbrage, however, as if it was a personal affront to her.

"What do you mean, 'strange'?"

"Nothing. It's just. Forget it."

Sir Will glanced back to Hunter for advice. He was after all the original travelling companion of this strange woman, even if Sir Will and Grape seemed to have bonded pretty tightly in a short time. Hunter cleared his throat.

"We're all just a little tired and hungry. Is your uncle's place far away?"

Grape sulked a bit, crossing her arms and not saying anything for a few minutes as Sir Will drove the car uncomfortably down the main street. Delilah began to bark at a small poodle outside a well-kept little bakery until Hunter wrestled her inside and closed the window. They were definitely not inconspicuous. Finally Grape let her upset evaporate.

"Turn left here. He's about 3 miles down this road."

Sir Will diverted the car gratefully down a side road that meandered almost by accident into the middle of the landscape and became rougher within moments. Bottled civilisation receded into the distance and they were free again.

Hunter found himself relaxing, the space and the sun giving the encroaching wilderness that soft movie touch again.

"This is better," he murmured to nobody in particular.

Sir Will nodded, another moment passing between them. Hunter preferred it when it was just Grape and himself. Sir Will seemed to notice his brow furrow in the back mirror.

Then Grape pointed ahead through the window.

"That's it there, the small building ahead."

A small almost-white building cautiously peered out of the trees. Sir Will approached slowly even as Grape tapped the seat with her soft fingers rapidly. It was a one-storey dwelling with outhouse attached. A sprawling outdoor cage lay in front with a mess of pigs sitting heavily in the mud. One in particular was slumped motionless and looked like it might be dead. A field stretched out behind the house, but the surrounding copse was heavy with overgrown trees. Wild.

Hunter and Sir Will exchanged looks even as Grape was leaping out and moving to the building, eyes wide and excited. She reached the front door and had placed her hand delicately on the splintered door when it was jerked open. Sir Will and Hunter couldn't see past her but the inside of the house was dark. A bony figure stood inside the shadows, almost only visible by his presence. Grape froze, body shaking, then she stepped in and tentatively hugged the shape. The figure didn't return the hug but stepped backwards with Grape attached like a limpet and shut the door. It happened so fast even Delilah wasn't ready to react.

Sir Will parked the car at an angle to the house and Hunter got out, dirty mud softening beneath his weight. The door remained closed with Grape inside. Delilah bounded out of the car and raced eagerly for the pigs until a sharp whistle from Sir Will dragged her back. The trio stood there, examining their surroundings and deciding on their next move when Grape suddenly appeared in front of them. She was pale and shivering even though it was hot and humid outside.

"Everything OK, Grape?" Hunter asked gently.

She nodded back to him, then shook her head, then nodded again, then looked at her feet, not sure where to place her gaze.

"My uncle. He's ... he's different."

She turned on her heel and made for the rear of the house. They followed. The back door swung on its hinges and Grape tentatively held it open for them to go inside.

Hunter went first and saw her uncle standing there.

"What ... do you ... fucking want?"

His voice was weak and insincere but had a deliberate slowness that made him unnaturally imposing. His movements were jerky and uncertain but violent in the way that he finished them. He reached for a coffee cup as if afraid it didn't exist, then grabbed at it aggressively. His hand went white from the effort, and he drank with the thirst of a dying man.

Sir Will stood by the doorway, eyes wild, left hand clutching Delilah's collar, right hand balled up nervously.

Grape's uncle looked at Hunter, eyes darting around and through him as if he was transparent. He was frightened and secure at the same time, confident in his living space but afraid of everything that wasn't him. A once-strong man reduced to insecure bones and failing muscle.

"Well, sir ... Grape ..." Hunter began, trying to hold eye contact.

"Who ... the fuck ... is Grape?"

"Sorry – Star?"

"Who ... the fuck ... is Star? Are you Star?"

"No, sir, I'm Hunter."

"What kind ... of a fucking name ... is Hunter? And who ... is that strange fucker?" He aimed his head aggressively at Sir Will.

"That's Sir Will."

"Sir Will? Is this ... a fucking ... joke?"

He threw the word 'fucking' around like a vitriolic mace, aiming it into their faces with a smattering of spittle.

Grape sat in the corner, cowed and broken.

Hunter stood up taller.

"We came here cos we wanted to buy some weed?"

"I don't ... have any. So I think ... you should ... fuck off, and leave Angelica here ... with me. You're not going to run off ... again ... are you?" His eyes were daggers into her face as he spoke to Grape.

Grape mumbled under her breath, then looked up at the man she had idolised only minutes before.

"I didn't run away. You sent me with a delivery."

Her uncle blinked as if this was news to him, then he recovered and slammed the cup down on the table.

"What fucking ... delivery? Why ... would I send you out on a ... delivery?"

"Because Anabelle May and Cherie never came back. Remember?"

Her uncle fell silent. The cup had cracked open so when he withdrew his hand to run it through his sweaty hair it crumbled apart into sharp chunky pieces. He stared at the broken pottery for a long time. When he looked up he was afraid.

"I don't know ... who the fuck ... Annabelle May is."

His voice was soft and trembled as it hit the air. He knew something was wrong. Hunter felt a deep well of sympathy for this man but there was nothing that he could do. Then

Delilah went crazy and the moment was broken. Sir Will struggled to control her but she bucked in his hands, fearful of everything around her. She lunged forward and Grape's uncle was startled. He fell on his ass, then pulled himself mournfully into the corner. He stared at the empty space in front of them and became still. Sir Will dragged the furious Delilah outside, happy to leave the room, and Grape and Hunter eventually followed.

Grape twirled her hair between her fingers rapidly, sitting on the hard ground in front of the pigs. Hunter sat slightly behind her, watching her at an angle. It felt like she needed the falsehood of personal space. The pigs grunted indifferently, noses intermittently buried in the muck. Sir Will brought Delilah into the fields to get some exercise and calm her down. Grape's chest was fluttering like a little bird. Her voice was low and soft so Hunter strained to hear her.

"He wasn't always like this. He was different before he fell. The fall changed him. He never saw a doctor. His head swelled up like a melon but then it got better. He was different then, not like he is now. I try and remember him how he was, the good him, then when I see him again it's like I've forgotten how he was. I want to remember him in the good way, you know?

"Sure."

Hunter wondered could he remember his mother that way. No, definitely not. Had somebody found her body yet or was it still lying where he had left it? Maybe all the drugs in her body had already embalmed her from the inside out. That would be nice. If her worst imperfections in life made her perfect in death. He resolved to pretend like that had happened. He refocused on Grape who was blinking rapidly at her feet, hair swishing around so fast between her fingers that it sent a little breeze his way which was oddly comforting. She was exactly like a gentle grazing cow, but cute and sexy in an awkward way that confused him. He found himself getting hard and shifted his legs to hide it even though he wanted to show it to her. Maybe sex would make them both feel better. Since he had sex with Sophie Durango it was on his mind all the time. He was wondering what Grape looked like naked even as she brought her face up to him, eyes wide and fearful.

"What will we do?"

"About what?" He wasn't paying attention.

"About my uncle?"

Hunter was silent. He didn't want to stay here and he didn't want to have to help Grape with her uncle, but he needed the money from the weed and he didn't want to be mean. He liked Grape even if he wouldn't admit it. He looked past her to the sky where it owned the world above the trees. The sky was simple. It changed colour, allowed clouds and planes to cross its borders, let some rain fall from its belly, and every morning and evening was lit up like a firework display from the sun. But it was a constant. Always there. He liked that about the sky. It had a profound depth but was reliable. Grape was staring at him.

"I don't think we should do anything," he announced finally.

It seemed like that was what she wanted to hear. Or maybe she just wanted to hear anything from him. Her body shook and then she was still but kept her eyes trained on him like he was an exotic animal in the zoo.

"Why are you looking at the sky?"

"It relaxes me."

"I like that." She followed his eyes into the sky

Grape and Hunter stared at the sky for a while, letting the deep blue haze wash over them and clear their minds. Grape was calming, her eyes full and free. She shuffled on her ass until she was next to him and leaned over to kiss his cheek. Then she dropped her head on his shoulder and was still.

Delilah barked in a fading rage behind them, pushing both herself and Sir Will into a torpor.

Twenty-Six

There was a stash of weed hidden behind the outhouse where Grape's uncle had been growing the plants. The plants looked like they had taken the brunt of a whirlwind of rage, and were now mostly trampled into the mud. The survivors were dried into whispered husks and brittle leaves that lifted from the ground with the movement of the air. They gathered up everything that they could find and stuffed it all inside a duffel bag. It was strong stuff so it stank heavily.

They went back to the front of the house. The pigs followed their every move, eyes piercing their bodies with hope. Hunter could see the ribs poking out from one of the smaller ones. She stared at him with deep melancholy eyes. It felt incorrect to see a skinny pig. He moved to the gate and put his hand over the latch but Grape stopped him.

"They're his pigs. You can't let them go. He loves them."

Hunter didn't care enough either way. Delilah was stalking around the wire mesh like a panther, willing with all her heart for Sir Will to give the order and let her loose amongst these gormless creatures. Sir Will was strangely silent and contemplative, almost unaware, his movements operating on reflex.

Grape cooked food for them all that night, and her uncle stood in the kitchen doorway watching her cautiously. His skinny body was taut as a bow and his hands constantly shook. He seemed unable to tell them to leave, but let them know how unhappy he was with a constant twitching of the facial muscles that yearned to twist into a bark.

They ate in silence, all four at the table, Delilah at Sir Will's feet. Grape said a stilted grace as if she was expecting to be stopped at any moment. Her words calmed the atmosphere so that it was almost nice. This man would die soon, Hunter knew, but he didn't care. Death had followed him around so much recently that he wasn't even sure it had any importance anymore in his life.

Eventually they needed to sleep. Grape retired to her bedroom, and Hunter and Sir Will made camp in the spartan dining room that was dominated by a dirty old couch. Her uncle stalked them from a few feet away. He hadn't said another word since the first interaction. The windows were boarded up from the inside with peeling cardboard and chipped wood pressed up against the glass, giving the place a prison-cell feel. Sir Will took the couch and Delilah curled up under his arm. Hunter sat on the floor against the wall, eyes averted to his feet. Grape's uncle stood in the shadow of the doorway, shifting from one foot to the next.

Eventually Hunter addressed him, looking directly into his vacant eyes.

"Are you OK?" he asked carefully.

There was a silent vacuum in the room and Hunter's words hung over it like a canopy. Grape's uncle opened his mouth, stuck his tongue out, bit on it and wrung his hands in pain.

"Fuck off ... and get out ... of my house," he said finally, each word painful.

"We're leaving tomorrow."

"Fucking ... good."

"Grape is worried about you."

"Who ... the fuck ... is Grape?"

"I mean Angelica."

Her uncle tasted the air with his tongue, then hid it.

Angelica. That name didn't fit Grape, it wasn't her, but then he wasn't actually sure who Grape really was so he couldn't be sure. Meeting her uncle explained everything and nothing.

When Hunter looked up he saw her uncle was crying a little. Hunter didn't feel anything for him.

"Your pigs are starving," he continued.

Grape's uncle didn't respond. He rocked back and forth on his heels, crying softly. Eventually he ran out of tears and, stepping out of the shadows, he stared at Hunter.

"Do you ... want to fucking ... help me?" he rasped.

"Help you do what?"

"Something ... fucking important."

"What is it?"

Her uncle didn't respond but slipped into the darkness of the house. There was the scraping of the front door being eased open and laden footsteps pressing into the night's flesh. Hunter wasn't inclined to follow. He lay with his back against the wall and pulled his knees against his chest. He had closed his eyes to sleep when he heard the first squeal. Neither Sir Will nor Delilah had noticed. Hunter jerked to his feet and ran to the door.

The cold air hit his face like a wet slap and it took a moment for him to focus in the heavy night air. Eventually shapes and shadows became entities, moving amidst a sea of noise and a glint of metal. Screaming pigs raced in every direction that was clean of the twirling reaper in their midst. Grape's uncle was dancing and gliding like a ballerina through the unfortunate animals, a long knife in his left hand flashing in and out like a beautiful death sickle. The halogen from the house lit him up like a spectre. He was light on his feet, bony ankles carrying him across the mud like a floating waif of death. Hunter was paralysed, feet planted in the mud, the desperate yelps of pain from the suffering animals evaporating around him. It was almost beautiful to watch. The white of the moon peering like a voyeur from behind the clouds cast the skinny figure covered in red blood as an angel.

Grape came by his side, her soft body trembling with shock. Then Sir Will appeared with Delilah. They were all transfixed, unable to comprehend what was going on, but accepting that it was happening. Delilah sat back on her haunches, confused that she hadn't been allowed earlier to do what this perplexing man was doing now.

Eventually Sir Will spoke the first words he had uttered since they had walked in the door.

"I think I would have liked him, in another time. I think he would have been interesting."

Hunter couldn't argue with him. The knife still flashed up and down in a glinting arc of death. He was surprisingly adept with the blade and the pigs died quickly, their meagre bodies piling up rapidly until suddenly there was no life in any of them. It was almost disappointing when it was finished.

When the last pig had been murdered her uncle looked straight at Grape, his eyes clearer now. He locked his gaze onto hers and didn't blink.

"It was ... time ... for the pigs ... to die."

Then he dropped the knife to the ground, bent his knees and gently placed his hands lovingly on each pig, whispering each name in turn and closing their eyes reverentially.

Grape's knees gave out and she dropped into Hunter's arms like a roll of heavy cloth.

"I'd better take her inside," he whispered to Sir Will.

Sir Will nodded and looked at the bloodied figure talking sweet nothings to his dead pigs.

"What about him?"

"I think it's best to let him do what he wants."

"I'll sleep upstairs with you guys if that's cool?"

"Probably not gonna sleep much."

"Yeah, you're right, he's got that knife."

Hunter carried Grape upstairs as gently as he could, her limp feet knocking on the banisters in a soothing tap-tap rhythm. Grape's room was warm and inviting, at odds with the rest of the house. There was a tidy closet in one corner, a rocking chair in another and then one wall from floor to ceiling filled with shelves. On each shelf sat a bundle of stuffed toys, each one different from the last, no two even remotely similar. Then there was the bed, and that was it.

Hunter lifted the motionless Grape into the bed, pulled the sheets over her and curled up behind her. Sir Will carried a rug into the room, laid it on the floor then saw the teddies. He walked to the shelves and examined them with soft hands. Delilah took position at the closed door, eyes and ears alert. They could still hear the soft voice from outside sweetly whispering the eulogies and for some reason it was comforting.

They awoke to the sound of singing, the morning having just cracked through the dawn. Grape woke first and the swivel of her body awoke Hunter who promptly fell out of the bed on to the floor. Sir Will started and was on his feet in a blur, ready for defence. Hunter shook his groggy head at him and Sir Will unclenched his balled-up fists. Delilah didn't wake.

"He's singing. He doesn't sing," Grape announced.

Grape scrambled out the door before Hunter could say anything. He wondered if she would remember what had happened last night. She had probably locked it away already. He got the feeling that's what she did with most things and finding the key to that lock would be a dangerous business.

Her uncle was singing hymns in front of nine marked graves, one each for the body of one of his pigs. Grape walked up behind him and took his hand but he shook her away. He glared at her angrily, then softened and let the mood of singing overtake him again. He didn't look like he had slept and the stench of dried pigs' blood weighed heavily in the air. Sir Will and Hunter stood warily by the door.

"Seems an awful shame to bury them – we could have had bacon for breakfast," Sir Will said dryly.

The violence seemed to have awoken Sir Will from his stupor and he was now filled with a resigned wit. Life was going to happen around him no matter what he did and he had apparently accepted that. Hunter took in the bizarre sight of Grape next to her crazy uncle singing hymns to a bunch of massacred pigs and pondered on what his father would have made of it.

The sun was still fresh to this new day and wasn't quite warmed up yet. Hunter wished that he could have a shower and watch some television eating Oreos and juice for the day. Everything else was hard work. Maybe they could do that. Then Grape's uncle stopped singing and noticed the boys' presence as if for the first time.

"Who ... the fuck ... are you two?"

"We ... it doesn't matter." Hunter hadn't the energy.

"If you came ... for my fucking ... pigs ... you're too late ... they're all dead now."

"We can see that."

Her uncle marched up, eyes flirting with every part of them but without any real menace. Even so the boys tensed. He trembled a little, then his eyes glazed again and he drifted past them into the house as if they didn't exist. Grape had turned to them when her uncle marched back out the door, brushing the two boys aside. Grape reached out her hand to touch him but he ignored her and got into their car.

They watched him transfixed. Then the engine started.

"I left the keys, on the table ..." Sir Will trailed off.

Her uncle put his foot to the gas and abruptly drove off, arrowing onto the road. They hadn't expected that.

"He just took our car." Sir Will was almost amused.

"Fuck." Hunter was dumbfounded. "And I left my backpack in it."

"You think he's going to come back?"

Hunter shrugged. Nobody could know the answer.

"He won't come back," Grape said sadly.

"I think we should probably leave," Sir Will said.

"Yeah. Grape, get your stuff, we're leaving."

"He wasn't always like this," she said.

"I believe you."

Grape walked inside and Hunter stretched out his back. Everything was messed up, but even still it seemed to make sense somehow.

Grape was back outside quickly, the duffel bag of weed in one hand, her canvas bag in the other and a stuffed backpack on her back. She was ready to leave.

"I'm never coming back," she announced to them both, back tall, head held up as if awaiting them to challenge her new idea.

"Fine by me. You got a problem with that, Sir Will?"

"No, man. I think that's the best idea you've ever had, Grape."

Grape smiled, pleased that they agreed, and strode forward onto the dirt road opposite. Hunter and Sir Will followed in her wake. Delilah dawdled behind, still unhappy that they were leaving perfectly edible morsels beneath the cold dirt. Then Sir Will rubbed her head softly and she forgot about anything else but her loyalty.

The sun was lazily stretching itself out to its full height when they reached the freeway again, having skirted past the town on a side road. The freeway was Sir Will's domain and he smiled as he gave them a brief introduction to hitchhiking.

"Always wave down the fastest cars, the ones breaking the speed limit – they're usually driving alone and will pick you up because it's something to do. Slow cars never stop, they're too afraid, that's why they drive slow. Trucks are dangerous, too many basket cases drive them, and keep an eye out for cop cars cos they get pissed at hitchhikers." There was twinkle in his eye again now that they were back and moving within his domain.

With the lesson over they walked in single file, switching up the front-to-rear order so that they could take turns in the art of waving down a ride. They had been walking for almost an hour when Sir Will hailed down a speeding pickup truck. It stopped about twenty feet further down the road from them and Sir Will approached to within a few feet from the vehicle, keeping his hand out ready to warn them if it was a bad situation.

The pickup was being driven by a middle-aged man with sharp eyes, balding around the pate and a little underweight. He nodded to Will who then beckoned to the others.

The man gave Hunter a hard look and couldn't hide the intensity of his glare at Grape.

"Where you kids going?" His voice was nasal.

"Wherever you are, sir," Sir Will replied.

"Well, I'm going to Vegas – you wanna go there?"

"Can't see any reason not to."

"We're not going to Vegas," Hunter said.

Grape turned and smiled at him sweetly.

"I've never been to Vegas."

Sir Will nodded in agreement but Hunter shook his head – it sounded like a bad idea. The driver stuck out his chin.

"You getting the fuck in or not?"

Hunter's mouth opened to object but Grape pressed into him and kissed him gently on the lips. Her lips were soft and wet, like Sophie Durango's had been. He had never been to Vegas – what was the harm in it? It was closer to

Los Angeles at least. It was all taking too long though. Sophie Durango seemed even further from his grasp. But Vegas. Why not?

"Please, Hunter?" Grape said demurely and he deferred.

They stuffed themselves into the car like a bunch of ripening tomatoes, bodies folding into each other. Then the pickup roared into life and took them on the road towards Las Vegas.

Twenty-Seven

The light hurt his eyes wonderfully. There were lights everywhere. The screams of people high on drugs, booze, money, sex and life suffocated him. Sir Will couldn't take the white noise and fell to his knees. As Hunter watched him collapse and Grape run to his side he suddenly remembered the first time that he had properly understood the word love.

He didn't know why he thought of that right then, even as Sir Will had a panic attack, grabbed the flesh of his face tightly between his fingers and rolled his eyes in his head like a dying fawn. Even as Grape reached an arm around Sir Will's tender shaking body, a hand prising Delilah's frightened tongue away from smothering the poor boy.

But he did.

He remembered when his father told his mother that he loved her in front of Hunter. She had laughed at him in that mocking way that she reserved for whenever she was emotionally threatened. Even Hunter knew this about her from an early age. His father knew it better than anybody and always persisted with his affection until eventually she scrambled away from his grasp. This time she had left the room, searching for solace in a bottle or a wrap, casting a glance at Hunter as she left.

Hunter lay on the floor, eyes fixed on the flickering television screen, but his father knew he was watching what was going on in the reflection. When the blacks were at their blackest it was a perfect mirror.

His father slumped into the couch and opened a beer, then spoke out loud to Hunter and nobody in particular.

"Never fall in love. It's a waste of your time. It's not true. You may think you're in love, but you just want to fuck. Remember that, even as you're holding her tight and she's whispering sweet things into your ear, one hand on your balls, the other stroking your cheek, it's not love, it's just sex. Never fall in love cos it's not real and she'll never love you back."

That was his father's breaking point, at the same time as Hunter heard him say he loved her.

Hunter was nine years old but he remembered every flickering reflection of his father's face, angst hewn deeply into his dying soul, the noise of the television merely a butterfly's wings in the background. His father's anguished drone continued unabated.

"Never fall in love because it's a made-up word. You're not in love when you grab a girl by the ass, or you kiss her lips, you're not even in love when you hold her hand, that's only the world trying to fool you into doing stupid things. The only love is the love between a man and his son. Don't ever forget that. Not between a man and a woman."

His father drank beer until he passed out and Hunter

had stared rigidly at the television set, too afraid to move. Eventually his father began to snore and Hunter slipped out of the room and deep into the protective covers of his bed. He could hear the drone of his father's chesty rumbles mixing with the desperate tears of his mother in the next room. As he lay in the darkness he resolved to never fall in love. Or to even care about another person.

Then he met Sophie Durango.

As he climaxed inside Sophie Durango he thought of nothing else but how magnificent the world was. How he wanted nothing else in his life but for that moment to continue unabated forever. He looked at her. She stared back with those crazy eyes of hers and he was swept away by her focus, afraid and certain at the same time. He thought of his father's words. "Never fall in love." But what did his father know? Besides his father was dead and had left him nothing but memories of inadequate advice.

He found himself laughing at the irony of it all. His father, so convincing in his dismissal of love, had unwittingly propelled Hunter on a quest for love. He liked how fucked up it was.

"What is wrong with you? He's dying."

Grape was staring at him accusingly, Sir Will cocooned in her arms like a creature that meant nothing to the outside world. She dragged him against the wall, away from the herds on the street. Delilah whipped around in bedraggled circular movements, biting at the air anxiously. Hunter felt detached from it all.

It had been a quick journey to Vegas, and the driver, eager for silence, turned up the radio to drown out all but the most determined of thoughts. Then he dropped them into the very epicentre of the main Vegas strip. Hunter thought it was incredible – the smell of sex, drugs and debauchery filling the air like a winged temptress.

"Hunter!" Grape implored.

He moved to Grape's side, skipping through the stream of people, lifted Sir Will's shivering head up off his chest and slapped him. Twice.

On the second slap Delilah growled protectively for her master but Hunter shot her a look and she backed down. The second slap drew a yelp of indignation from Grape but Sir Will's eyes cleared and he stared at Hunter with something akin to hatred. Then he softened, remembered their bond, and began to cry. Hunter preferred the panic attack to the crying, or whatever it was.

Sir Will sniffled. "I'm sorry. Too much information. A sensory overload."

"A what?" Grape asked.

Hunter turned away as Sir Will explained to Grape in a bleating voice what a sensory overload was. There were people everywhere, the kind of people with too much money and alcohol in their system, the kind of people who would eagerly smoke their way through Grape's duffel bag of weed. Some watched what was happening as they passed with a vague interest but most didn't give a fuck, too immersed in their own adventures. He wanted to join them. A Greyhound bus passed by and he saw a reflection of himself on it, heading directly for Sophie Durango. It was overwhelming.

Grape was by his side. She pressed against him awkwardly, her soft body comforting against his hip. He could feel her eyes upon him but kept his eyes in front, even as the street bustled around him in crazy beautiful chaos.

"Sir Will needs to rest, somewhere away from all … this."

She said it distastefully, but for the first time since he had been robbed and beaten up Hunter felt alive. Like a man. This was the place for things to happen. He could feel it. He was in charge now. They all knew it, even Delilah. For all the bond steeled between himself and Sir Will, it was only a temporary alliance. He hoped that Sir Will knew that. He felt ashamed then, for he liked Sir Will in a way.

The flashing lights were draining now. It was constant. Oppressive. He needed to sleep. He suddenly saw Grape's uncle slaughtering the pigs like he had been slicing up ripe tomatoes and he felt ill. Crazy beautiful chaos that had no end. They should all get some rest. He looked at Grape. She needed him to tell her what to do, her gentle doe's eyes were pure and trusting. He was a good person, wasn't he? Why did he like it whenever she looked vulnerable? Would Grape feel as good as Sophie Durango? He wanted to fuck Grape to find out. Maybe then he would be more of a man for when he met Sophie Durango again. The energy of the strip filled him with something dark and mysterious. He was invigorated. He was a different person. He felt like none of it mattered. Who cared? Grape turned away to lift the distressed Sir Will to his feet and he took in the round shape of her ass as it swayed from one side to the other with the movement of her hips. He liked Las Vegas. It felt dangerous.

Twenty-Eight

It was a nice motel. Most motels were generally the same, the only difference being how stained the sheets were or the colour of the outside wall. Maybe yellow, maybe blue. This one was surprisingly clean. It was a true Vegas motel, replete with slot machines on each floor, the basic requirement for round-the-clock gambling. They navigated past the slots to a ground-floor room near the back of the motel. It was dark here and a reprieve from the mayhem.

Sir Will took the bed furthest from the door, curled up with Delilah and was instantly asleep, his body quivering intermittently.

The one remaining bed beckoned to Hunter and Grape like a gaping void of possibility. Or of conflict. Could he have sex with her with Sir Will in the room? Grape looked at him, eyes wide, as if she knew what he was thinking and he felt ashamed. They needed to sleep. His limbs were heavy and he really just wanted to curl up and let his mind drift. Then she pulled off her blouse, her heavy breasts almost spilling out of her bra. Fuck.

He didn't say anything but undressed quickly himself got under the covers so that he could watch her step out of her clothes until she was in her underwear like before. Her eyebrows were arched in a permanent state of anxiety. She turned off the lights and followed him under the sheets.

They lay there like that for a few minutes, Grape facing away from him, arms protectively in front of her breasts, knees up against her belly. Hunter lay lightly curled behind her, careful to avoid touching her. Then Grape sighed and stuck her ass into him. He instinctively recoiled from the touch and she trembled as if being rejected so he quickly grabbed her tightly and held her into him. This was about as far as he knew what to do. As a sexual fantasy it was so much different. He felt like a child.

"Are we going to have sex?"

Her voice was low but still broke a little.

His own mouth was dry and he had to wet his lips before he spoke. "I don't know."

"I've never had sex before."

Was she lying? He had been there in the house watching the dead old man when she was outside making noises.

"What about with that man before, when ..."

"No. We didn't do anything. That was Star anyway. I'm not her anymore. I'm Grape now."

Her voice sounded innocent and she was convincing.

"Still, maybe we shouldn't," he said.

"Do you not want to because it's my first time? I've done things as Star. Sort of. Not really though. Never as Grape."

She was confusing him now. He didn't know how to take the lead. Sophie Durango had led him and he had followed.

"That's not it. I do want to. But maybe we shouldn't

with Sir Will in the room."

"OK."

"We should probably sleep."

"OK."

Grape fell silent and Hunter lay there, trying his best not to breathe too loudly. His heart was beating in his chest and his lungs weren't filling with air properly. Everything felt strained. Then just when he thought she might be sleeping Grape spoke again.

"What's it like?"

"What?"

Her breath squeezed out of her in small awkward spurts.

"Sex. What's sex like?"

"It's … nice."

"Really, like what?"

"What?"

"Nice like what?"

Hunter didn't really know. It had only been that one time with Sophie Durango. That had been enough to make him believe he knew it all. It was enough for any boy. But it wasn't and he knew it wasn't. Even now he was afraid of being so close to Grape.

He hesitated and she felt it. She was as docile and confused as a pet sometimes but she sometimes she just knew things. Her voice softened as though addressing a child.

"We don't have to talk about it."

"No, we can. I mean."

"You don't want to have sex with me."

"I do."

He blurted that out too quickly and for some reason he knew that it made him less attractive to her. He felt less attractive to himself. She fell silent and he struggled to regain his composure. What happened to wanting to fuck her even with Sir Will in the corner?

Sir Will's silhouette gently lifted up and down with the rise of his chest as did Delilah's beside him.

"It's like ice cream. Warm ice cream."

Grape turned to him with a stupid smile on her face, nose touching his.

"I like warm ice cream."

"Well, yeah, kinda, a bit."

"What else?"

Her cheeks were flushing a little and he felt the heat off her body reach out and threaten to smother him.

"It's just warm, soft, lovely, I dunno ..."

She seemed disappointed but her hand grabbed him and he jolted, a burning spear in his belly. Her eyes had changed, they seemed darker. Knowing.

"What else?"

He suddenly felt empowered. He was a man.

"It's happiness, and anger, and confusion, beautiful confusion."

He had no idea what he was saying but her hand was on him now, moving with every word and he grabbed her, slipping his hand below the waist of her panties. They grappled with each other, both afraid to move away lest the moment they had would be lost. It felt primal and secure, safe and dangerous all at the same time.

Her mouth was touching his but they didn't kiss, it felt like the moment might be broken, they had crossed into a territory with no rules and no way to leave or come back. The only thing they could do was destroy it. They grabbed and tugged and pulled, warm, wet, hard, happy anger.

They stared at each other but looked beyond the other, seeing nothing but their own pleasure, and then they both climaxed. He knew nothing about the climaxes of women but it seemed to happen when it was supposed to, so for Hunter that's the way it always was and for Grape it was something more.

They slowly pulled away from each other, and like sycophantic mirrors they lay side by side. Hunter wanted nothing more than to be alone, to let the intense soft feelings wash beyond him. He was full and famished at the same time. Grape wanted to bury herself in his body, to trap herself beneath the skin of his skin, to be a part of his thoughts, and to share her own. He began to roll away and she rolled into him, turning so that her back was to him and pulling his arm over her belly. He let her do it. She wasn't facing him so he didn't have to let her see his thoughts even though he didn't know what they were yet.

He hated himself. She was no longer sexy and her belly lay in his hand like a self-satisfied animal, heaving in and out smugly. He wanted to be alone, to understand himself but it was cosy inside the duvet and easier to stay where he was.

"That was better than ice cream," she whispered.

"Yep."

"I think we should do that again."

"Yep."

"I always imagined what it would be like. I would see people doing it, on the television, and wonder what it felt like. Did you ever wonder that?"

"Yep."

"Sometimes I would close my eyes but I didn't know what it felt like, so I couldn't think about it. Have you ..."

She fell silent and his innards bellowed at him. He knew what she was about to say. And she knew his answer.

"You did this with that girl, didn't you?"

"Sophie Durango."

It felt strange to say her name out loud, and when he did he wanted to savour it more, to let it roll off his tongue. Grape pushed his hand off her and scooted away.

She didn't say anything but her shoulder muscles bunched together like a wall. He sighed and turned onto his other side, sleep quickly over taking him. He was in Las Vegas and he had just had his second sexual experience and this time he wasn't in love with the girl. His father would have been proud. Maybe.

He gently thought of Sophie Durango and wondered how many sexual experiences she had enjoyed. Did it matter to him? Probably not. When he saw her again nothing else would matter because everything else would fade away and it just be Cat and Sophie. He wouldn't tell her that he was called Hunter, or what had happened. He would only tell her that he loved her. It seemed that he loved her more every day. That must be what love was. The noises outside of Vegas bleating like an animal skipped around him like a glorious nightmare until he fell asleep.

Twenty-Nine

The boys got up, sweating in their clothes. The shower was weak and tepid but a shower in the morning was always a luxury no matter how it was taken. The air was hot and humid anyway and they wouldn't have wanted it to be too hot.

Grape rooted in the bag of spare clothes she had gathered when leaving her uncle's and pulled out a white blouse and a blue wraparound skirt.

They staggered past the pupil-searing sun and wandered into the breakfast room for some cold coffee and stale croissants. Grape had a warm yoghurt and ignored Hunter while Sir Will fed Delilah quietly, still immersed in his own morose thoughts. Then a switch flipped inside of him and his face cracked with a skin-creasing smile. He had good teeth. Hunter wondered if his family missed him. Even though they might hate him he was lucky to have a family and Hunter felt a pang of jealousy. He wanted to call somebody, to let them know about his mother. The thought of her solitary body filling up that painful house with the smell of death was uncomfortable so he forgot about it and focused on the eager words streaming off Sir Will's face.

Delilah slapped her tail from side to side, thrilled at her master's enthusiasm.

"... we could make enough cash to get a big car and drive the fuck to where we want, buy what we want ... it's perfect!"

"What is?" Hunter asked.

"Sir Will was telling us his plan to make us rich," Grape sneered back at him. It wasn't like her to sneer.

Hunter ignored her and looked at his comrade.

"A plan to get rich, Sir Will?"

"Yeah, Hunter man, we're in Vegas. I don't even know how or why, but we are here, so there must be a reason. We can win big, really big, get enough money to do what we want! All we need is a plan, man."

"Yeah. That's a good idea." Hunter was doubtful.

"I know, man, I know."

"What's the plan?"

"It's simple."

Sir Will slapped his hand down on the table like he was already declaring a winning hand in poker. An older man in the far corner, battered by life, gave them a weary look of sympathy and resentment. Croissant flakes dotted his greying beard and he made no effort to remove them.

Sir Will was apparently having a moment of fate and deep insight. This was the moment for all of them and he couldn't let them ignore it. He whispered the basic gambling plan to them, then rose to his feet majestically, arms spread and Delilah barked her encouragement.

"Let's go!"

"I don't know ..." Grape began.

"Yes, you do, Grapefruit. Yes, you do."

His eyes sparkled and it was impossible not to get swept up in his eagerness. With somebody like Sir Will anything could happen. They were in Las Vegas and here was where they were supposed to be all along. Sir Will almost ran for the door. Hunter found himself rising to his feet despite his misgivings.

They galloped behind him, racing out along the streets towards the main casino strip like three idiots, broke and thirsty for money, Delilah circling them and yelping. People stared but they didn't care – they were going to win and win big. They didn't even need to know where they were going. They simply followed the streams of people and traffic, the neon lights still bright in the daylight. This was destiny.

There is nothing in the world that can't be bought with money. Hunter didn't need to be told that, he knew it as well as he knew how to eat and sleep and breathe. It was the human materialistic condition. Fight for your place, make money to keep it and then expect to own it forever. That's what he knew and nobody could convince him otherwise. Sir Will and Grape held hands as they eagerly skipped towards their new financial destiny, feet dancing along the concrete. Her ass leapt and bounced and he wanted to grab it. With money there is nothing in the world that can't be bought. Except love. Although maybe even love. Hunter carried the duffel bag of weed on his back like a Viking prize. If you bought love with money did it matter where the money came from? Nobody saw your sweaty history in the grubby crease of a twenty-dollar bill, but they respected what that bill could do for them. Las Vegas and her corporeal promises reared her beautiful ugly head up into the empty skies and he was drawn into her embrace. Money and love. That's all he wanted.

They sauntered into the first casino like they owned the place. They were quickly removed for having a dog, being dressed like tramps and having no money to buy poker chips. In their eagerness the cold reality of needing money to make money had escaped them. Grape scuffled her feet but Sir Will wasn't fazed.

"The weed. We will sell the weed, use the money for some new clothes, buy chips, win more chips, become rich. Simple!"

Hunter ground his teeth together uneasily. If they sold all the weed and the plan didn't work then he had no way of getting to Los Angeles to find Sophie Durango, a destiny that was becoming muddied more and more each day. He looked to Grape for support.

"We shouldn't sell all of it," he said. "We should keep some."

He expected her to side with him. After all they had travelled together since the beginning, and now they had experienced something sexual together. They were bound.

Her face was blank and unreadable.

Sir Will waved his hands in the air, searching for attention like a puppet on steroids.

"No, man, no, we have to do it all – it's a big plan, our plan of destiny, we have no choice but to do it all – it's what the universe is telling us to do – we have to respond."

Sir Will paused to catch his breath. Grape's hard docile eyes fell upon Hunter and through him. She reached for the bag.

"It's mine anyway."

Hunter meekly felt her rough touch with a shiver of annoyance.

"You said you would give me the money to get to –"

"To find that girl. Sure. But we have to win first. What's more important, the universe or some girl?" she snorted and ripped the bag off him.

His arm twisted a little and anger flared but he let it pass. She saw it flare however and glared, as if he had committed the greatest crime in the world. Maybe he had. Her face was a fury, and seemed to scream Sophie Durango's name at him. Then she turned to Sir Will and triumphantly handed him the duffel bag. He took it out of her trembling hands gently, confused at what was going on and wishing that he could know. Hunter pretended there was something in his teeth.

"There you go, Sir Will. Why don't you keep the bag and let's make our money to get rich?" Grape genuflected.

Sir Will smiled at her benevolently, then held the bag aloft above his head like a television show prize and screamed at the top of his lungs.

"Let's get fucking rich!"

Hunter waited for Sir Will's masquerade to stop – his face hurt from pretending to smile. When Sir Will was satisfied that he had made enough of a scene he skipped away and beckoned for them to follow. Today was a terribly exciting thing. Until it was over it was filled with the possibility of sweet success. Hunter wondered sourly what its end would bring and how long it would take.

Thirty

"Get out."

"Why, man, why?"

"I don't need a reason."

Grape pushed past Sir Will and stood under the security guard's face, her nose barely level with his chest. Her eyes glowered with a delicate rage.

"Yes, you do. You need to give us a reason or else we're not leaving."

The security man seemed momentarily taken aback by the soft little ball of aggression, then after examining her was maybe a little smitten. Grape had that way with people. Something about her eyes. He reached out and touched her hand but she shrugged him off like she had been stung and his eyes went cold again.

"You have to leave because I'm telling you to."

"We have chips in there, man!" Sir Will protested.

"I don't care."

"They're our chips!"

"Not anymore."

Sir Will attempted to rush past him but a brawny arm flicked out and clattered him dead-centre in the chest, knocking him backwards.

"Don't try that again, boy, or there will be trouble."

Hunter was a few steps back, holding Delilah by her collar. The security man pointed at the dog.

"You better get rid of that thing or put her somewhere before you get yourselves locked up. I'm being nice, and don't ya'll forget it."

Hunter whistled at his companions and they reluctantly turned and followed him out on the strip. When you look like you don't belong, people feel threatened.

They had sold half their weed quite quickly, most to a bunch of college kids on a stag party with more alcohol in their bloodstream than sense. Then they had marched into the Bellagio, Hunter getting the chips, and made a beeline for the roulette wheel. They had put down $100 immediately on red and lost it, but then won it right back on the second spin. They played on, winning, losing. Then Delilah jumped up onto the table, scattering chips and drinks. Sir Will thought it was hilarious. They were fucking high rollers with the universe behind them. Unfortunately, the universe hadn't told anybody else. Security had definitely missed the memo and the next thing they knew they were dragged outside unceremoniously.

Hunter got them each a Coke and they sat on the pavement to recharge and get their enthusiasm back. Sir Will fed Delilah from his Coke can, letting her slobber over it delightedly. The sugar seemed to re-animate him.

"That was a test man, a test of our backbone. We go back in again, and we go back in again *hard*."

Grape was subdued despite her bravado. She patted Delilah a little then spoke up.

"I don't want to lose everything. That was $500 gone so quickly. I never sold that much in one day before, and now we have nothing. I don't know what to make of it."

"But we won $300 in a heartbeat, so easily!" Sir Will countered, enjoying his attempts to be right.

"And lost it!"

"Doesn't matter, we won as well. We were on a winning streak."

Hunter wondered had Sir Will gone a little mad. Since Grape's uncle had slaughtered the pigs in front of them he seemed affected, something behind his eyes was bouncing but never alighting long enough to be discerned, and he was either too quiet or too heightened. It made Hunter uncomfortable. Sir Will's eyes were wild again as he described how they would win this time. Maybe he had always been this way – they hardly knew him. His hands wreaked havoc in the air.

"All we do is stick on red. Red, red, red – then at the right moment when we feel it change we go to black, black, black. If we get it right we can keep winning, it goes like that, it's a mathematical pattern."

Hunter rubbed some dead skin off his forearm and looked at him dryly.

"You know the mathematical pattern?"

"Yeah, sure, man, it's easy. Almost too easy, that's why people don't trust it, cos it's so easy it makes them mistrust it, don't you see?"

"Not really."

"You're not really looking, man, you gotta really look."

Hunter sighed and pulled the skin so hard it ripped the

nice pink flesh underneath. Blood welled up in a little pool then dribbled down his arm. Sir Will stared at the blood, something flashed in his eyes, then he was on his feet again. He was beginning to wear both of them down – Hunter could feel Grape's desire waning with Sir Will's increasing fervour. Maybe he had taken something – he probably had drugs that neither of them knew about.

"Let's go, man, let's go!"

Sir Will grabbed the duffel bag from Grape and started off down the street, searching for some eager patrons of weed. His slender frame dodged through the crowds like a snake-charmer. Grape sneaked a glance at Hunter and he smiled benignly at her but she pouted and looked away, not ready to make up just yet. She stubbornly chased after Sir Will and Hunter followed. He could already feel the day's possibilities fading away. He knew now that it was going to end badly, there was no way it couldn't. It had the feeling of dark fate but he didn't have the energy to fight it. He just wanted it to be over so he could figure out another way to get to Los Angeles and find Sophie Durango. Maybe it was time to leave Grape and Sir Will behind.

He caught up with them as Sir Will was negotiating a transaction with some hippie-looking dudes in the shade of a Starbucks. They shied away on Hunter's arrival but Sir Will hushed them with a wave of his hyper limbs and they completed the purchase. They bought half of what they had left without batting an eyelid. Did everybody just have money to burn in Vegas? Sir Will showed the money to Grape like it was gold dust, then shoved it into his pants. He was the de facto leader here now and Hunter and Grape were just along for the ride. Sir Will's eyes combed through the crowds and in moments he had spotted his next customers. Before the hour was out the weed was all sold, and they were $635 to the good, ready to pour their souls into the unforgiving belly of Las Vegas to digest and regurgitate at will. Outside the Cosmopolitan hotel Hunter addressed the dog.

"We can't bring Delilah inside."

"Then one of us has to stay with her." Sir Will shrugged.

"She's your dog."

'But I'm the one who knows the system."

"It's not difficult – red, red, red, then black, black, black. We can figure it out."

"It's all about the timing, man."

"Well, then what will we do?"

Grape looked at them both and took the dog from Sir Will's grasp.

"I'll stay with Delilah."

"Are you sure?" Hunter asked.

"Yep. She likes me and I like her. I think she understands me better than I understand myself."

There wasn't a whole lot to say to that, so Hunter nodded.

"OK then, you and me, Sir Will."

"Brilliant, we are gonna run the fucking place, man!"

Sir Will's wild eyes devoured the world around them, challenging it to disagree but the world didn't care about him anymore than it cared about anybody else. He clapped Hunter on the shoulder and led him off towards the heart of the Cosmopolitan, shouting over his shoulder at Grape.

"Wait for us here, Grapefruit, we won't be more than an hour! Even mathematics has a time limit!"

Hunter didn't quite think an hour was accurate but then the Cosmopolitan reared up in front of them like some beautiful crystalline thing from his imagination and he forgot about anything else. He walked and stared, walked and stared, walked and stared. Silver reflections slid his roving eye around and around before he found himself standing beside a roulette table, chips in hand as Sir Will screamed at the table like he was at the races. They were both served vodka tonics with too much vodka and too little tonic and soon he found himself screaming just as loudly. Smoke filled the air, and the possibility of being rich quivered in everybody's veins. It was all here. All was possible. Everything that they ever wanted.

Too soon they were down to the last $100. Sir Will devoured another vodka and concentrated on watching the roulette spin. Hunter felt everybody's eyes upon them. They were kids in a man's world. Nothing was possible for kids like them. Hunter put his hand on Sir Will's shoulder, conscious of the smug half-grins upon them.

"I think we should quit while we have something left."

"No."

Sir Will didn't look at him, but kept his eyes glued to the tiny white ball that span and span. Hunter could feel everything spilling away. The little white ball taunting him.

"$100 on number 14!" Sir Will declared.

Hunter knew it was over. Just like that. The fervour and the rush hadn't even lasted twenty minutes. It was over before it had even properly begun. The little white ball spun gently around in its final throes and Hunter wondered how it had come to this. He hated himself for trusting Sir Will.

Then the white ball landed on number 14.

The other gamblers reluctantly cheered, but their faces betrayed their irritation. Sir Will grabbed Hunter and kissed him. He tasted of vodka and cigarettes. He stacked the chips obsessively in a neat little pile and began again.

"Trust in the system," he panted.

They were up, then down, then up, up again, then down and then all of a sudden they were up $3,500. Cheers and groans, kisses and vodka. It didn't even make any sense. None of it stopped long enough to allow it to be savored. It was momentary and instantaneous. The hour was abruptly up and true to his word Sir Will grabbed Hunter like the world was about to end and dragged him outside, cashing the chips on the way like a hyperactive child at Christmas. Hunter didn't even notice the looks that the staff gave them as they rushed outside into the searing heat, light burning their darkly adjusted eyes. They had won $3500. An obscene sum. He didn't even know how to begin counting that much money in his head.

When they came out Grape was nowhere to be found. Hunter scoured the outside world which seemed disappointing after the opulence of the arena inside.

"We told her to stay here. Right here."

Sir Will was about cry, the money forgotten, emotions on edge.

"Right here, that's what I said, wasn't it?" he yelled.

"Yeah, sure, but she'll be back."

Hunter wasn't convinced. He had that sinking feeling in his belly again, the one which tormented him because it was always right. He began to feel the beginnings of the fear that he had when Grape had gone missing at the bus depot, but tried to rationalise that surely she would be back. She had to be.

"Maybe Delilah was thirsty," he offered.

"Don't blame Delilah."

Sir Will was becoming hard work, face twisting and

turning to scan and rescan the streets. Hunter took the money out of his hand easily while his attention was elsewhere and put it carefully in his pocket, where he checked and rechecked it constantly, worried it might dissolve through the fabric and disappear.

They walked along the strip, desperately searching through the myopic heave of bodies, avoiding the gleaming edifices grinning down around them. The weight of the money weighed Hunter down like a great stone in his pocket.

Then they saw her.

On the apex of a bridge leading into the Caribbean Hotel she was singing and clapping. Delilah lay at her feet, an empty coffee cup between her ordered legs.

Hunter and Sir Will approached with something like morbid fascination. She was dancing and spinning, her skirt swirling, half-talking half-singing an obscure song that had no beginning and no end. People stood and watched her, captivated by something that none of them understood. She seemed to glow, her skin reflecting the sun like a creature that didn't belong in Vegas. She was pure. People placed bills into Delilah's unwitting collection cup and she barked at them to back off. Then Grape thanked them in the song, half-singing, half-talking, the endless song that didn't seem to need a chorus, but just kept going incessantly, almost like Grape herself.

Sir Will rushed to join the party, leaping upon Grape like a fervent locust, spinning her around and singing loudly, out of tune but too eager to care. Then he sat down beside his dog and began tapping out a beat on his knees and the ground, flowing effortlessly into Grape's meaningless song.

A bigger crowd formed and suddenly it was everything

that mattered in Vegas. Hunter watched on the outskirts, fingering the money in his hand, stroking the dirty notes and watching every movement of Grape's tender body. He wished that Sophie Durango was here to join in this feeling of joy that he had. Life couldn't get better than this, and he wished that she could be here to experience it with him. He would bring her here and this would happen again and she would fall in love with him.

Grape caught his eye and she smiled, the turmoil she felt having dissipated with the joy of her music. She was everything and nothing at the same time. Then his hand touched something odd in his pocket and he pulled it out. It was the card that the Biker had given him, of his friend who ran a club in Vegas. He had pocketed it without ever thinking it would be useful. Now they were in Vegas. They had to go, he just knew. It all made too much sense not to. He played out the beat on his knees as Grape and Sir Will threw their energies into the wind and made the crowd happy. Everything and nothing all at once.

Thirty-One

Bang!
Bang!
Bang!

The music hit him on the side of the head like a loving hammer, not quite hard enough to knock him down and not quite soft enough to let him dismiss the pain. He couldn't hear anything but noise, if noise was just a thing in itself.

Grape was dancing again, only this time she wasn't singing, just swaying with the beat. Her skin was flushed with red and her blouse was stained with sweat. Her body gyrated to the deep bass. This was what a real nightclub felt like.

They were initially refused at the door but Hunter asked for the name on the card. A huge imposing figure, the sort that would be friends with the Biker, strolled out balls first like he owned the place. Turned out that he did. Hunter told him the story, innocently believing that this giant of a man would care. He smirked at him, seemingly taken in by Hunter's naivety, then charged them $50 each and took Delilah to stay in the locker room. They didn't care – they needed to celebrate and for once Sir Will seemed content to let Delilah out of his sight. The sight and sound of willing chaotic bodies unfurling their anguish under the low lights through the door appealed to his darkness. She protested and strained to follow them but he bent down and whispered in her ear, running his hands along the back of her head. Once calm she was led away, ears flat against her skull.

Sir Will was writhing beside him, groin pressing against Hunter's ass every so often as if by an innocent mistake, but Hunter knew what he was doing. He stepped away to create some distance between them. Sir Will took Grape's hips in his hands, ground himself against her ass and Hunter wondered if he wasn't gay after all. Grape pushed back into him, grinding like girls on MTV get paid handsomely for and covertly flicked her eyes up at him. This was what a real nightclub felt like. Boundaries were pushed without consequence.

Hunter needed another drink so he left them to whatever games they were playing and pushed a path to the bar.

"Two shots of tequila, please."

"What?"

He had to raise his voice to be heard and almost screamed.

"Two shots of tequila."

"Sure."

The bar girl was cute. Her long blonde hair was tied into a perfect ponytail, dark eye make-up, rouged lips, breasts tight against her lowcut top. Every inch of her designed to make you want to buy drinks just to get her attention. Buy a drink and I may fuck you, her body lied. It worked every time. Hunter knocked back the shots quickly, the burning in his throat giving him shivers, and indicated two more. He just wanted to feel her smile upon him. Maybe she meant it for him, why wouldn't she, could probably smell his winnings. He was getting closer to Sophie Durango now, could almost taste her breath upon his skin. He was further than ever but he knew the dichotomy of that – he was physically further but felt closer and had experience on his side against his previous innocence. Why did every woman make him think of Sophie Durango? There was breath on his cheek from a man in a suit, eyes glazed and oblivious to the world. Hunter turned away from his stink, drank the next two shots and plunged back into the crowd for his companions.

Grape had her hands in Sir Will's hair and was gyrating on his knee like it was the last thing left on this earth for her to experience. He felt a bolt of jealousy, which pissed him off more than the actual jealousy. They were both high and drunk. Sir Will had procured some little red tablets once inside the club. There wasn't any need to ask why or where from, it was just accepted. Grape was nervous but Sir Will plied her with alcohol and then she was willing and pliable to try it out. Hunter took them without question because it was Vegas and that's what you were supposed to do. He spun around slowly and took it all in. A wall of flesh, sweat and sex filled every angle and crevasse. There was nowhere to sit and just be alone. Human chaos. Eyes, hips, curves and muscles filled his vision, bonding with the beating music bouncing inside his skull. Grape and Sir Will were two writhing snakes becoming a singular. It was too much. Bile rose from the pit of his belly. He felt dizzy and stumbled forward, looking for the entrance. He was overwhelmed with an urge to find Delilah – they should never have left her. He couldn't remember the owner's name again, where was the card? His hands were wet. He scrabbled around in his pockets and pushed it out into the damp air where he promptly dropped it. Before he could bend down to pick it up there were feet in front and behind and he was pushed forward and then carried away. He might as well have dropped it into the sea. No matter, he would surely recognise him. He made his way outside, a concentrated grin upon his face, left hand still clutching the precious bills, brain melting into itself from the drugs.

There were still people waiting to get in even at this late hour. He nodded at them proudly, belly full of tequila, head full of acid, aware that they must all be jealous of him. He was a god, a Las Vegas Conqueror. Why did he even need Grape or Sir Will? He had money and spirit. He should leave now and find Sophie Durango. Maybe she was even inside, why wouldn't she be, that would make sense, it was fate after all, they were in love. Nearly in love. He looked around frantically for her, scanning every face, trying to see past the tight skirts and layers of make-up for her sharp beautiful features. He paused. He had never seen so many gorgeous women in one place – surely there couldn't be this many in the world?

"Hey, buddy, you alright?"

Hunter turned to the voice of a large bouncer with a clinically shaved head. His eyes latched onto him like a predator, willing him to run so he could pounce.

"I'm good. Yep. Yeah. Fine."

"You sure?"

"Yeah yeah yeah."

"If you're too drunk you can't go back inside."

Inside. Grape and Sir Will. Delilah. He had come outside looking for Delilah. He needed to find her.

"Delilah."

"What's that buddy, your girlfriend?"

"Delilah. The dog."

"What dog?"

"Our dog. Not my dog, but Sir Will's dog. Nice dog. Barks a lot. We left her with your boss. The big guy. My biker friend. I had a card. I lost it. Where is the dog?"

The bouncer stared at Hunter, a smirk forming. He was the type that liked fucking with drunk kids. He probably remembered the dog but wasn't inclined to get her anytime soon. The night was long and he needed entertainment.

"You want the dog?"

"Yeah."

"You know we gotta charge you for her?"

"Huh?"

"You have to pay us for her, you were told that."

"No no no, you're keeping her safe."

"For $200 we sure are."

Fuck. Hunter was losing his vision, everything swam. Maybe four tequilas so quickly was a bad idea. His head hurt. And his feet, why did his feet hurt? He needed to get Delilah, it was the most important thing in the world right now. He reached into his pocket for his money. It was OK, he could pay $200 because he was rich, and Delilah needed to be saved.

"You got the $200, buddy?"

"Yeah, yeah, yeah, I won big, I own Las Vegas, I'm gonna bring Sophie Durango here."

"That's great. The $200?"

Hunter pulled his wad of notes out in a flurry of masculinity, and the Bouncer's eyes lit up greedily. Nobody cares about anybody else in Vegas. Hunter began counting out the $50 bills slowly, losing count after two.

"Let me help you with that, buddy?"

Before Hunter could say no the bouncer swiped the notes from his hand. He waited, swaying, eyes closing as the man clapped his shoulder.

"I'll get your dog now, don't worry."

"OK."

Hunter held out his hand stupidly, waiting for the money to be passed back. Some notes softly hit his palm and he closed it quickly. The wad felt smaller this time, lighter. No matter, he had some. Some was better than none. If he could keep his eyes closed then everything would hurt less.

Delilah barked at him.

"Hey, Delilah!"

The dog pulled away from the man holding her and eager to be released from her prison cascaded into Hunter, knocking him off his feet. He struggled to his feet, pushing her wet face off him. The bouncer stood over him, still smirking.

"You can't come back inside now, buddy."

"My friends are still inside."

"Too bad."

The bouncer turned away and strode towards the crowd, holding his hand up to indicate that two more were to be allowed in. Hunter thought about arguing but Delilah seemed like the most important thing in his world right now. He wondered if Sophie Durango liked dogs. Maybe they could get a dog together. He'd like that.

The entrance to the club was inside the Wynn hotel, and Hunter strolled out into the lobby, Delilah trotting alongside him. Some people stared, but it was Vegas and if one person accepted it then it appeared to be OK with everybody. There was a row of slot machines to Hunter's left. He stopped for a minute and stared at them. The spinning fruits were hypnotic. Fuck it, he was on a winning streak, he should give it a few spins. Who knew, maybe he would get lucky and he could even get enough money to fly to LA. Maybe he had enough money now anyway – he wasn't sure how much a flight to Los Angeles would cost.

The stool was comfortable. His ass melted into it, designed to encourage you to stay longer. He passed some bills through the machine, not even sure what he was putting inside. All he knew was that he was winning big and he owned Las Vegas. Delilah whined beside him. He gave her a warm smile, rubbed her ears and then focused on trying to make a bunch of red cherries line up with some other bunches of red cherries. It was a very delicate business, the button had to be pushed at the perfect time. Maybe there was a system, mathematical. He scrunched his eyes tightly shut and tried to imagine that he could see floating numbers in his head like Russell Crowe in *A Beautiful Mind*. Delilah whined again. Then he fell asleep.

Thirty-Two

When he woke up it was apparently early morning, judging by the smell of eggs in the restaurant across the hallway. You couldn't really tell because there was no sense of time inside the casinos. The slot machine blinked eagerly, a happy red light indicating that he had an abundance of credit left. He automatically began to press buttons and had played almost twelve games straight before he remembered Delilah. His head hurt. He looked around. The dog was gone.

"Delilah?"

Hunter panicked and fell off the chair, then gathered himself together. Maybe he had only been asleep for a few minutes – surely she couldn't have gone far? He began walking through the casino slowly, calling her name out softly, partly to avoid attention and partly because his brain was pounding against his skull like a jackhammer.

"Delilah? Hey girl, where you at? Delilah!"

The further he ventured into the casino the more he

encountered stereotypes of people, cliches upon cliches, people upon people. Most were either drunk and confused or sad-eyed and focused, drifting through the glamorous chaos. Then without warning the slot machines and roulette tables ended and he found himself standing in the pathetically vast reception. Sunlight streamed through the glass and illuminated the dome-like structure into a giant reflected sun. His mouth was dry. Where the fuck was Delilah?

He marched up to the reception where a slender brunette with long hair down her back like a polite waterfall looked at him suspiciously. She was too beautiful to be suspicious.

"Can I help you, sir?"

Hunter coughed to clear his ravaged throat and she visibly shrank back. He became aware that he was still in the same clothes and hoped that smell wasn't him.

"Yes. I. Uh, well. Have you seen a dog?"

The pretty receptionist didn't even blink. This was the least strange request that she had heard all morning.

"A dog? What kind of dog?"

"A German Shepherd. Nice-looking dog. She, uh, well, I had her inside, and –"

"You had her inside? Inside the hotel?"

"Yep."

"Are you a guest here, sir?"

"No. But I was in the nightclub, my friends are still there."

Now the receptionist blinked and indicated a grand old clock above her head which appeared ostensibly for show but actually worked. Its face glowered 2.20pm. Now it was Hunter's turn to blink.

"The club closed ten hours ago, at 4am, sir."

"Oh. Yeah. Shit. I fell asleep at the slots."

"With your dog?"

"Yes."

"And when you woke up your dog was gone?"

"It's not actually my dog."

"Whose dog is it?"

"My friend's – Sir Will."

"Where is 'Sir Will'?"

"Well, I'm not sure but he was with my friend Grape."

"Sir, I'm going to stop you – I haven't seen any dog."

"But maybe in the lost property?"

"We don't keep dogs in the lost property."

"But, maybe?"

"Sir. If you want to get your friend, 'Sir Will', to come by maybe he can find the dog, but I think you should leave, get a coffee, have a shower and find your friends."

"I can't leave without Delilah."

"Who's Delilah?"

"The dog."

"I think it's best if you leave, sir."

The receptionist really was pretty. Even though her tone was condescending, she was warming to this odd character in front of her and Hunter found himself dissolving into her soft eyes. He wanted to tell her everything. It all came pouring out. Her eyes were open and green.

"Delilah, that's the dog's name. It's myself, Sir Will, Grape and Delilah, we're travelling to Los Angeles after we get rich to find Sophie Durango because I might be falling in love and Sir Will has been kicked out of his home because he's gay, and Grape's uncle sells weed but when we met him he killed all of his pigs with a knife, and then we got a lift here and won lots of money but I think I might have lost some, and now the dog is missing. I don't know. I have to get to Los Angeles. Oh, and my mum died last week and I've not told anybody yet."

Hunter suddenly felt like crying. He wasn't sure why, he hadn't felt any sort of emotion in a long time, but now it was overwhelming and it raced out of him. His body began to shake involuntarily and he could feel the outer layers of his face shaking. Tears welled up and threatened to roll down his cheeks. He held his head up straight to hold them back.

The pretty receptionist was out of her depth. She smiled at him uncertainly, taking in his show of emotion.

"Eh, sir, I'm sorry, but I, well, I don't ..."

"But you have to help me ..."

"Well, I want to, maybe I could ..."

On cue a nerdy angry man in a slick suit approached, having watched the interaction from across the room. This de facto manager took his place beside the pretty brunette who immediately switched to her ice-cold work demeanour. He stared at Hunter as one does at a cockroach that's wandered into your living space.

"Everything OK here, Lily?" he asked coldly.

"Yes, sir, of course. This gentleman was just lost and he's now leaving."

She shot Hunter a warning look and he nodded inanely, careful to keep his head straight. She didn't owe him anything. He scraped away some of his tears and headed for the searing sun. He suddenly hated the sun and wished he could find a dark corner filled with blackness to curl up in and get lost in. Where was Delilah? He felt terrible. He had lost Sir Will's dog. Where were Grape and Sir Will? It was all fucked. He put his hand in his pocket and stroked the bills but there wasn't hardly anything left. The bundle was now slim and soft.

He had fucked up. He was never going to find Sophie Durango. He didn't even know where in Los Angeles she was. He hadn't wanted to admit that to anybody, not even himself, but he had no idea where he was going to go once he got there. He didn't even know if Sophie Durango was her real name. He had been too afraid to check in case she had been lying, or wasn't even from Los Angeles. He was trusting the fact that he had no choice, and as long as he didn't know then he could stay with the hope. Maybe he never even wanted to get there and was creating reasons to never get there. He needed to tell somebody about his dead mother.

He walked back to the motel quickly, refusing to get some water as a self-imposed punishment for losing Delilah.

Grape was sitting on the wall opposite the motel waiting for him. She didn't see him until his shadow gave her shade from the beating sun. She stood and without saying a word slapped him hard.

"Why did you leave us?" Her eyes were fire.

It didn't hurt, but the gesture stung.

"I don't know."

"Where is Delilah?"

"I don't know."

"What?"

"I don't know."

Grape was furious until she couldn't be any more furious. Then the fire died and she was disappointed. Her head hung in defeat and her body slumped a little. He preferred her fury.

"Sir Will had a panic attack. We came out and were told that you took Delilah. We thought you were back at the motel, but you were nowhere. You had all the money and the dog. Sir Will thought you had left without us. I told him that you would never do that. Would you do that?"

Her voice had softened, a little lost girl again, needing his reassurance. The companionship of Sir Will had given her some extra confidence, lifted her spirits and she had revelled in the subtle attention of the two young men. Now alone with just Hunter she was vulnerable again. Maybe she had just hidden it for a while. Hunter faced her. He felt jealous of her protection of Sir Will. The memory of the night was imprinted in his brain.

"Did you fuck Sir Will?" he said slowly.

"What??"

"Did you fuck Sir Will?"

"He's gay."

"So? He was grabbing your ass."

"Cos he's gay."

"Did you fuck him or not?"

"No."

Grape scowled, no longer the little girl, but a judged woman. Her eyes shone with passion.

"I wouldn't fuck him anyway."

"OK."

"Did you fuck that girl from Los Angeles?"

Hunter wasn't expecting her to turn that around onto him. He averted his eyes upwards, letting the sun create white spots in his pupils, then when it hurt too much he looked down at her. The pain made him dizzy and he tried to pretend that he hadn't heard her.

"Where is Sir Will?"

"He's gone to report that Delilah is missing. Do you know where she is?"

"No. She's lost."

He felt ashamed. There was nobody to blame but himself. He had fucked up. Maybe he should have left with Delilah and the money – he had that opportunity and he spurned it. Sophie Durango would have liked Delilah. Grape's pained eyes burrowed into his chest. It hurt. Dogs went missing all the time – what if they never found her again?

"I'm sure she's fine, they find dogs all the time," he said.

Hunter smiled as he spoke, not believing what he was saying. Grape looked doubtful, but she wanted to believe. She stood up, her soft body rearranging itself with gravity into something graceful. She looked more than a woman each day to him. He remembered the feeling of wetness, the warmth of her body, the rough nervousness. As if reading his thoughts, she scolded him.

"You should never have left us! That wasn't nice."

"I know. Sorry."

"We almost got into a fight. I was frightened. I thought you had left me."

"No."

"Did you think about leaving?'

"No."

She nodded, satisfied with his answer.

He wasn't really lying and it seemed to make both of them feel better. They fell into step together, Grape leading the way. He didn't ask if they had checked out of the motel – there were no possessions to pick up anyway apart from Grape's backpack with some clothes in it and it seemed she wasn't bothered about that. Grape had small feet but they seemed to glide across the ground sometimes like a dancing fairy, then she would get self-conscious about being elegant in the world and stumble. She didn't notice how light on her feet she was right now.

"He didn't tell me where he was going. He left in a rush, something about finding the police station. I don't know where that is."

"I guess if we walk we will find it."

"OK."

They walked like that for a while, aimlessly marching down block after block, eyes open for both Sir Will and Delilah and a cop station but secretly enjoying the silence. It was nice, just the two of them again. Hunter watched her out of the corner of his eye and as if feeling his gaze Grape muttered under her breath.

"Hunter and the Grape."

"Huh?"

"Just our names. The two of us on an adventure."

"Right."

She didn't seem that distressed about Sir Will and Delilah anymore. Maybe she was getting tired of his antics too, or last night had been too much for her. Then with joy he realised that Sir Will would have been too distraught over Delilah to do anything with Grape. He had prevented something happening. Why did he care though?

Sophie Durango. Sophie Durango. Sophie Durango.

He closed his eyes to picture her face, and tried to recall when he was inside of her. He could only remember Grape's warmth all around him. Fuck.

"Are you trying to remember where you left Delilah?"

Grape was watching him. He floundered.

"I lost most of the money."

She shrugged, as if she had already anticipated that, then said nothing more.

They walked up and down the strip until finally Hunter asked for directions and they found the police station.

Sir Will was outside it. Of course he was.

"Sir Will!"

Grape ran to him like a long-lost lover, arms outstretched gratefully, which irritated Hunter. Sir Will was sitting on the ground and didn't look up. His eyes were glazed and he appeared high.

Grape wrapped herself around him like a comforting blanket but his body was taut as a bow and didn't react. When Hunter stood over him, trying to conceal his own inner turmoil, Sir Will looked up. His eyes were blank. Nothing. What had he taken? He must be high. He had never looked this way. His face was pale and drawn, with some blood vessels spotting on the surface of his forehead. His acne was bad, eyes dry and empty, chapped lips ripped and bleeding. When he spoke his voice was weak and whispery. Was he dying?

"They have Delilah."

"Great! I knew we could find her."

"They've impounded her as a stray. They've already taken her away this morning. If I want her back then I have to pay a fine."

"A fine?"

"Yeah, man. A fine, and a fee to release her. Do you still have the money?"

Hunter hesitated but Grape looked at him, her wide cow eyes imploring. Sir Will emanated death. If they didn't get Delilah back he might just roll over and die. The thought vaguely fascinated Hunter. Would Sir Will die like the pigs and make some grunting death noises, or would he be silent like Hunter's mother and just roll over and sleep? He couldn't know unless it happened.

"Hunter?" Grape was firm.

He automatically wanted to fight it, to tell her to fuck herself. But she was right. She was getting a control over him.

"I'll go fix it."

Sir Will grabbed his leg as he made to move past, his pathetic fingers barely able to grip. Hunter stopped moving in case he broke the skinny hand.

"You're a true friend, Hunter."

The benign way that Grape clutched onto Sir Will like he was a small pet made it clear that nothing sexual had happened between them so Hunter could like Sir Will again. He reached down and squeezed the bony hand gently. He wondered would his hands be so clammy if he died. He shook away the thought and went inside the police station.

The money was light in his pocket, and when he took it out he was barely aware it existed in his hand.

"It's $600, son."

Hunter had $734. After this there was nothing. It was all his fault yet nobody was blaming him. The policeman took the money and gave him a form to sign. Hunter stated that he was the dog's owner. It was just easier that way rather than bring Sir Will in and have him explain the importance of his name. It didn't matter anyway, it was just a name. Then the office cop delivered the coup de grace to his day.

"You have to pick her up at the Moapa Valley pound."

"Huh? Why?"

"We send some big dogs there that's why, when there's no room here."

"Where is that?"

"Use a map."

"We don't have a car."

"I'm sure you'll figure it out."

People hated you when you didn't have any money. Hunter had always known that, but some things become more certain than others and knowledge isn't the same as experience.

Moapa was about 60 miles away. Hunter found it on the huge map covering the wall opposite the reception. The map was so big it must have been hiding something ugly behind it, bullet holes and the outline of a dead guy maybe. Why else have such a huge map stretching across the wall?

He walked outside to his friends, fingering the remaining money cautiously. He could lie and tell them that he had nothing left. Tell them that Delilah was expensive, maybe say that she bit somebody and that he hadn't lost her at all, in fact he was the victim in it all.

Sir Will's hopeful eyes scanned him for deceit. Hunter's muscles froze and he found himself hating the idea of himself.

"We have to go to Moapa. She cost over a $1000 bucks."

Sir Will chuckled. "She's an expensive dog, they must know how special she is."

Grape nodded in agreement.

"You have to pay for the best."

Were they both stupid? Hunter looked from one to the other, checking their reactions to see if they were mocking him. Nothing.

Sir Will got to his feet, with Grape supporting him. He was so frail. For the first time Hunter examined him. He really examined him, and noticed how thin he was. Not slender, but bony. He was a wisp of a human being. Nobody could survive being that thin for very long. Sir Will unrolled his spidery body into the warm healing air and stepped forward.

"Let's bring Delilah home."

Thirty-Three

How it was then was how it would never be again. Somebody might have said that once or he had read it and as Hunter stared out the window of the bus going in the opposite direction to Los Angeles he thought about what it meant. What would Sophie Durango think about it all? He wanted to tell her the story of the last few days. Or maybe he wouldn't and he would just forget that any of it had ever happened.

He looked behind him through the gap between the seats of the bus, twisting his neck awkwardly, to where Sir Will's head lay in Grape's lap. Her hand lightly stroked loose strands of hair away from his eyes. He had physically suffered incredibly in the 18 hours since Delilah had gone missing, to such an extent that Hunter struggled to quell the disgust he felt at his pathetic state of self-immolation. Or maybe his spirit was simply crushed because without Delilah he had nothing. Grape and Hunter were freshly passing spirits, transitory in nature to his world. Delilah was his only constant. But then neither Hunter nor Grape had anybody else in the world, so fuck his selfishness. Sir Will mumbled into Grape's knees, as if aware of Hunter's thoughts. Hunter turned away – the eyes were the entry to his soul but his scowl was obvious. Sir Will didn't seem to harbour any anger towards Hunter for losing the money or the dog. Hunter found himself hating Sir Will for that. Sir Will mumbled his wet mouth into Grape's grubby blouse. They all needed a wash and a change of clothes. It wasn't romantic anymore, it was disgusting.

"I found her as a puppy. She had been abandoned, left for dead in a bag in the street. Who would leave such a beautiful animal to die? My dad didn't want me to keep her, but he relented because of her spirit. She had a spirit he said he had never seen in any dog before because of her will to live. When I was kicked out it was like she understood me, she knew what I was going through. We are kindred spirits who have both suffered."

Hunter was tempted to remark that Sir Will's parents hadn't tried to kill him so it wasn't the same, but he held his tongue.

Sir Will's plaintive voice continued. "How much longer till we get there?"

"Maybe 45 minutes."

"I don't know what I would do without her ..."

"It'll be fine."

Grape stroked him and Sir Will stopped speaking to enjoy her tender affection. She would be a great mother someday, if a little crazy. Maybe you needed to be a little crazy to be a mother. Hunter wished that he could have seen his mother when she was younger. She would have been very beautiful, he knew. Not because of her physical looks but because she had a spark about her that electrified the air. The way that when you touch a metal surface sometimes an electric current passes through and surprises you. His mother would have been like that. Surprising and intangible and ultimately wild. His father had understood that. A heart attack had killed him suddenly but Hunter didn't remember much about his death. Life around that time became a blurry montage of moments, everything around them was blank. Whenever he tried to recall anything his head would hurt and clouds covered the remembered images. Sophie Durango would make everything alright. Grape touched his shoulder.

He glanced at her, keeping his mouth closed. She was close to him and his breath stank. He was hungry.

Grape was worried. "Sir Will is sleeping."

"So?"

"I don't want to wake him."

"Then don't."

"I need to move – my legs are sore."

Hunter stared at her for a moment longer than he should. Her lips were soft and full today, her eyes wide and vulnerable. He wanted to kiss her.

"Just move him off you. I doubt he'll even notice."

"He seems so delicate."

"Yeah."

Grape tried to shuffle her legs but stopped when Sir Will's head rolled on her knees.

"Do you think we'll get Delilah back?" she said.

"I'm sure."

"I don't care that much."

Hunter looked at Grape. Her face was tense, almost waiting to be chastised for not caring.

"Why don't you care?"

"She's just a dog. I had a dog once. It died. They all die, and they're usually trouble."

"Delilah was nice though. I thought you liked animals?"

"No. I don't like animals much. I thought I did. I used to like my uncle's pigs. Not anymore. I've changed my mind."

"You're allowed to do that."

"Don't tell Sir Will. I don't hate her or anything. I just don't care that much."

"I won't say anything."

"Thanks."

Grape stayed there, inches from his face, only the dirty gap between the seats separating them. He held his breath then had to finally exhale. When he inhaled he tasted her breath. Hers was also stale so he didn't feel so bad. She examined him, searching him for a reaction. Then she blushed but didn't break her gaze.

"I liked it."

"What?"

She sucked on her bottom lip.

"The other night, with you. I liked it. I want to do it again."

Hunter felt like a man. Here was a woman asking to do sexual things with him on a bus from Las Vegas. This was what life was all about. His cheeks flushed and Grape saw. Her eyes sparkled, a private conversation passing between them quietly. Then Sir Will moved in Grape's lap.

"Delilah," he mumbled.

He sat up, eyes wet and blurred, mouth hanging open like an idiot.

"Where's Delilah?"

Hunter hated him for breaking the moment. Grape

hugged him, stroking his hair back and let him nuzzle into her chest like a stupid baby. Hunter let his eyes drift out the window again. They were nearly there. He hoped they found Delilah, he liked that dog. He doubted if Grape really was so unconcerned. Maybe her uncle killing the pigs was affecting her. She had no idea how to fit in. Where did any of them fit in? He looked back at her. She cradled Sir Will, comforting him despite the discomfort to herself. Not many people were like that. He certainly wasn't. He shouldn't have left his mother like that. He hadn't even pulled the sheets over her face, just left her there. That was an odd thing to do. Would his father have been disappointed in him? What did her face look like now? Did that even matter?

The bus pulled off the freeway into the town of Moapa. Delilah had better be here – he couldn't stand Sir Will's whining anymore.

Thirty-Four

They clambered off the bus, Sir Will hanging off Grape like a ruined war survivor. Hunter took point, determined to get to their destination before annoyance swept over him and he helped Sir Will understand what real physical pain actually was. Sir Will kept delaying the party with some muscular complaint so their pace was slow. Grape was stoic as she helped him. Finally they approached a cheery animal shelter with cute paintings of cats and dogs on the outside walls. Like a creche. Sir Will gazed upon it with all the enthusiasm of coming upon a concentration camp.

"They put her here? Oh fuck, man, fuck, poor Delilah! She won't know what's been going on, fuck, this is awful."

"She's a dog, I'm sure she's fine."

Hunter couldn't help himself anymore. The paintings really were quite cheery. It was a pity that dogs couldn't see in colour and appreciate the vista on the walls. Sir Will stared at him, searching for betrayal.

"But this place, man, this place. My parents wouldn't

even send me here."

Whatever. Hunter ignored his pleas and marched into the little reception office. It was flanked by a small courtyard in the sun and an open patio guarded by a stone statue of the happiest dog to ever exist. The effect was calming and by the time he was facing the overweight receptionist he almost felt delighted to be there. There was nobody else around.

She lifted her heavy lids to the sky and examined him, nose crinkling. Her voice sang with the weight of alcohol and coffee.

"Can I help you, son?"

"I'm here to get a dog."

"That's a nice start. We do dogs."

"Great."

Hunter displayed the creased documents he had paid a precious sum for and pushed them under the woman's plump face. The folds of her skin dribbled down her skull with the mocking laughter of gravity. She hummed as she read the documents from cover to cover, even the index at the bottom when she really didn't need to. Maybe she wasn't really reading it all. Finally she scooped her rolling face back up at him, fingers heavily crushing the thin paper.

"And are you the owner of the dog, Delilah?"

"Yes. No. Well, sure."

"That doesn't sound very convincing to me?"

"I don't own her. Does anybody actually own a dog?"

"Every dog is owned by somebody. Unless it's illegal. You're not trying to illegally take a dog now, are you?"

Hunter shook his head, flapped a bit and stuck his head back outside.

"Sir Will, get in here."

He turned back with a shrug. She smiled at him like a benign cancer. Sir Will hobbled inside, making as much effort to appear like he was dying of a broken heart as was physically possible.

"Delilah? Is she here?"

"She might be, for her owner."

"Oh, ma'am, yes, I'm her owner. I'm Sir William Blake."

The fat woman stuck her tongue out roughly, letting it taste the freedom of tepid air, then swallowed it.

"Really?"

"Yes, ma'am."

"I'm Joan of Arc, nice to meet you."

Sir Will stumbled towards her, hyperventilating through a fresh monologue about the virtues of his fucking dog.

What was Hunter doing here? Why wasn't he with Sophie Durango in Los Angeles right now? This was all Sophie Durango's fault. If she had only waited for him. The fat woman held up her hand to silence Sir Will's pitiful moaning and caught Hunter's attention.

"I don't care about these wonderful stories of you and this dog. Just tell me who the owner is and you can take her."

"You mean she's here?"

"Yes."

Sir Will looked around frantically, expecting to see Delilah staring at them from some glass window, watching them like an episode of *Big Brother* and judging the state of Sir Will's love. He wouldn't let her down. He began yelling plaintively.

"Delilah! DE-LI-LAH?"

"Could you please make him stop?" the woman sighed.

"Sure."

Hunter walked towards Sir Will and slapped him. He hit him harder than he meant but Sir Will turned into the blow at the wrong time. It only connected with his cheek but the sound was deafening even if it far outweighed the force. Sir Will froze and stared at Hunter with tears in his eyes.

"Man?"

"Just chill the fuck out and we can get her. OK?"

"OK, man. OK. I'm sorry, man."

He turned to the fat woman to apologise but she held a chubby hand up remarkably quickly to stop him.

"It says here that the owner is Hunter."

"No, no, it's me. Sir William Blake."

"Fine. But the name on the form says 'Hunter'. Is he not the owner?"

"No. I am."

"Who is Hunter?"

"I am."

The fat woman was getting annoyed now.

"You're Hunter? But you don't own the dog?"

"No. He does."

"But your name is on the form."

"I paid for her release. Although it was partly with Sir Will's money."

"So your name is here, but you don't own the dog?"

"Technically yes and no, but it's not a big deal – it's his dog."

The fat woman licked her lips from the inside, sticking them out like a donkey, sneezed, then shrugged.

"I can only give the dog to the owner, and since you're not the owner then I can't give you the dog."

"But my name is on the form!"

"But you have said that it's not your dog, and that this

man here, Sir William Whatever, is the owner, but his name is not on the form."

"That doesn't matter."

"I don't have the jurisdiction to deal with this, it must be dealt with by the officer who signed these papers. So you will have to fix this with him and come back to me."

"That's in Las Vegas?"

"Fine."

"That's not fine. We just came from there."

"So go back. I'll still be here, so will your dog."

"This is ridiculous."

Sir Will watched the conversation back and forth between Hunter and the woman like a confused child, waiting for the pain to be over.

"Well, that's all I can do, I'm sorry. Now please leave."

"Seriously?"

"If you don't leave I'm going to call the cops. There's a button here at my hand. I press it and you all go to jail."

She held her hand just above the desk dramatically even though none of them believed her.

"I just want Delilah back. She needs me."

The fat woman scoffed at Sir Will.

"I'm sure Delilah can survive one more day without your companionship. She's a dog, they're very durable. Now please leave or I'll have to press the button."

Sir Will moved like liquid water. All the energy saved up in his body from barely moving for himself over the last 18 hours released in one movement and he propelled himself towards the door behind her leading to the dog kennels. His mouth was open in a giant 'O', but no sound came out, just the idea of his beloved's name.

"*Stop right now!*" the fat woman screamed hoarsely,

voice breaking, but he was already pushing through the door even as she jabbed her hand up and down on her imaginary panic button.

Hunter and Grape ran after Sir Will, not sure what else to do. The woman made a grab at Hunter, her weight knocking against his hips, but he skirted her like a pro footballer, proud of himself as he did so.

Sir Will fell as he burst through the doors, his legs confusing themselves and the initial burst of energy expended. Hunter picked him up and they scrambled across the floor, the fat woman following red-faced and exasperated.

"There she is! There she is!" Sir Will cheered.

Sure enough Delilah was sitting happily in the far cage, watching the commotion with veiled interest. When she saw Sir Will she stretched and wagged her tail, none the worse for wear. Sir Will literally fell upon the cage and tore at it with his feeble fingers. His harassed worry worked Delilah into a frenzy so she began frantically barking, setting off every other dog in the room. He finally succeeded in releasing the door clasp and Delilah tore through the door into Sir Will's arms and knocked his slim frame to the floor with her enthusiasm. He laughed with joy as she slobbered all over him, eyes welling up and even Hunter paused and felt something as he watched.

The fat woman caught up with them, her red face ready to burst, but she stopped when she saw the tears in Will's eyes. Then she snapped out of it and jabbed a finger in Hunter's direction.

"The cops are going to get all of you!"

She was about to continue but then Sir Will was beside her, and before she could react he embraced her lovingly, his charming voice whispering softly into her ear.

"Delilah is the only thing that I have in the world. Thank you for keeping her safe for me. I would die without her."

The fat woman began to shake, her fingers first, then her hands, then her entire body quivered. Sir Will beckoned Delilah over and she put her muzzle into the fat woman's hand reverentially as Sir Will clutched her.

"Nobody ever thanks me for looking after the dogs. They just, they're always so rude, like it's my fault ..." She trailed off.

"I know, ma'am, and I'm sorry if I was out of order. I wasn't myself without Delilah, I was quite lost. I appreciate what you do and your help."

The fat woman shrank before their eyes, letting herself sink deeper in the skinny man's arms. Her voice was small and lost.

"I didn't really contact the police, I just wanted to scare you. I have dogs. I love dogs. Most places don't care for them, but I do, that's why I try to take them from places like Vegas where they just don't care. I care, I love them all. People are so mean to their animals and just leave them in terrible places. I try to have a protocol to protect the animals."

"I know. I know."

Sir Will and Delilah clutched the woman between them and Grape held Hunter's hand and for a few moments everything was beautiful between them all.

Thirty-Five

Sir Will was something close to his old self. They sat on the wall across the street from the dog pound, hoping that the day would tell them what to do next. Sir Will walked along the wall on his toes like a circus clown, pulling faces introspectively. Delilah followed his every movement. Then when he had expended enough energy he sat down again, suddenly morose. He looked at Hunter.

"Thanks, man."

Hunter shook himself from the light daze he had melted into.

"For what?"

"You got Delilah back. You got us here, you did it all. I was all over the place, my head was a mess, I couldn't handle it. I'm ashamed. You took control."

"It was my fault."

"No, man, no. No blame ever, it just happened. Life happened. It was a test for all of us."

Hunter wished Sir Will would shut the fuck up

sometimes, and just agree that he had fucked up. The pseudo-hippy-everything-is-all-right attitude really pissed him off but he smiled anyway. At least Will wasn't moaning.

"I'm glad we got her back."

Sir Will clasped his shoulder, then Grape chimed in brightly.

"You guys should be blood brothers. We all should."

They looked at her, a beaming smile tearing her face apart as if it was the greatest idea that she'd ever had.

"Like in the movies. Blood brothers for life. It shows how we're all family."

"I don't know, Grape."

"Sure we should."

Hunter had always secretly wanted to do it. He pulled out his pocket knife. Grape moved to the ground between them, creating a secret circle and Delilah lay at Sir Will's feet with disinterest. Grape shivered with excitement as she outlined the rules.

"So we all cut ourselves on our palm until a drop of blood spills onto the ground, then we each press our bloody palms together, shaking hands. It makes us blood brothers. We share blood, like friendly vampires."

Grape nodded for Hunter to begin and he flicked the blade open, then pressed the sharp metal against his palm. He looked to Grape for encouragement. Cutting yourself was frightening because what if he cut too deeply? It was exciting at the same time though and he found his belly tightening. Then he closed his hand around the knife and sliced in and down. Pain seared through his arm and he winced but didn't make a sound. Grape's eyes penetrated his soul as she watched him, eager to make this commitment. The blood welled up in his palm and escaped gently. They all watched as he turned his palm to face the ground and a drop slowly detached itself and fell to the earth.

"My turn."

Grape took the knife from Hunter, took a deep breath and then quickly sliced into her hand. They could all feel the flesh rip, and Hunter was certain that she had cut too deeply. Her face flushed and went white. Then she opened her palm to reveal the long strip of blood decorating her skin. Drops quickly threw themselves to the earth chasing gravity and she looked up at Hunter. He nodded and they reached for each other like children disobeying social mores. Hunter's hand clasped Grape's, feeling the odd mixture of cold sweat and warm sticky liquid against his own slippery skin. They held hands tightly and let raw flesh rub flesh. He looked into her eyes and wondered was she imagining the same thing as he was. He half expected a rush of energy to pass between them or to see her thoughts but nothing happened. When they took their hands away the blood from both of them was smeared across their tender palms.

Grape laughed, rocked back on her heels and looked at Sir Will who had been forgotten. Grape offered him the knife with her clean hand. He stared at her for a long time without looking at the small blade hanging in the air, but looked at her, without feeling, just looking. Delilah flattened her head to the concrete. His voice was a floating whisper.

"I don't want to."

Grape scoffed at him, her eyes light.

"Oh, stop being a baby, it's just a little cut."

"No."

"You have to. Hurry up before the cuts dry up."

"I'm sorry, but no."

Grape looked hurt, her eagerness melting into insecurity.

"Don't you want to be blood brothers with us? Do you not like us enough?"

"Course, Grape man, but not now."

Grape flared with anger and grabbed Sir Will's hand to cut him herself. He reared up and away, his hand lifting away from hers but she was upon him, one hand on the knife, the other scrabbling for his palm.

"Gimme your hand, Sir Will!"

"Stop it, Grape, stop it!"

Grape wasn't going to be stopped. Her teeth were gritted in determination and she overpowered him through sheer force of will. Delilah thought it was a game and watched nonplussed on the ground until a flailing foot caught her on the head and she leapt away to safety. Grape got Sir Will's hand clear and raised the knife up as if she was about to skewer him in victory.

"Get the fuck off me!"

The force of his voice stopped her and in the moment of hesitation he kicked her off with his knee, pushing her onto the ground.

Sir Will sprang to his feet. His face twisted in pain and his mouth trembled.

"I don't want to do it, man – I don't want to fucking do it!"

Hunter opened his mouth to speak but Sir Will turned on him furiously.

"I might have a disease, alright? I might have a fucking disease. Yeah, yeah, let's talk about how I might have a fucking disease. Well, I fucking might, I just might, and that's just the fucking way it is."

Hunter was silent. Grape gathered herself off the concrete silently, holding her hand to her belly, the bloodied knife flung a few feet away.

Sir Will continued. "I slept with a guy, my friend – OK, we fucked, and we didn't use protection or shit. They say, they all say, you read it everywhere how you get diseases and shit if you do it with a guy, and it's in your blood. So I don't know, I might do, I just might, but maybe I don't but I don't know, man, I just fucking don't know. My dad said I did, he fucking said I had a disease now. He said lots of fucking things that I don't care about – but that thing he said, what if he's right? So I don't know, but it makes sense if I did cos that's how shit always happens. It always happens to the good people, right? The good people are the ones that life fucks up when it's bored and needs something to amuse it. Fuck Life. Fuck you, Life!"

Exhausted from this diatribe he slumped to his knees, head hanging low. Hunter moved to Sir Will and clasped his shoulder.

"It's cool. I doubt you have anything to worry about, but it's not a big deal. Forget what your dad said."

"How do you know?"

"I just do."

"But he said that everybody who was gay had a disease. What if he's right?"

"He's not. You're fine."

Grape nodded in support.

"And I won't tell Life what you said about her."

"Why is Life a 'her'?"

"Because she's too beautiful to be a man."

Despite himself Sir Will laughed. Grape moved to them and squatted down, and they hugged gently, the three of them.

"I'm sorry for being irrational. I just ..."

"It's OK."

"I really want to be a blood brother."

"No, you don't, it hurts like hell," Hunter said.

Grape nodded, clutching her hand tighter so that Hunter noticed.

"You OK?"

"Sure."

"Show me your hand?"

"No."

"Show me your hand, Grape."

Hunter's tone was soft but firm, exactly how Grape had wanted him to be. She gingerly held her hand out to him and he scowled. The knife had cut across the bottom of her palm when she had fallen.

"We need to get that bandaged."

"I'll be fine."

"No. You won't."

Sir Will looked aghast at Grape's torn skin.

"Grape man, I'm so sorry, I just ... oh man!"

Grape waved away his protestations.

Hunter got to his feet. How was it that he was taking charge? But he was because if he didn't then nobody would.

"Let's go eat."

He lifted Grape up and looked at Sir Will – maybe he had some great ideas like before to steal some food. But he was barely holding himself together as it was.

Grape held her hand back against her chest, wrapping it in the lower folds of her dirty blouse.

They needed to get to a pharmacy. They also needed clothes, food, a shower and sleep but they didn't have the money for all that and the bus to Los Angeles. Hunter sighed, aware of the staleness of the clothes on his skin. Food first. Everything else later. Sophie Durango flickered in his mind again, the sharpness of her features exciting him. He had to get back on track.

There was a Mexican a block away. They made their way there and sat down to order and eat in silence.

"Want some more?"

Grape was looking at him. "I don't want the rest of mine."

She offered her half-eaten burrito to him, pushing her plate across the table.

Sir Will picked at his food slowly. They hadn't said a word since they had sat down, too focused on eating.

Hunter looked at Grape and saw Sophie Durango.

"Want some more?"

Sophie Durango giggled as she spoke, her clever eyes winking at him every time she blinked. Her hand held out the fries. His mouth was full, cheeks bulging. He shook his head.

"I'm good."

"Sure."

The sun caught her eyes as she spoke and the world stopped. The coffee shop was full. Or was it empty? He wasn't sure. Details. Clouds. Sophie Durango reached out and grabbed his hand in hers. He was falling in love. She smiled then, a shy little girl's smile and his chest filled.

"Hunter?"

Sophie Durango never called him Hunter. Grape waved her hand in front of his face. Her eyes were wide and unblinking. He smiled at her but she knew what he was thinking.

"So what should we do now, blood brother?"

Her voice emphasised 'blood brother' to remind him. It was whatever he wanted it to be though. He cleared his throat but it felt heavy. How can your throat feel heavy? Grape's eyes were big and wide and blue. Very blue. His mother's eyes had been blue. They had never faded even when her spirit had waned against the fetid air of life that surrounded her. He had to be honest with them.

"I need to go to Los Angeles."

Grape nodded, refusing to show her disappointment.

"Delilah has always wanted to go to Los Angeles, isn't that right, girl?" Sir Will chimed in.

Delilah lapped the air feverishly, hoping to catch somebody's skin, and slapped her tail against the ground.

"I don't know if I want to go to Los Angeles." Grape spoke firmly, enunciating each word clearly, eyes set on Hunter.

He looked away. "Let's get some sleep first. I'm tired."

"No. Let's get the bus back to Vegas today. No time like the present – otherwise we're just wasting our time," Grape countered.

She started eating the rest of her burrito with her injured hand, chomping on each mouthful with a slow certainty, not showing any pain. Hunter didn't care. Her eyes didn't wink at him like Sophie Durango's.

Sir Will looked at him, certain that he was missing something important, then gave up. They all looked in different directions and had different thoughts.

Thirty-Six

Las Vegas was upon Hunter. The air seemed heavier today. They had found Delilah but now Grape felt like a weight around him. There was too much going on, too many people, too much distraction wherever he looked. Even through the glass of the window it was overpowering. Was Las Vegas always this way, pulling you into initial ecstasy then killing you after?

The bus groaned into the depot and Delilah leapt forward, Sir Will behind her. They had sat at the front of the bus, with Grape and Hunter taking the last available double seats near the back. They could see Delilah's tail whacking the floor throughout the short journey but Sir Will never looked back to them, lost in his own head space. Hunter waited for Grape to get off, staying in the seat as long as possible, his limbs heavy. Eventually he slipped off the bus to confront her standing deep in the crowd, head turning frantically left and right. Hunter joined her. His teeth felt fuzzy, maybe he should buy a toothbrush. He wanted a shower before getting on another bus. It was only 7 hours to Los Angeles, but his feet were itchy and the skin on his inner thighs was chaffing.

"Where did he go?" Grape spoke aloud, more to herself.

"Who?"

"Sir Will. He's not here. *Sir Will! Where are you?*"

People milled around like flustered butterflies, changing direction with the moving winds of the crowd. If you stood still the pack would break around you as a rock in a stream. Once you moved you were accosted. Sir Will must be somewhere in the crowd. Maybe he had joined the stream.

Grape cupped her hands together and yelled across the depot. "*Sir Will! Delilah!*"

People looked at her but she didn't care and nobody told her to stop. Hunter stood by patiently.

"*Sir Will! Delilah! Sir Will!*"

Nothing. Grape licked her lips, walked to a bench a few feet to the right against the wall and sat down to examine the faces of the world passing by. After a few moments Hunter followed her.

"Guess we have to just wait until he comes back."

Hunter knew he wasn't coming back. He knew Grape knew it too but they would have to wait it out. Minutes passed, then more minutes and then they had been sitting there for an hour, just the two of them, Hunter and the Grape, waiting for the strange boy who had left them.

"He's not coming back," he said.

"I know."

"Then why are we still sitting here?"

"I'm waiting for you to leave too."

"Why would I leave?"

"Because you're going to Los Angeles and everybody always leaves me. I expect it, but I'm OK with it. I'm used to it."

"We're blood brothers," he said, half-hearted.

She looked back at him, eyes steady.

"Sir Will didn't do it so it doesn't count just between us."

He held up his palm to show her the dried scab that proved otherwise but she had turned her attention to the strangers floating past.

They were silent for a while. Hunter was aware of a slight pulsing in his belly – he would need to pee soon but if he got up and left he might never see Grape again. They both knew it. The moment he let her out of his sight she would disappear forever.

"I have to go to Los Angeles."

"I know. You've said."

She held herself with a straight-backed elegance when she was upset, her ungainly awkwardness replaced by a steely grace.

"Are you still coming with me?"

"No."

"Please."

"Why?"

Why did he want her to come? Maybe he just didn't want to be alone, he had gotten used to having company, having friends. It was a nice feeling that he didn't want to lose. That must be it. He blamed the loneliness.

"Because you're my friend. I don't have any friends."

"Where is your family?"

She turned into him, wide stern eyes affixed on his reaction, appraising his pauses, seeing into his brain. He met her gaze even though he hated it.

"Why?"

"You've never told me anything. Tell me."

"Albuquerque."

"Do you want to go back?"

"No."

"Why did you come with me to the old man's house?"

"I don't know. Why did you go there?"

"Because I wanted to," she said defiantly.

He nodded and licked his lips which she studied. Then he began talking. It seemed as good a time as any to be honest with her.

"My mom is dead. She died on the day I left. I found her on the bed. She wasn't breathing. I didn't know what to do and I didn't really care anymore. So I left."

"That was the day we met?"

"Yeah."

Grape wasn't in the mood for a sob story and her hard eyes informed him of that.

"My uncle killed himself."

"You don't know that."

"Yes, I do."

"We saw him drive away – we don't know what he did."

"I do. It's what he wanted. He was crazy."

"I was there too, I saw him, but I don't know if he wanted to kill himself."

People pushed around them uncomfortably close, legs, feet, hips, bags, faces. A lady stumbled into them, her feet too slow for her flustered brain, her elbow hitting Hunter on the back of the head but he hardly felt it.

Grape's eyes bored into him like a heavy drill.

"He told me he was going to kill himself. When I first went in. It's the first thing that he said to me."

Hunter wasn't expecting that.

"Why didn't you tell me, I was there."

"Just because you were there doesn't mean that I owe you anything. You know nothing about me."

"OK."

Grape seemed on the verge of shouting – her face was going red and she bit her lip so hard it began to bleed.

"Where is your dad?" she asked abruptly.

"Dead."

"You have any brothers or sisters?

"Nope."

Grape didn't blink but her wide eyes softened a little and she stopped biting her lip. Hunter stared right back at her. He wasn't sure what he felt.

"I'm sorry about your mom," she said at last.

"It's cool. I'm sorry about your uncle."

"Is she still there?"

"Where?"

"Where you left her?"

"Maybe. I guess."

"That's weird."

"Maybe."

"You should go back to her."

"Why?"

"She's your mother."

"I don't want to."

"You have to."

"I don't have to do anything."

Grape nodded, sighed, closed her eyes, exhaled and her little body shivered. Hunter watched as she then took his hand in hers, pressing their blood-brother hands against each other, the scabs scraping a little, the large Band-Aid strip on her wound rough. She didn't do anything with it, she just held it. He felt detached, floating above these two people having a strange conversation about death. Still strangers until a moment ago. People looked at them as they walked by. One man approached to sit and rest his weary frame but their intensity unnerved him and he hesitated, hovering just outside their sphere, then moved on.

Hunter examined the faces of all the people who passed by, the ones who stared at them, and the ones who ignored them. They were all the same. Cliches, stereotypes, faces from a million television programmes, adverts, historical events. Different races, shapes, sizes, but all the same. All bustling through Las Vegas in a search for their own unoriginal story to add to their meagre life that wasn't even lucky enough to be a footnote in the sprawling womb of the world.

Hunter and Grape were the two most important people in this universe right now. They were different. He felt it. He wasn't sure if he cared either way but he felt it and that was important. Special. Grape didn't speak and she watched with clinical bemusement as tears began rolling down his cheeks, leaving little tracks on his skin where they crept through the dirt. He didn't stop staring at her and she didn't move, just held his hand as the tears let themselves out. Once they came he didn't feel anything, just an awkward fascination with it all. His tears made it less real and that was nice. Crying in a public place had never made sense to him – his father wouldn't have approved. Never fall in love, he had said. Never care. Tears were the sole reserve of women and children. The last time he had cried was before his father died. He hadn't cried when his father had died. Clouds and pictures. He had kept his feelings bottled up because he knew that was what his father would have wanted. He hadn't cried in years and years and years. Now all the tears that had been stored and dried up and restocked flew down his sullen cheeks like a giddy spring waterfall, wet and eager.

The last time he had cried had been when Tommy Giddings smacked him from one side of the street to the other. His father watched it all through the window from inside the house and let it happen. Hunter hadn't hit him back, just cried and cried and cried. His father watched him sit on his ass on the wet ground crying little children's tears as Tommy had laughed and laughed and kept hitting him like a cat playing with a mouse. Then when Tommy got bored and walked away his father had still let him sit there, his tears mingling with the wet ground. Eventually Hunter stumbled home to find his father sitting in a chair watching from the window. He didn't say anything, but Hunter knew he had been watching the entire time.

"Clean yourself up," his father had said calmly.

He never cried after that. He would always remember his father sitting stoic in that chair, limbs stiff and unmoving, face impassive, as if even his blood was still, pausing its ritualistic beat to allow its host this uninterrupted quiet.

But as he sat there opposite Grape he couldn't picture his father on the chair because to do so would mean picturing his house and he couldn't go back inside his house in his mind because his dead mother was lying there and he couldn't bear to go back. He had to move forward to Los Angeles and to Sophie Durango. He had to fall in love, prove his father wrong. Then he could return and bury his mother, do so many things. If he still wanted to. Maybe he wouldn't want to. He knew that his soul screamed with desire for him to forget it all. Nothing mattered if it wasn't there. Everything is nothing. The tears were beginning to make his face itchy.

"You're lucky."

Hunter stopped crying, probably because there was nothing left to cry. He looked into Grape's deeply cut eyes. Blue. He liked blue. Everybody likes blue though.

"What?" he asked.

"I never knew my parents. You're lucky."

"Why?"

"At least you feel something for your parents, good or bad. My mother died when I was born. Giving birth to me. Nobody knew who my father was. Nobody cared enough to find out. My uncle looked after me. Nobody cared if he did or not, so he did. It made no difference to anybody else. Nothing I've done has ever made any difference to anybody."

"I'm sorry."

"It doesn't matter. My uncle always told me that the only person who will look after you is yourself."

"Do you believe that?"

"Perhaps."

Hunter's palm was sweaty, suddenly self-conscious. Grape looked out into the crowd, challenging them. Her voice was controlled, like her face. A woman. She gripped his hand.

"I'll come to Los Angeles with you," she said to the crowd.

"Why?"

"Because I've decided to come."

"OK."

"To help you find that girl."

"OK."

That was it. They were going to Los Angeles, Grape wasn't going to leave and Hunter was going to find Sophie Durango. Sophie Durango. Her name rolled off the tongue. He was glad that he had cried now and not in front of Sophie Durango. Now it was out of his system and he vowed to not let it happen again. His belly hurt and he needed to pee.

He stood up and she scrambled to her feet too.

The universe parted for them as they walked to the bathrooms. People skipped around them, eyes averted for fear of Hunter's tearstained face becoming a part of their own reality. He didn't care because Grape didn't care and there was something powerful about that. He was somehow glad that Sir Will and Delilah had gone. He hoped that they would be alright, but it wasn't his business anymore. Sir Will had made his own decision to leave and that was that. Thinking about it wouldn't change the reality of it. If they came upon him again then it would be different but now it was just Hunter and the Grape again. Now they would go to Los Angeles and find Sophie Durango. All he had to do now was figure out where to look. He read somewhere that Los Angeles had over 10 million people stocked through its veins. He wasn't sure if that was accurate but he had some searching to do. Until now he hadn't considered how he was going to do that, he had just assumed that it would happen, but when Sir Will had disappeared he became aware that he had no way of finding him again. What if Sophie Durango proved just as elusive? He pushed the thought from his mind and focused on Grape's hand on his. Blood brothers. It was something that his mother would have done. Stupid and romantic and his father would never have approved.

Thirty-Seven

Los Angeles. The home of Sophie Durango. Los Angeles was everywhere. Sophie Durango somewhere within. He could taste the soft metallic texture of the air, hear the gentle drone of surrounding traffic, feel the pulsing beat of optimistic souls in his fingers. It was intoxicating. The heat wasn't overpowering like Albuquerque in the summer but dry with a cooling breeze from the sea. Hunter had never seen the sea. How far away was it? Grape stood beside him in a reverie of her own. The bus hadn't left them anywhere interesting, unless bus depots hold a hidden secret, but they were here, in the city. Grape had no reason to care about it, but even she felt it: that something in the air that only certain big cities have. An intangible electricity that wrapped around you like a gentle voyeur, teasing and probing and whispering sweet possibilities into your ear like a playful lover.

"I want to see the sea." Grape spoke softly, afraid to break the spell on them both.

"Me too. Let's find the sea first."

"I want to walk in, up to my waist so my feet look transparent and fake like in the movies."

"Let's do that."

Hunter walked out on the street and looked around him. He had no idea what to do next so finding the sea first seemed like a good starting point. He stood staring down the yawning boulevard, Grape a few feet behind him. Then a yellow cab waiting for needy travelers spotted them and pulled up alongside, glass rolling down as it stopped. The stern face of a young man old beyond his time stared out at him through the open window. His left hand was draped casually across the steering wheel, the roots of a tree each ending in a name sprawling across his wrist and finishing on each finger.

"You need a taxi, eh?"

The man spoke with a thick accent, a heavy inflection on each word and his eyes were loaded with darkness. Hunter nodded slowly, perturbed by the man's intensity. Opening the passenger door for Grape first, just like he'd seen in the films of his childhood, he spoke to the driver as he clambered into the back.

"We want to go to the sea."

The man grimaced at them.

"The sea – to see what, eh?" He chuckled at his own joke.

"Just the sea."

"You want see the beach, eh?"

"No, the sea, the real sea."

The man stared at Hunter then broke into a soft grin.

"You never see the sea before, eh?"

Hunter shook his head and Grape did the same when the

268

taxi man cast his eyes over to her. His eyes lingered on her for a few moments, poring over her breasts and having those illicit thoughts that dangerous men have over gentle women. She shifted her hips against the hard seat and he twitched as if she had rubbed her ass against him and not the seat.

Hunter broke the spell by closing the door loudly. The man looked at him with a soft grin that was bewitching and terrifying at the same time.

"Off to see the sea eh? Let's go see it then, eh."

He laughed to himself and took off, another speck in the city's arteries.

They weren't actually that far from the sea, the bus depot having left them near the bottom of downtown.

The taxi driver drove in an absolute fury, muttering threateningly in exasperation at his own terrible driving, switching to his native language to curse roughly.

Grape didn't care, her eyes fixated on the city streaking past her.

"Where's the stars?"

"What stars? You said you want sea? Stars is at nighttime, eh."

"The stars in the street."

"The Hollywood stars, eh?"

"Yes."

"In Hollywood, eh. This is downtown, we go to Venice, eh."

"What's Venice?"

"The place that people who don't know where to go end up at to see the sea, eh."

The man laughed to himself and began to sing a made-up tune of going "to the sea to see the sea cos that's where the sea will be if you see what I see". Despite its bad lyrics and lack of a discernible beat Hunter found himself humming along and then it became an impromptu singsong. The man grinned at him with his cloaked eyes, and Grape joined in. Grape couldn't sing but she gamely destroyed the made-up high notes.

"Where you from then, eh?"

"Albuquerque. You know it?"

"Ah yes, eh, yes. I been there. I from Russia, eh."

"Russia?" Grape's eyes widened at the mention of such an exotic place. "Russia is so far away," she said.

"Yes, yes, yes, it is – you know Russia, eh?"

"I've heard of it. It's always in the James Bond movies."

"Ah yes, Bond, James Bond, ha eh, ha. Mother Russia, she doesn't want me anymore."

"Your mother – why?"

"No, Mother Russia – she is my country, but she doesn't like me."

"Oh. What happened for you to upset an entire country?"

The Russian stared at Grape, even as he changed lanes and broke the speed limit on the freeway. His eyes slit darkly and looked aggressively pained. Grape held his gaze in that unassuming way she had that was so attractive and made men confused as to whether they wanted to fuck her or protect her from the world.

"I did bad things. Things I can't take back. Now Mother Russia has aborted me. I am the child she wishes didn't happen. I am her mistake."

"What did you do?"

The Russian licked his lips, then hesitated, suddenly vulnerable.

"I was an addict. I did heroin. I did speed balls of heroin.

Many balls. Every day. For a long time, eh, and it fucked me up, fucked me up many times cos I had to do bad things to get my fix, you know, eh – it's not cheap, eh, it's not cheap at all. In Russia if you get caught they do bad things to you. If you don't get caught you're a god."

"Did you get caught?"

"Not for many times, eh."

"But then you did eventually?"

The Russian's eyes sparkled. "I got caught but they didn't catch me, eh."

"What's heroin like?"

He became very serious and for a moment forgot that the road existed, it seemed.

"It's like bad things. Imagine many bad things rolled into a ball. That's heroin. All the bad things I did in life come from heroin. Bad things happened. You don't let heroin into your life – she's a devil, eh."

The taxi turned off onto Lincoln approaching Venice and the Russian stopped talking, maybe remembering the old times, both good and bad. Grape looked back out the window. Los Angeles seemed so sweeping and grand. Billboards for television shows and movies peered down upon them with judgement, daring them to not want to be there alongside them. Join us up here they seemed to whisper, we know you want to.

Hunter felt uncomfortable. How would he find Sophie Durango in a place like this? She had seemed so close and now was beginning to feel distant again. Maybe he never actually expected to get here, but now that he was here he had to find her. If he didn't then where was he going to go? His belly tightened and he felt cold. What if he couldn't find her, what would he do then? The thought was too grave to contemplate.

The taxi drove along Lincoln through Mar Vista and suddenly there it was, the horizon visible on their left, then the marina and the blue waters dancing back at them.

Grape whispered to him. "The sea ... there it is ..."

"Fuck, wow."

The Russian spotted their awe and laughed at them. A big heavy laugh.

"Ah yeah, eh, the sea, eh. She's a beautiful mistress, the sea. She can teach you many things. Can you swim, eh?"

"Yes," Grape said quickly.

Hunter looked at Grape in surprise – how could she swim? He certainly didn't doubt it. Grape would only say that she could do something if she actually could, but for some reason he hadn't expected her to be able to.

The sun framed her profile in the window, the wind lifting her hair around her face in tempting circles. He wanted to feel her hand around him again, to feel the warmth of her wet softness, the tender shiver of her lips against his. But he was in Los Angeles now, too close to Sophie Durango and Grape wouldn't understand. He couldn't do that to her. Even in his naive state he knew enough to know not to do that. That didn't mean he couldn't be tempted in his mind.

As the taxi approached the beach, it slowed to let Grape stick her head out the window, arching her back as she did. Hunter stripped her in his mind. The Russian did the same. Neither spoke but gazed at her curved body with admiration. Maybe she was aware of it or maybe she wasn't, but she closed her eyes and drank in the smell of the sea on her skin, the light smattering of salt that was carried on the wind. Seagulls swept overhead in that languid commanding way of theirs and she giggled, overcome with the joy of freedom that the sea offers. Freedom and possibility. The men were drunk with the possibility of sex and for a moment it was all the same and they were all happy.

The Russian pulled up along 18th Ave, parking directly in front of the beach. Grape got out slowly, the blue of the sky melting into the sea rendering her speechless. It was a warm soft perfect day in LA, the day that makes movies span generations if captured on celluloid. She swayed towards the beach, stepping across the walkway and then onto the hot sand. She took her time, removing her shoes slowly, then her socks. Her bare feet accentuated the soft curves of her legs enticingly.

Hunter remained in the car with the Russian, both enjoying her enjoyment.

Then the Russian turned his eyes to Hunter.

"Girlfriend?"

"Huh?"

"She is your girlfriend, no, eh?"

"Oh. No. I don't know."

"A man should know, eh."

"I don't."

"You're not a smart man. A smart man knows when something should be his, eh."

Hunter found himself getting irritated with the Russian but the man's eyes were soft and he calmed himself.

"How much money do you got, eh?"

"Are you going to rob me?"

"Ha! No, you don't have enough to rob, eh, you're too poor to rob, haha! No, tell me, eh, I'm just curious."

"Enough."

The Russian smiled at Hunter's defensive reaction, then his smile hardened.

"Take care out here. It's not a good place for people like you that know nothing. It eats people up, people like you, and her. She most of all. This place loves girls like her, and without you she won't last very long. Trust me."

"We'll be fine."

"Maybe. Maybe not. But just because you think something doesn't mean that it's true. Even if you hope for something, that doesn't mean that it's real, eh."

"What are you talking about?"

"You know what I mean. Think about my words. This taxi ride. It's free. It's my gift to you, my gift to help you. From Mother Russia. But people don't give gifts out here. They want something, eh."

"What do you want?"

The Russian smiled and Hunter knew he could have whatever he wanted and had done so before. This man's secrets were darker than the night. He pulled down the neck of his sweater to reveal clutches of snakes pouring up his neck as if understanding Hunter's thoughts.

"I used to take what I want when I needed it, or even when I didn't. Now I don't. I don't need anything. I have a son, he's all I want. Another time I would want her. And your money. Yes, eh, and I would have her, but now, no. Now I feel something else, eh, and I am only telling you this to help you. Listen, learn and be careful what people tell you. Even me, eh, don't believe me because on a different day I might have lied to you and taken everything that you have in this world. People have colours and they change day by day, eh."

Hunter nodded and the Russian smiled like the father he was. His eyes were more mysterious than threatening now.

"You're a nice boy, nice and smart. Be smart. Go run onto the beach and forget anything I said until tomorrow, eh. Today go and be free and be happy that you're free and can run along the beach if you want to. But tomorrow remember what I told you."

The Russian cancelled the meter and put his hand out. Hunter shook it, feeling the man's strength pumping through his veins. They held the shake for a moment, then Hunter let go and got out of the car to follow Grape onto the sand. The Russian honked his horn and she turned slowly to wave at him, the sun back-lighting her like a film star against the deep blue of the sky.

The sea beckoned behind them, and they turned into her embrace. Walking through the soft sandy grains neither spoke but kept their gaze fixated on the sea. It was so beautiful. Cresting waves broke onto the shore like a living painting. The horizon rolled out beyond to touch the sky with its fingers. Everything seemed possible. Sophie Durango. He was here. He was here and he was going to find her, but first he had to let the sea roll over his feet and feel the pleasure of freedom.

He took off his socks and shoes, rolled up his jeans and caught up with Grape who had walked a few feet ahead. She smiled back at him and continued drifting to the sea. Nobody else on the beach existed as they made for the Pacific, eyes fixated on her gentle lapping mouth. Gulls and indignant little birds scattered out of their way begrudgingly. Then suddenly the sea was upon them. They watched the first wave approach their feet in slow motion, then its cold hard wetness flowed over their feet and whispered against their naked ankles. Magic. They both felt it.

"Hunter and the Grape," she whispered.

"Hunter and the Grape."

"We found the sea."

"Yeah."

"Do you miss being called Cat?"

"Do you miss being called Star?"

Grape smiled at him and he smiled back, then without warning she pushed him playfully. Off balance he fell to his knees in the water but before he could leap back at her she was stripping off her skirt and blouse and throwing them back onto the sand. In seconds she stood there in her sensible underwear, a soft vision of curves and lonely loveliness. She giggled shyly then ran at the sea violently, chasing the spray as it whipped up around her. She didn't stop when the water was up around her waist, she only slowed a little and kept moving, the water swirling up around her. It was at her chest before Hunter had removed his own clothes and bounded after her. He screeched as the cold water hit his balls and sent shivers through his spine, then he reached her and dived towards her little frame. She saw him too late and they tumbled under the water, cold filling their heads and salt rearranging the taste in their mouths. He wrapped his arms around her waist and pulled her through the liquid with him. Surfacing with a scream Grape smacked water towards him in mock rage. He retaliated and then they were tossing and turning through the sea's glassy surface like puppies on an adventure. The sea seemed to get warmer the longer he was inside it and Hunter forgot about anything else but these moments. The moments when they splashed half naked in the sea like two errant children whilst people on the beach watched with jealousy and shame that it wasn't them prancing through the water with their lover.

Thirty-Eight

The sun quickly dried their bodies but the wet underwear clung to them for much longer. The absurdity of not having any changes of clothes or even enough money to get new ones made Hunter smile. But it was a resentful little smile of reality. They had $87 between them. That wasn't going to last very long. Grape lay back in the sand, arms outstretched, making a protective sand angel.

"What's your wish in life, Hunter?"

"What do you mean?"

"What do you wish for above everything else?"

He considered her words. Everything was relative to the moment.

"Money. I wish for money, to not have to think about it."

"Hmmm."

"What's yours then?"

"To be happy. To just be happy. To feel as happy as I do now forever. Isn't that all there is?"

"I guess."

"I think if you decide to be happy then, you are."

"Hmmmm."

Grape squinted at the sun, then sat up and looked at the sea again as if it might evaporate and disappear from her life forever if she looked away for too long.

"What's her name?"

"Who?"

"This girl – I've forgotten her name?"

Hunter didn't respond immediately, he knew that she hadn't forgotten, but Grape waited for him, staring protectively at the sea and eventually he responded, the words catching in his throat.

"Sophie Durango."

Grape repeated the name to herself quietly. Hunter felt as if he had betrayed them both.

"Is she beautiful?" she asked blandly.

"I guess."

"She either is or she isn't."

"Yes, she is then."

"That's good."

"Why?"

"Because every woman should be beautiful."

Hunter looked away and scraped some grains of sand off his arm where they had stuck between the hairs.

"Why do you want to know?"

"I'm curious. You came all the way to Los Angeles to find her and I came with you so I want to know what she's like. Tell me about her. Tell me about her when the sun is warm and my feet are wet from the sea and I won't get jealous."

"Why would you get jealous?"

Grape turned to him but said nothing, just looked at him until he couldn't hold her gaze and he had to look away.

He spoke to the sand at his feet, with Grape listening if she wanted to. She leaned her head on her arm, eyes closed, sun on her face as he spoke about her. She didn't bat an eyelid or scrunch her face and tighten her fists. She felt nothing because to her, right now on the sand in the sun by the sea, Sophie Durango didn't exist and never would. Later she would tear at her hair, let wetness blur her eyes, feel a pain in her chest and attribute it to everything other than what is was but right now she was too happy to be unhappy over anything. The beauty of Hunter's honesty with her almost overpowered the nature of what he was talking about.

"She's got brown hair, light brown, with a little bit of red. And small pretty bright eyes that seem to look through everything, but not just look, they sort of, I don't know, dance through everything. She's small and thin, with long fingers and soft lips."

Hunter trailed off. What else could he say? He wasn't going to mention the feel of her breasts in his hands or the taste of her mouth. He had described her sort of similar to Grape in a way, but also in a way somebody the complete opposite.

"What's she like?"

"Like I just said."

"As a person. Is she happy or sad?"

"I don't know."

"Why not?"

"I just don't … happy, I guess."

Grape didn't ask anything more and Hunter didn't offer. Sophie Durango was hard to describe. In his mind she was clear but in words she made little sense, a translucent mirage that he couldn't catch with prose. Clouds and pictures. Besides, whenever he remembered Sophie Durango he was merging her with Grape. He needed to see her again, to remind himself of what he thought he knew.

"She sounds lovely."

Hunter knew that Grape didn't mean that, but it didn't matter what Grape thought.

"Maybe I'll fall in love in Los Angeles like you."

"I'm not in love."

"If you came all the way to Los Angeles then you're in love, Hunter."

Grape said things sometimes that surprised him. The sun warmed her belly and she turned over to let it heat her ass and back. Staring at the roundness of her ass in the air made him uncomfortable so he looked out at the sea. Sophie Durango, where was she? How was he going to find her now that he was here? He had to find her or Grape would judge him, even if she was judging him silently anyway. It all felt so difficult all of a sudden, difficult and confusing. Why was he so obsessed with Sophie Durango? Was he in love or not? He could be. Grape's ass wiggled a little as she moved in the sand to get comfortable. What had the Russian seen that he didn't? The seagulls drifted overheard lazily and he wished he could fly like they did, simple and carefree above the ocean.

"I'm hungry."

"You're always hungry."

He threw some sand at her playfully and she giggled in mock disgust then threw some back. He grabbed at her and fell off balance half on top of her. They grappled for a while, until he was on top of her, pressing her arms behind her head into the sand in rough play fighting. He stopped, breathless, his naked belly against hers, painfully aware of the slender nature of the fabric of their underwear between them. She opened her mouth just a little, letting her breath slap against his mouth. The gulls circled overhead silently and the only noise was the gentle lapping of the waves behind them. Hunter didn't say anything but slowly lifted himself off her. Grape laughed out loud, too loud. Hunter looked away and began to get dressed, the beach his own private room. He felt sad. When Grape did the same there was something slightly lewd about it and Hunter jealously caught every passing man's eye who wandered past, even trying to outstare the surfers who watched her as they drifted on dying waves. Grape took her time getting her clothes on, teasing her sexuality both for him and for anybody who cared to watch. There had been a moment and he had let it pass and now she wasn't his anymore, if she ever had potentially been.

When she was fully clothed they wandered along the beach, strolling up onto the boardwalk that ran from Marina Del Rey up into Santa Monica. The energy was palpable. Homeless people decorated the street and the beach running alongside it like they were part of it, melding into the dirty sand like fixated territorial guardians. Hunter got some stark glances off some of them and one muttered disgustedly to him even as he pushed a shopping cart with his belongings across the cracked concrete.

"Why didn't you call me? You promised to call me, boy."

Hunter was about to respond but the man had already carried on walking, trying to accost the next person within range. Grape strode a few feet ahead of him, bare feet slipping across the ground like a dancer. She seemed to fit here, like an easy piece in a jigsaw. Everywhere there were musicians and painters along the beach opposite shops and bars. It felt alive.

They stopped to buy some juice and sandwiches without talking, then ate them on a bench beside a tanned man with long dreads playing bongos. His dog held a cup for donations around his neck. He carried the same air as Sir Will might, if Sir Will lived that long. Hunter doubted he would. The air was thick with uncertainty.

"You guys smoke?"

The bongo player was staring at them. Or at Grape. She nodded.

"Cool, man, cool. You wanna smoke with me? Get a little high?"

Grape nodded again. The man pulled out a little bag of weed and some skins and began to roll openly, doing it on his knees with short quick flicks of his wrist, the joint finished in a few moments. Grape and Hunter moved closer to him, he lit it, took a slow drag and stuck it in Grape's mouth.

"You're going to enjoy this shit – it's mellow, man."

"My uncle grows the smoothest stuff."

"Oh yeah?"

"Yeah. He's dead now."

"Shiiit, man, sorry."

"It's OK."

"You kids just get here?"

"Yeah, today."

"Fresh off the boat?"

"No, we got a bus."

"Yeah, man, exactly."

Hunter took the joint off Grape and used it as his cue to muscle in on the conversation. The bongo player looked at him with a cracked smile, broken teeth winking at him from odd angles.

"Good joint, man," Hunter said, trying to be cool.

"What you kids doing in LA?"

"Stuff."

The hippy nodded, then flicked his eyes back to Grape.

"Lot of kids come here to do 'stuff'."

"Yeah?"

"Yeah. Never works out. You gotta have a plan, man, be the man with the plan!"

He tapped his head as he inhaled, reinforcing the plan idea, then taking a long toke off the joint he began playing the bongos again. His hands whipped up and down in a blur of chaotic energy with no discernible purpose but it was still soothing.

Hunter lay back on the grassy sand, letting the bass of the beat rumble in his bones and the weed take over his senses. He was here, in Los Angeles, and tomorrow he was going to find Sophie Durango. The thought scared him. It was real now but what if she didn't want to see him? She hadn't waited for him. He had dismissed any fears about that before, excusing her and blaming himself. Now a tendril of doubt wormed through his skin. He felt uncomfortable. The weed was strong and his vision was blurring. He felt dizzy. No. Sophie Durango wanted to see him. This was the way it was supposed to be. He hadn't confronted the possibility of anything other than her embracing his journey to find her as a wondrously romantic gesture. He hadn't actually faced down the reality of what he was doing at all. There couldn't be any futility to this quest because he never allowed it to blossom into anything beyond the certainty of what it was. The thought settled him and his head stopped spinning. There was nothing else but Sophie Durango, there couldn't be anything else because to consider anything else was impossible anymore. He felt calm again.

Grape watched Hunter from the corner of her eye even as the stoner played his bongos, touched her arm and let his eyes roam across her face. He never looked at her breasts or hips, keeping as much eye contact with her as possible. It was disconcerting but strangely polite and she liked it. He had a wiry body, with a long neck and a nice jaw, clean eyes and hands. He was worldly. Weed didn't affect her much – she had smoked so much of it with her uncle that it didn't change the world for her. Everything got a little slower but she approached the world at a sedate pace anyway.

Hunter had opened his eyes, that intense look when he was considering Sophie Durango stilling his movement. He looked at her and his eyes changed. She was going to have to leave him now before he found her. There was no other way. They had to separate. The thought made her sad. Hunter's eyes pierced her own and she was transfixed. Then the stoner grabbed her arm and pulled her up onto the concrete, imploring her to dance for his music.

"Dance, girl, dance like it's always tomorrow!" he exhorted.

Grape responded graciously, moving her hips and ass like she knew he would like, flickering her eyes to Hunter intermittently. He watched her for a few minutes, even as the crowd gathered and she picked up her pace, letting the tremor of the beat wash away her shyness. Hunter stood up awkwardly, his muscles fighting the action, and he wandered unsteadily to the beach. She watched him turn his back on her and drift to the water's edge, each step taking him further and further away from her.

The tempo of the beat increased and people began to clap. She altered her movements to the clapping, stomping her bare feet on the ground. A crowd gathered and she looked at each of their faces in turn. One by one they were each the same, wanting something more from what they could see around them than what they were going to get. Grape understood that. Nobody here was satisfied with what they held in their hands. Hunter was each of them and they were Hunter. The only thing that could happen was a breaking of their hope. The bongo stopped playing and she turned her back on the beach and began to walk. Her body felt tired but that didn't matter anymore. Nothing mattered except being alone again.

The water ran through the digits of Hunter's wrinkled feet like a thief, stealing the essence of his soul and sweeping it out into the Pacific. He could hear that the beat had stopped and he knew that Grape had disappeared into the crowd the same way that you knew somebody was watching you. You could feel it, and when they had stopped you didn't feel it anymore. He felt nothing but the cool breeze on his skin and the lightness of the weed in his head. Tomorrow might as well be today. Sophie Durango was all that mattered and he was Cat again.

Thirty-Nine

He stood at the phone box, examining the grime on the earpiece. Stale urine stained the ground and cluttered the air. Ripped pictures of half-naked women and adverts cluttered up the glass panes, patiently waiting for his heart to stop beating so fast, to swallow his attention.

After some punitive research he now had three addresses and two phone numbers for where Sophie Durango possibly lived. She wasn't on Facebook when he had joined to find her. There were a couple of girls named Sophie Durango but none were her. Maybe she had a different name, or like him she didn't have the inclination to share her life through a computer. His father had been old-fashioned and his mother wasn't wealthy enough to have a choice. Even in school he had eschewed communicating over the web, which made him more of a pariah than anything his insolent introspection could have achieved. There were programs and places you could find somebody though, and getting the addresses for the various Sophie

Durangos living in Los Angeles hadn't been hard through the internet.

Every time he looked at the paper in his hand and attempted to dial the first number his heart rallied against his chest with such power that he could taste the blood in his cheeks. Be a man, he whispered to himself. He grimaced at an arrogant green alien cartoon advertising car insurance, grabbed the receiver and tossed in a quarter before his heart could catch up. Without the time to change his mind there was quickly a sound from the earpiece. He couldn't stop now.

The dial tone took an age, clicking slowly from a distance, then abruptly there was a strained female voice on the other end.

"Hello?"

"Sophie Durango?"

Hunter could barely squeeze the words out, so concentrated on speaking that he didn't hear the other voice.

"Who's this?"

"Sophie Durango?" he repeated with a whine.

"There might be a Sophie here but who are you that's asking?"

"Sophie Durango?" Hunter wheezed again, eyes closed.

"Stop saying my name like that."

Hunter caught himself from repeating it then listened.

"If you don't tell me who you are then I'm going to hang up."

"No, no, no, don't hang up, please – I won't be able to call again."

There was a silence and Hunter felt the blood in his face throb uncomfortably. Then there was a cracked coughing, that hard wet sound of blocked mucous being dislodged that even over the phone made you squirm a little.

"Why are you looking for Sophie Durango?"

"I'm her friend. I need to talk to her."

"Well, I'm Sophie Durango. Do I know you?"

"I don't know."

But it wasn't her. The voice on the other line was old and fed up, a long life audible in her aged tones.

"How old is Sophie Durango?" the woman who was not Sophie Durango teased.

"Nineteen. Sophie Durango is nineteen."

"Ha! I wish I was nineteen. I'm seventy-three, sonny. You have the wrong Sophie Durango."

"Oh."

There was a crackling silence for a moment and Hunter wondered if he could simply hang up. His hand hovered over the end-call button.

"I wish I was still nineteen though. How old are you?"

"Eighteen."

"I remember when I was nineteen. All the boys liked me then. Boys used to chase me down the street, can you believe that?"

Hunter didn't say anything.

"Why don't you have this girl's cell phone? Everybody has a cell phone these days?"

"I just don't."

"She didn't give it to you then?"

"I was late to meet her, so she left."

"Ah. Men are always late. Well, sonny, I hope you find her and, if you do, tell her that she has a reputation to uphold as a fellow Sophie Durango to not take any shit from the world."

"I'll tell her."

"Good. I hope she's as beautiful as me, for your sake!"

The old woman cackled down the phone and then hung up.

Hunter put down the receiver and looked at his paper. There was only one other number left to call and two addresses. The list seemed tiny and insignificant. What if none of these were her? He placed another quarter against the slot and let it fall in gently, the clatter of its journey taking his hopes with it. The dial tone began its tedious approach.

"Yep?"

A thick deep southern male accent barked at him. Hunter was composed this time.

"Hi. I want to speak to Sophie Durango?"

"Why?"

"I'm her friend."

"Who are you?"

"Hunter. I mean no, I'm Cat. Tell her it's Cat."

"This a joke?"

"No. My name is Cat."

"Sophie isn't here right now. I'll her that you rang. Bye."

"Wait, wait, does she live there?"

"Of course she lives here – you just rang her home, didn't you?"

"Is this Sophie nineteen?"

"What?"

"Is she nineteen years old? She's not eighty or anything like that, is she?"

"Who the fuck are you, kid?"

"I just want to make sure that I got the right number, that's all."

"No, she's not eighty and, yes, she's nineteen. Now I'll tell her that you rang and if she has your number then she can call you back."

"Wait, she doesn't have my –"

The phone went dead. He knew where she lived. Sophie Durango. He had her address and he knew how to find her. She was close. Achingly close.

He stepped out of the phone box and looked around for Grape to tell her but she wasn't there. He was alone. He should have felt elated. He knew where Sophie Durango lived, he knew where to find her and it had been so easy, but there was nobody to tell. He liked Grape's irritation whenever she noticed that he was thinking about her – for some reason it let him pretend that it wasn't important how she felt. Her anger about Sophie Durango made it easier to ignore the reality of her existence. He wasn't sure why that was, it just was.

The sky was blood-red, casting a heavy glow across the streets. People flecked the dirty ground like slowly morphing creatures, drifting with the eve of the light towards sanctuary. He couldn't go tonight. Tomorrow. Like he had said to Grape. He would find Sophie Durango tomorrow.

He wandered across the Venice boardwalk with no purpose. Maybe he would find Grape. If he did he didn't know what to say to her. He had wanted to be rid of her for so long, and now that he was he didn't feel satisfied. He didn't yearn for her, but her soft body and quiet gentle eyes had made him feel comforted. He felt that he had to protect her so that stopped him from thinking about protecting himself. He had felt alone his entire life without being bothered, but after Grape, and even Sir Will and Delilah, now that he was alone again he felt uncomfortable. It was nice having somebody care about him. Now he was alone again. But Sophie Durango would change all that.

The boardwalk was emptying. The little shops with their loud music, flashy colours, intoxicating tattoo-parlour signs and gaudy shirts were being swept, shutters pulling down, doors closing. The hot visceral wind of earlier in the day was fading with the light and it was getting cold. A basketball court still harboured a heavy-hitting game so he sat on the bleachers opposite and watched the play. It was a ferocious and skillful exhibition of release. A relentless sweating drive to forget anything else but the ball and the hoop. One particular player stood out. At least a head taller than the rest, his skin blacker than the night, hands as big as feet, he shovelled his way through the game like a madman, eyes pouring out of his head. Hunter stared at him mesmerised until a smaller player had the temerity to steal the ball. The huge man's fist came down in a surge of anger, smashing the smaller man's head into his neck and dropping him to the ground. The play stopped and the players swarmed around him. There was some light jostling but nobody had the balls to confront him properly. They moaned from all angles in a building drone until eventually, overpowered by the weight of feeling, he threw his hands up in the air and made for the bleachers. He sat beside Hunter, his bulk rattling the seats. Hunter was caught up in observing the ugly beauty of his size when the man glowered at him.

"Whatcha fuckin' looking at, boy?"

"Nothing."

"Better be fuckin' nothin'."

The giant stared like a predator at the court, and Hunter

followed his gaze out to where the game was recommencing awkwardly. The fallen man was still groggy but desperate to show his masculinity by playing. The giant appraised Hunter, his eyes scanning him up and down. Hunter remembered the advice that the Russian had given him so he got to his feet but the giant's voice was a wall.

"Where you from?"

"Nowhere."

"You afraid of me?"

"A little."

The giant nodded but didn't smile, his heavy muscles shaking with each deep breath, ready to spring. Hunter looked at his feet then stepped off the bleachers, never more painfully aware of the whiteness of his skin and his own mortality.

The sun disappeared over the horizon, letting night take over. Hunter carried on walking the boardwalk with nowhere else to go but he didn't feel the cold. He needed to get some sleep, but with nowhere to go decided to just keep walking. The moving would occupy his anxious brain at least. When the sun next rose Hunter was going to see Sophie Durango. That was the only certainty in his world.

Forty

He didn't have a plan. He stood motionless outside the small house in Long Beach where Sophie Durango lived, hands trembling by his sides. His back had never been so straight.

He had eventually dozed on the beach that night, sitting against the wall at the bottom of the bleachers in front of the outdoor athletics area in the sand, watching the tramps scrabbling around muttering to themselves. None approached him. He had sat there in the shadows thinking of nothing, clearing his mind of any thoughts. Not his mother, his father or Sophie Durango. Nothing. The air was clear. At one stage he had begun slipping into sleep when there was the sound of sex beside him. Unaware of his quiet presence a young couple had started fucking in the sand. He watched them for a short while until he found their animalistic grinding annoying and he had moved away to the other side of the bleachers. They were beyond reality on drugs or alcohol and never noticed him.

He had awoken gently with the sun and the gradual building of activity on the boardwalk, so he walked to the sea to clean himself off with a swim, enjoying the fragile idea of being a traveller, an explorer. Pretending that he was on an adventure released him from examining his thoughts. The sea was already flecked with surfers, riding the waves like ballerinas. He watched them until he got cold, hoping that they would fall or that a shark might emerge from the froth and devour them. He cast his eye across the beach for Grape but she was nowhere to be seen. Probably for the best.

When the cold sea had defeated him, he stole a towel off the beach from one of the little piles of belongings that people left as they surfed and swam or did yoga, and visited the public showers which were by the basketball courts.

Then he had walked to a bare-skinned man in grimy shorts seated across from a bicycle rental shop. It was nestled in a side street leading off the boardwalk, amateurish cobblestones lumping the uneven ground. The beach front was slowly coming alive around them.

Hunter coughed to announce himself.

"I need directions, please?"

The man lounged back in an old canvas chair, head tilted to the sky, eyes half open, hands touching the ground.

"Yeah?" He didn't look up. "To where?"

Despite failing to actually check it on a map in his enthusiastic yet fearful search, Hunter knew the address by heart, the letters seared into his mind. He gripped the paper with whitened knuckles, almost afraid to speak the words out loud in case they then ceased to exist. He stuck the open piece of paper under the man's nose and waited. The man slowly opened his eyes, sucked on his teeth, found something of interest, picked it out with his tongue, then spat the offending lump of food onto the ground. When that ritual was complete he took the paper in his long fingers.

"Long Beach. Hmmmm. Long Beach."

"Yeah, where is it?"

The man smiled, then languidly sat up and opened his eyes fully, stretching the skin around his wet pupils painfully to examine the kid in front of him.

"That way."

He stretched a long arm out and pointed loosely down the beach.

"Is it far?"

"Yep."

"Can I walk?"

"You can walk anywhere if you want to."

"Should I walk?"

"No."

"How do I get there?"

"Drive."

"I don't have a car."

"Hmmmm. Cycle. Take you a few hours."

Hunter looked across the uneven concrete of the side street at the rows of bikes laid out. The man winked at him, leaned back until his head was parallel with the skies, and closed his eyes.

Hunter made a decision.

"Thanks."

"Uh-huh."

Hunter walked around the corner, stood rigidly beside the wall, then when it seemed like the man was asleep padded slowly to the bikes. He felt a shiver of fear, and a little embarrassment, but pictured Sophie Durango in his mind to stop the shaking of his hands. Keeping his eyes on the skeletal man, he grabbed the nearest bike casually, pretending to be only perusing the wares. The man's head remained flat against the canvas, eyes closed, motionless. Taking care for the wheels not to make any noise, Hunter led his prize away and around the corner, marvelling at his temerity.

The cycle had been long and people didn't seem to like being asked for directions in Los Angeles, their eyes openly judging his dirty clothes and his tourist beach bike but he didn't care. As the morning wore on he had become more and more certain of what he was doing. The process of moving towards his goal didn't allow for any uncertainty. He was about to find Sophie Durango and he was so close that he could taste her again. If he shut his eyes the image of her face sprang into his mind, the softness of her mouth against his, the taut feeling of her skin under his hands, the eager smell of her sex. He cycled harder.

Sophie Durango.

Now he was standing outside a large house in Long Beach California, trying to pluck up the courage to walk in and demand to see her. It was a nice house, clean walls, large yard, extension on the roof. It was almost copied from a suburban television show: 2.5 children, a dog and a jeep. Hunter felt a little intimidated by its perfection.

"What are you doing?" a female voice asked behind him.

He startled, so focused on his own actions as to be unaware of life outside the sphere of his breath. A little girl was looking at him with tiny eyes squeezing past her oversized bangs. She leaned on her bike coyly in a pose that made him think she was imitating some music video.

"Nothing."

"Why are you just standing there staring? You look silly."

"I'm fine."

Hunter turned his head back towards the house but the little girl stayed where she was, eyes trained on him and it was distracting him from his mission.

"What?" he asked.

"I'm not doing anything, officer." She threw her hands up in mock surprise. "I'm just minding my own business." She recited lines from some TV show with remarkable dexterity, her face mimicking fake sincerity.

Hunter softened, cracking his knuckles to loosen the tension in his limbs. She waited for him to say something.

"I'm waiting for somebody," he offered to her finally.

"Who?"

"A friend."

The little girl looked thoughtful, as if this was gravely important information that must be considered deeply.

"I've never seen you before."

"And I've never seen *you* before."

"Well, I'm the gatekeeper. Who are you?"

"Really? The gatekeeper of where?"

"Here. There. Everywhere. This is my house and if you want to see a friend then you have to ask my permission first. Only the gatekeeper can let you enter. Although you're not my friend so you must be Sophie's friend. You can be my friend if you want. Do you want to be my friend?"

Hunter was talking to Sophie Durango's sister. She had a sister. When he looked closer he saw that they had the same eyes, the same nose, the same confident character. The little girl arched an eyebrow just like Sophie Durango did.

"Well, do you want to be my friend?"

"Sure."

"*Aaaaaaaaaaahahahahha! I don't want to be your friend!*" the little girl screeched loudly, pulling a face of mock indignation.

She jumped on her bike and rushed past him into the driveway. The front door was partly ajar and the little girl dropped her bike to the lawn with a loud clatter, still shrieking.

"*Sophie, Sophie, Sophie! There's a boy here, he's really weird and he wants to be my friend. Aaaaaahahahahahhaaa!*"

Hunter couldn't move. The world around him ceased to exist as a tunnel grew in front of his eyes trailing to the front door. He took a step forward, unable to see where he was walking, fixated on the door, unblinking. He would tell Sophie Durango everything, he longed to tell her everything. To kiss her. To tell her that he loved her. He didn't even know what would happen then. He just knew that this was the moment. Another step forward.

The door swept open and then there she was.

Forty-One

Sophie Durango stepped out from the shadows of her home and into the shared daylight where he resided. They were breathing the same air, feeling the same sun on their cheeks, standing on the same ground. "Sophie Durango." Her name whispered past his lips cautiously like an escaping convict.

She looked at him. Those slitted cat eyes immediately suspicious, her slender body facing the world solidly in defiance of everything. Her lips parted in confusion as she drew in his face.

"Sophie? Sophie Durango?" His voice croaked.

"Yeah?"

"It's Hunter. I mean, it's Cat."

"Who?"

She didn't recognise him. He blinked and felt himself falling.

"Cat. Cat from Albuquerque."

There was a moment when she stared right through him in the way that only she could do and he didn't exist. Then her brow furrowed, desperately trying to place him. The world made no sense anymore. He was a lie to her cat eyes. Then she exclaimed a little firmly.

"Oh yeah, right. OK. Cool."

He stood there, uncertain if he should move to her. She didn't make any gesture towards him, just raised an eyebrow in that mocking way that he found so sexy, expecting the world to justify its presence to her. He couldn't breathe so he walked forward again just for something to do. If he kept moving everything would be OK. When he was inches from her she understood his intention and turned her face to the side so that his lips brushed against her cheek.

"I told you he was weird."

Her little sister was watching them behind the screen door with the same mocking face that Sophie Durango had perfected.

"What are ya doing?" Sophie Durango asked.

"I just thought ... I dunno."

Cat stumbled back inside himself, feeling himself physically shrink into a vortex. Sophie Durango's lip began to curl maliciously, then stopped as she appraised his tattered state.

"Gimme a sec. Wait out here – sit over there."

She jerked her head to a bench under the window and watched him until he sat down on it before going back inside and shutting the door. He could hear scattered voices inside but couldn't make anything out. His head felt as if it was going to drown him with the gravity of its confusion. A careless balloon filled with the weight of his world. He had found Sophie Durango. Everything had been about this moment, about finding her, and she didn't seem to care. It wasn't right, it was disjointed. Her voice broke his thoughts.

"Hey. Cat, right?"

She was standing in front of him, the sun silhouetting her from behind so that he had to squint. Even the sunlight was eager to grant her dominion over him.

"Yeah."

"Let's go for a walk. My dad will be back soon and I don't want him to see you."

"Oh. OK."

Cat got to his feet gingerly. Everything hurt. He was Cat again and Hunter had never existed. He looked at the vision in front of him and tried to picture her as before but he couldn't remember anything. Clouds and nothing else. She was in front of him now so the past shouldn't matter but it so clearly did. The past had never been so important. It felt wrong. He reached for her hand as he followed her out onto the street but she skillfully lifted her fingers away and kept her distance.

Nothing felt right.

Forty-Two

"You followed me here?"

Sophie Durango stared at him. Her feminine curves were at war with the tight belly-top and pants she wore, straining for freedom. She looked like Hunter had remembered she had looked, or had imagined she looked. He needed to smell her skin to be sure that it was real. He needed something more tangible.

They were sitting on a crumbling wall around the corner a few blocks away from her house. She seemed more comfortable here, the slightly stiff way that she moved at the house having melted away into the graceful smoothness that he remembered. She looked at him, soft voice and gentle cat eyes scanning his face.

"Yeah. I did. I followed you," he said proudly.

"Why?"

Hunter was confused by the question.

"Why wouldn't I?"

Sophie Durango didn't seem to have an answer for that.

She bit her lip, suddenly uncomfortable, and took out a cigarette. He watched her smoke in silence, two cigarettes quickly, one following the other. He was still reeling from the reality of what was happening. It had been a long journey to this moment. The excitement he felt was tempered by how cool she was being with him, but then she had always had that air of detachment about her, and he didn't really know her that well. His memories were clouded in any case. She would thaw eventually. He was in no rush. He had nowhere else to go. This, right now, this moment, sitting on a wall with a pensive, chain-smoking Sophie Durango was all that was real for him. Almost real.

When she had finally finished a third cigarette and mashed it into the dirt with her heel, she looked directly at him.

"Why did you call yourself Hunter?"

"Uh. I was given a new name."

"By who?"

"A girl. A person that I travelled with. It's silly, my name is Cat."

Sophie Durango nodded.

"Who was this girl?"

"It doesn't matter. I was coming here, to Los Angeles, she was coming here also. We travelled together. It's a long story. I want to tell it to you though. I want to tell you lots of things."

Sophie Durango smiled passively. She looked up at the sky, around them, to the ground, to the distance, as if there was something profoundly interesting drifting around them, just dangling forever out of reach but infinitely more fascinating that what was happening on the wall.

"I have a boyfriend," she said finally.

Hunter blinked. He had never considered that. That didn't make any sense. He must have misheard her.

"What?"

"I have a boyfriend," she repeated perfunctorily.

He stared back at her, stoney-faced. His cheeks felt like paper stretching over sharp bone, ready to rip through his face.

"That doesn't make any sense."

"I always had a boyfriend."

"Even when we met?"

"Yeah."

Hunter closed his eyes, trying desperately to process this information. There had to be a way around this, it was simply another challenge. He had faced many challenges already. There was always a way. He recalled his father staring down at him, face hard and cold.

"There is never one way to do something, remember that. If something gets in your way then get the fuck around it. Get it the fuck out of the way."

His father had been drinking beer as he cajoled him in that rough manner he had developed the older he got. The bonnet of the car was lifted up, pieces of the car engine strewn across the ground like oily pieces of jigsaw. Hunter had to put it together because he had filled up the oil tank with a mixture of gas and water to see if he could try and save the environment. His father hadn't been amused and made him figure out a way to fix it as punishment. He threw his empty beer cans at the corner of the garden like a man owning his territory. Hunter had pleaded that there was no way to fix it. It was broken.

"Figure it out. There's always a fucking way," his father replied.

He wasn't sure if his father had meant to impart that nugget of life advice as he berated him to fix the engine. His memories were blurred. Maybe that had never happened. Maybe with Sophie Durango it was all different and he had imagined it all. What if he had imagined it all? No. He hadn't. Sophie Durango was staring at him. He had seen her naked. Clouds and pictures. He finally spoke and for the first time since he arrived at her house he was certain.

"I'll figure it out."

"What?"

"Your boyfriend. I'll figure it out."

Sophie Durango shook her head and lit another cigarette.

"How are you going to figure it out?"

"I'll think of something."

"You're not listening. I like my boyfriend."

"Doesn't matter."

"Yes, it does."

"Then why? With us? Why, what happened?"

Sophie Durango shrugged her shoulders.

"You seemed sweet."

"That's it? I seemed sweet?"

She suddenly seemed unsure. A flash of the teenage girl that she was.

"Yeah. I guess. I dunno. I didn't think you would come all the way to LA. But, look, it's not that long of a journey anyway. Although it's creepy that you were able to find me so easily. I wonder if we're being filmed right now?"

She looked around in mock apprehension. He could see where her sister had acquired the playful mannerisms from. Hunter didn't understand. Her mocking way was frustrating now that he needed her to be serious. She wavered under the intensity of his look.

"I just mean, that maybe they know everything, and nothing is secret anymore ..."

She trailed off and dragged the life out of her cigarette.

Hunter was overcome with a desperate urge to get drunk. Either kiss her and forget about this conversation or get really fucked up and then figure the rest out. Sophie Durango touched his shoulder gently.

"I have to go. I'm sorry."

"Wait, you can't."

"I can. I'm going to. Just get the bus back to Albuquerque and forget about me. Nice seeing you again, Hunter. I like that name better than Cat. It suits you."

She stood up smoothly, balancing on her little feet like an exotic bird.

He couldn't let her leave. He grabbed her hand.

"My mother died."

Her hand shivered in his touch. She looked like she didn't believe him, but his eyes pleaded with her.

"Oh. I'm sorry."

"That's why I was late to meet you that day."

"Because of your mother?"

"Yes."

"When? Oh, in the diner."

"So I couldn't come to meet you on time."

"Oh, wow. I'm sorry."

"Yeah, you left without me."

"Well, you never came."

"So you just left with another guy?"

Sophie Durango went silent, but her face hardened.

Hunter looked at her, eyes wide and impassioned, and gripped her hand harder. He had come too far to let her go.

"I was late to see you because of my mother. I had to

help her. She was sick. Then I never saw you again. She died. I found her."

"Look, we only met once, we don't really know each other."

"I've not told anybody else."

That last part was sort of a lie, he had told Grape, but that wasn't important right now. He didn't want to tarnish the importance of Sophie Durango having this information.

Sophie Durango paused in the air, her body flattening against gravity. This was new territory for her.

"When did she die?"

Hunter didn't respond immediately. There was a lump growing in his throat and he couldn't breathe. His head swam. A pain began in the back of his skull and spread outwards like a swarm of bees. His mother. He wished he could speak with her. When she was sober she would chat to him, her bright smile making light of everything. "It will all work out," she would say. It hadn't all worked out though. She was dead and she had left him. He was alone. Completely alone. He watched a tear blur his vision, then it slipped out, hitting the ground and splaying into tiny bits of infinity. Nothing.

Sophie Durango sat back down on the wall quietly as Hunter cried to himself. He didn't make any noise and his shoulders barely shook but tears of suppressed pain flowed through his body until he seemed to shrink a little before her. When he was finally spent his body gave a little shudder and then was still. The ground was wet with his tears.

She rested her hand upon his back.

"Where are you staying tonight?"

He shook his head, unable to speak.

"You can stay here tonight, but you can't tell anybody where we met or why you're here. Tell them that you're the cousin of my friend Jane. She's out of town. I'll tell them that you're waiting until she gets back and you're just stuck for somewhere to stay tonight."

Hunter wasn't sure if anything that Sophie Durango was saying mattered. His mother was dead. The world was a hard shallow place. His head hammered at him violently. He tried to stand but his legs buckled and he collapsed to his knees, a soft mass of blunt limbs and loose flesh. He fell to his back and lay there, supine to the world. The skies were clear. It wasn't like Albuquerque where you could almost taste the clouds on your tongue. Here the blue of the sky was vapid and empty and distant. His mother was dead. He wasn't sure why that mattered right now. Maybe it was the knowledge that he had nowhere else to go except back to her dead carcass. Sophie Durango hadn't said very much to him but what she had said was enough. He was an idiot. A fool. Chasing across the country to a girl who didn't exist except in his mind. Under the pretence of love. He wanted the world to open its maw and take him inside. To wrap its overbearing lips around him and devour him over and over until he didn't exist anymore.

Sophie Durango lit another cigarette and stared at the blue sky as if it was the most interesting thing in the world and waited for the boy at her feet to compose himself.

Forty-Three

There were two types of people in Hunter's eyes. People that he liked and people that he disliked. Sophie Durango's father fell firmly into the latter category. He had examined him with the assertive glare of an aspiring upper-middle-class father, trained to dismiss his daughter's suitors within a moment's analysis. His dry-cleaned shirt had stiffened when Sophie Durango had brought Hunter into the kitchen. His soft mouth rolled around his jaw gently as he spoke and his voice was pleasant enough, but it was his eyes that cut. They were as hard as glass, a wall which somebody like Hunter was never meant to clamber over.

Hunter felt acutely aware of the deficiencies of his own upbringing. This man made him feel inadequate simply by existing in the same physical space.

"Dad, this is Cat. He's a cousin of Jane's."

"Really?"

"Yes, Dad."

"He doesn't look like a cousin of Jane's."

Hunter's face was red from crying and his body felt numb. He didn't respond. Sophie Durango existed in a different realm.

"Well, he is. Jane is away so I said that he could stay tonight."

"Fine."

Sophie Durango's father drank a glass of water, rinsed the glass and placed it back perfectly on the shelf near the sink. Everything was clean and precise. The numbness in Hunter's body spread around him like a vacuum, sucking in everything around.

"Where are you from, Hunter? Are you in college?"

Her father didn't look at him when he spoke. Hunter didn't care enough to speak. It didn't matter. Sophie Durango took control. She was well equipped to handle her father.

"He's going to have a shower and get some sleep. He's been travelling a lot."

Her father nodded, unwilling to engage with his errant daughter, swept his blazer off the counter and disappeared out the door. The jeep outside started smoothly and backed out the driveway in a customary little circle that no doubt never varied.

The air felt warmer without his presence.

"Sorry about my dad – he's a bit protective."

Hunter nodded and turned around to take in the room. His mother would have loved it here. An alcove broke through the wall from the living-room-cum-kitchen to a hallway and from there Sophie Durango's little sister looked at him with wide perfect suspicious eyes.

"Why are you here?"

Hunter found his voice and felt the blood reverberate

through his body again.

"Because I have nowhere else to go."

"That's silly. Everybody has somewhere to go. You can go home."

Hunter felt his eyes welling up again and the little whelp grimaced with condescension.

Sophie Durango patted the couch in front of the flat-screen television and beckoned him over. It was a calm living room, filled with colour and packed carefully with furniture, toys, and nice lamps. The huge flat-screen television artfully dominated the room. It was playing cartoons.

Hunter sat down beside the love of his life and pulled himself together.

Sophie Durango looked at her little sister impatiently.

"Go to your room."

"No."

"Do it."

"I don't want to."

It was a routine ritual and even as she was spitting back the little girl meandered towards the rooms at the back of the house, giving Hunter one last dismissive look before she disappeared. Hunter let the couch swallow his tender body. The silence was nice. If Sophie Durango didn't talk then nothing more could change. Maybe they could stay like this. He didn't recognise the cartoon but the colours were comforting. He took a deep breath and focused.

"What was your mother like?" She was looking at him not the cartoon.

He didn't want to talk about his mother anymore. The cartoon was familiar now – he couldn't remember the name but there was a coyote in it. It used to make him laugh when he was younger. He took a breath, feeling safer.

"What's your boyfriend like?"

"I don't think we need to talk about him."

"Yes, we do."

"Talking isn't going to change anything."

"Why don't you want anybody to know that we met in Albuquerque?"

"Tell me about your mother."

Hunter ignored her and continued with his own line of direct questioning without removing his eyes from the cartoon. It gave him power somehow if he didn't look at her.

"Is it because nobody knows that you went and fucked other people?"

Sophie Durango hardened, but beneath the steel he could almost taste how fragile she was.

"I can kick you out at any time."

"I know. But is it the truth?"

"Yes."

"OK."

On the reflection in the television he saw her lean back into the couch beside him, kicking her feet under her ass in that sexy way that only girls can do. She pulled at her eyelashes reflectively.

"I was feeling lost. So I jumped on a bus to see my friend. Then I met you. Nobody knows that I went. I would prefer it if nobody knew."

"Have you done that before?"

"What?"

"Gone somewhere and met somebody?"

She didn't avert her gaze but something changed behind her long lashes.

"Yes. A few times."

"And you have always had a boyfriend every time?"

"Yes?"

"Why?"

"Why what?"

"Why do it?"

"I don't know."

The pain behind his eyes was almost gone. The Coyote was trying desperately to drop a rock on the Road Runner. He remembered the name now. Wile E. Coyote. The rock missed. It always missed. He felt like he understood the Coyote, felt sorry for him, they were kindred spirits. Pop music began to circulate in the air from the room behind them, pulsing through the walls.

Sophie Durango shifted her weight on the couch uncomfortably. Her face was pained and her lips pulled tight against her teeth.

"I'm sorry," she mumbled.

"Sure."

On the television the Coyote was fabricating his next plan.

"What are you going to do now?"

The way she asked he understood that she needed something. He wished he knew what. Grape would probably know.

"Do you love him?" he asked.

"Yeah."

"I don't believe you."

He never saw the slap coming. He only felt the sting after her hand withdrew back to her lap. Her body had remained perfectly still – only her arm shot out in a whipping motion. He was impressed by the speed. Her face remained impassive and it made him smile. He wasn't sure why but something about the slap made him feel in control. It was like with Grape – when she was at her most angry he felt empowered, a surety of touch in his extremities.

Finally he looked at Sophie Durango. There was the tiniest doubt in her furrowed face at what she had just done. It was a moment.

He leaned over and kissed her.

His lips pushed hers apart gently and his tongue slipped into her mouth before she could react. She fell back in the folds of the couch, his body covering hers, letting it happen. Her eyes closed as he stared deep into the creases of her lids. He was kissing Sophie Durango again. She tasted just as he had remembered, a mixture of wet peaches and cigarettes. He ground his groin against her in an aggressive manner that he never knew existed. He wasn't anybody anymore but a man wanting to fuck a woman.

"Ew! Gross! I'm telling Ryan!"

The voice of Sophie Durango's little sister cut through their ardour. The pop music had increased in volume when she had walked out of her bedroom door but neither had noticed. Timing was everything.

Sophie Durango pushed Hunter off her and squirmed off the couch, grabbing her sister by the cheeks aggressively.

"Don't you dare tell Ryan anything, you hear me?"

"It'll cost you."

The little girl grinned boldly back at her older sister, enjoying the game of brinkmanship. She'd played this before. Sophie Durango's grip didn't let up but she relented.

The Coyote missed the Road Runner again in the background.

"Fine. Whatever you want."

"I want your room."

"What the fuck?"

"Yep. Your room is bigger. I want it or else I'm telling Ryan."

Sophie Durango looked like she might crush the little girl in her hands. Then she shivered and began to laugh. It was a tentative giggle at first, then gradually it devoured her body, wracking through it like a wheezing cough. Her little sister laughed back with her and Hunter found himself enjoying it. It was the kind of laugh that made you happy even if you didn't understand why.

"You're a cheeky bitch."

"Yeah, I am a cheeky bitch. And you're gonna give me your room."

"That a promise? A fair exchange – room for secrets?"

"Pinky promise."

The two sisters, almost identical apart from the gap in their age, clasped the pinkies of their right hands, then hugged. Then Sophie Durango spun her sister around and pushed her out of the room.

"Now go back to your room and tomorrow we can start moving stuff."

"But I wanna do it now!"

"Do what I say or the deal's off."

"But."

"Do it."

"Fine."

Her little sister craned her neck over her shoulder at the last minute and blew Hunter an imaginary kiss which he caught in his hand. Then pain hit him between the eyes again and he sank back into the couch, breathing heavily and waiting for it to subside.

Sophie Durango sank to her knees on the floor, staring at the room in front of her. Hunter watched her and waited, taking deep breaths until his head was clear. She didn't look at him as she spoke.

"I want to know about your mother."

"Sure."

Satisfied, she picked herself up in one fluid movement, then gestured with a tilt of her head to her bedroom.

"He'll be gone for at least a few more hours, no time like the present."

It took a moment for Hunter to register what she meant but then she stepped away from him and began walking to the hallway leading to the back of the house. He scrambled to his feet. Took a breath to control himself and, as coolly as he could, he ambled down the corridor. The pop music began to blare louder as his footsteps bounced on soft carpet, each step massaging the hard arches of his feet through the old leather of his boots. Sophie Durango's ass swayed in front him, each cheek rising upwards like the moon with each gentle step. She had a skinny ass, not as gently round as Grape's. He liked Grape's ass. Then they were in her room.

It was large and comforting. The room of a girl. He had never been in a girl's room before. Except Grape's. He remained on the threshold. It smelled the way he had always imagined a girl's room would smell. The bed in the centre was bookended by a desk and a colourful beanbag. A large bay window was cloaked by a light pink drape, allowing light to filter in selectively. Bookshelves and posters and a large closet completed the room. The posters and decor were confusing, at odds with her dark clothes and abrasive personality. It made no sense. Just like her.

Sophie Duragno closed the door and he had no further time to appraise his surroundings when her teeth smacked against his and she dragged him onto the bed. The mattress gently lifted him back into the air as she climbed on top of him, taking control. He wondered should he do what he did before and push her back, make her feel like a woman, inconsequential to his manly wiles, but he felt like a boy again in her hands and let her direct him. It was easier this time, he was ready for it to happen and they were still half clothed by the time they began to fuck.

Then it was over.

Half-naked, in just stretched dark panties, the cheap elastic loosened from where he had pulled it down hard, Sophie Durango padded to the window, lifting it open so that a cool draught brushed through her hair. She sat on the beanbag, lit a cigarette and pulled it through her tender lips. The image of her smoking naked against the pale drapes was poetic. Hunter lay there and watched her. There was nothing else apart from these moments, he decided. He liked how it made no sense.

"Tell me about your mother."

She was nothing if not persistent. It seemed like a strange time to begin considering his mother but he felt more content than at any time in his entire life. He would have agreed to any request as long as he could stay where he was, in this room with her small pert breasts peeking at him when she turned her shoulders.

"She was strung out a lot. She was a good mother, but she had demons inside her. She loved me but couldn't love herself."

"Did you find her body?"

"Yeah."

"I watched my mother die. She had a heart attack. She was making me breakfast when it happened. One minute she was going about her day, pouring milk into my cereal and drinking coffee, then she was dead. Just like that."

"I'm sorry."

"It's OK. I was dating Ryan when she died. He's the only friend I still have who knew her. I find it hard to keep friends. That's why I can't break up with him. My dad won't talk about her and Stacy, my sister, she was too young to have any real memories. Ryan and me would hang from when we were very little. He remembers more about my mother than I do. When I get sad he tells me stories about her."

"Oh."

"I can't hurt Ryan. To hurt him feels like I would be betraying my mother."

"It's not the same."

"What do you know about that?"

Hunter was silent and Sophie Durango finished her cigarette, letting the ash fall to the floor, some of it catching in the draught and whispering away into the air. She seemed so small and thin now, some of the spark from before gone. There were tears in her eyes when she turned to him. He didn't like seeing her cry.

"Is there anybody that you talk to about things?" she inquired.

He shook his head. The only person he had ever really spoken to or felt close to was Grape and he had let her slip through his fingers like the ash in the breeze off Sophie Durango's cigarette.

"You need to be able to talk to somebody."

"I could talk to you."

Sophie Durango crept back onto the bed. Her face moved towards him like a doe-eyed snake. She kissed him gently and shook her head.

"No. I can't give you anything."

"I'm in love with you."

"No, you're not. I can tell. You think I'm something but I'm not. I'm just a girl, living with her dad and her sister, with a quiet boyfriend who doesn't question when I disappear for a few days and never explain where or why. That's all I am."

"That's all I want you to be."

"You're sweet, Hunter. You're too sweet."

She curled up in the crook of his arm and nuzzled her face in the warm smell of his armpit. When she was satiated with his musky scent she let her face press against him, lips feathering his skin. He didn't want to breathe in case it disturbed her head but after a minute he had to inhale and the movement of his chest jolted her upright and back to the present.

"We should get dressed before he comes back. Ryan might be with him. They work together sometimes. Ryan wants to work in the printing business. My dad is training him. If Ryan comes back then you can't stay with me."

"Where will I go?"

"I'm sure you will figure it out. I'm going to shower."

Without another word Sophie Durango unspooled herself from the bed, wrapped a dressing gown around her thin frame and moved to an ensuite bathroom that he hadn't noticed before.

He listened to the sound of the water from the shower as it beat upon the tiles, the sound changing when she stepped under its flow and it began hitting her body like rain on an umbrella. His head began to hurt again and there was a loneliness in his belly. He gradually became aware of his own nudity. He felt a chill from the breeze through the window. He hadn't eaten since the sandwich with Grape the day before. It all seemed so long ago. He felt a pang of guilt at the thought of Grape. Was she OK? Should he feel guilty for her? Surely all his feelings only existed for Sophie Durango? He could still care for Grape though. He had wanted to be rid of her for so long, to be alone with his thoughts, to find Sophie Durango. Now he had fucked her for the second time in his life and instead of being elated and ready to profess his prowess to the world, he felt a sadness that dragged his limbs deep into the soft cavity of the bed. The memories of both his dead mother and her dead mother hung heavy in the air. Stolid spectres floating above and between them like imperfect ghosts, neither real nor imaginary, just things that were. He wondered if he would ever find Grape again. If he didn't then maybe it didn't matter. Or maybe it did.

Forty-Four

His mother used to play James Brown when she cleaned. She hated cleaning, referring to it playfully as the devil's work, so to cheer herself up she would put on a different James Brown record each time and dance as she cleaned. Sometimes he would dance alongside her, whipping his skinny legs out into the air like he was flipping burgers with his feet. He was usually a poor excuse for a dancer but when James Brown played it felt different. It didn't matter how his body moved because everything was correct – there was no wrong way to move to a James Brown song. She never let him help her clean. He could watch and dance to entertain her but the cleaning was her job, something that she needed to own.

After his father died she gradually stopped playing James Brown as she compressed her body into smaller and tighter folds within her skin. Nothing had nurtured her like that music, but she refused to play it when she wasn't cleaning and she didn't have the energy to clean anymore. If he put it on in an attempt to lift her spirits, she would spin into a frenzy. So James Brown gradually drifted out of his world. He would turn it off if it ever came on the radio now, and if it was playing when he worked in the store he would hum a different tune loudly, ignoring anybody who told him to quieten. James Brown went from the source of the greatest joy between him and his mother to the blackest reminder of what had once been.

Sophie Durango had an old record player in her bedroom and when she emerged from the shower the first thing that she did was turn it on. "Get On Up" blasted happily from beat-up speakers, the music crackling and bassy. He closed his eyes and tried to remember his mother's smile and the times that they had danced together, but his vision was clouded by images of her screaming, plates shattering, eyes high and lost bulging out their strained sockets.

When he opened his eyes Sophie Durango was moving her hips as she dressed, mouthing along, feet circling the floor in gentle concentric patterns. Her dancing saddened him and he had to look away. His mother had a greater hold over him then he had ever realised.

"You should put on some clothes. I have to cook dinner. You hungry?" she said as she danced gently.

"Sure."

"You can stay for dinner."

Sophie Durango cooked some pasta and broccoli quickly and easily, and when it was ready called Stacey in. They sat together, Hunter and the two Durango sisters eating at a table. It almost felt comfortable.

Stacey was watching him eat, her eyes trained so intently on his mouth that he had to purse his lips together as he chewed to make sure nothing fell out. She made a face at him.

"Why do you eat funny?" she asked.

"I don't."

"You do, you squeeze your lips together like a duck."

"Well, you keep staring at me."

"That's cos you look like a duck."

"Maybe that's cos you keep staring at me."

"I told you he was weird."

Stacey looked triumphantly at Sophie Durango and stopped staring at Hunter to eat her pasta, bored now with anything else that he did.

The meal was simple but Hunter hadn't eaten in what felt like forever and the food swelled his belly pleasantly. He had to restrain himself from swallowing without chewing. Sophie Durango finished her portion and looked at Hunter's empty plate.

"Seconds?"

He was about to nod when the porch door slide open outside. There was moment when the silence held nothing but stillness. Then the front door was pushed open and her father walked in, followed by a tall wiry boy a few years older than Hunter. He had a tired frown etched into his face which deepened when he saw Hunter. Sophie Durango gave him a terse smile.

"Hey, Dad, Ryan. This is Hunter. His mom just died."

And just like that, Sophie Durango carefully destroyed any possibility of the aimless male posturing that might have disrupted everything. Nobody can make a stand to anybody whose mother has just died.

Then Stacey chimed in.

"And he's really weird. And they made out in her room."

Fuck.

Sophie Durango glared at her little sister.

"Stacey? What the fuck?"

"I'm just joking. Sorry, it seemed funny."

Ryan said nothing but sat down on the couch across the room. He seemed the morose sort, internalising everything. His carriage was stiff and his shoulder blades clicked as his back muscles bunched in on themselves. He looked beyond tired. Sophie Durango's father took off his blazer and folded it carefully over a chair then sat down on the table, biting his cheeks thoughtfully. The armpits of his shirt were stained with sweat. He was probably once a handsome man, thick eyebrows heavy over his eyes, large features with deep eyes that didn't let you know anything, but now a sourness floated around him and ruined his looks. Sophie Durango laid a plate of pasta in front of him and he began to eat slowly, eyes casually stroking across Hunter's face. When he had sated his initial appetite he smacked his lips together.

Sophie Durango moved to the couch and kissed her boyfriend on the forehead. Hunter felt like a trapped animal. Sophie Durango's father wiped his lips carefully on a napkin.

"Where are you from?" His voice was cold.

Hunter wished his own father were here. Then he wouldn't feel so vulnerable. Not having his father around anymore had left him with a constant feeling of inadequacy with older men. There was no challenge to their authority beyond what Hunter could muster. He felt like a child.

"Albuquerque."

Sophie Durango's father rolled that information around his brain, letting it sift through whatever else lived up there.

"You're the kid on the telephone."

Sophie Durango shot Hunter a look that warned him to deny everything. Hunter caught her glance from the corner of his eye and shook his head.

"No, sir, that wasn't me."

"Let me hear your voice."

"What?"

"Say 'Is Sophie Durango home?'."

"Why?"

"Just say it."

Hunter licked his lips. Ryan stared at him even as Sophie Durango laid her hand across his cheek. He felt a pang of sharp jealousy but kept his face clear. The jealously was hard and cutting. Clearing his throat, he suddenly laughed. He wasn't sure why he laughed but it seemed appropriate. He was jealous of a girl who wasn't even his. His father would have laughed. So he laughed, deeper than he had done in a long time. His laughter set off Stacey and she began to giggle excitedly, kicking her legs against the table leg for emphasis. One look from her father immediately silenced her but she kept grinning. Her father's eyes considered Hunter and saw everything.

"What's so funny?"

"Nothing, sir."

"Then why are you laughing?"

Hunter looked over at Sophie Durango stroking her boyfriend's cheek and suddenly he didn't care anymore.

"My mom just died and you're questioning me over whether or not I called you asking questions about your daughter."

"Was it you?"

"Yes, sir. Yes, it was."

Sophie Durango's eyes slit like a cat's, that destructive glare she had piercing the side of his skull.

"I did ring, yes, sir, because I hadn't been here before and I lost the address. I've been forgetting everything lately. That happens when your mother dies."

"So you came here to see my daughter from Albuquerque? Is that where you met her?"

Hunter held the older man's gaze. He wasn't anything to feel threatened by really. He was just a man who was trying to hold his family together.

"No, sir. I met her here in LA," he lied smoothly.

"How?"

Jane and her cousin, it seemed, were out of the picture.

"My uncle lives here, sir. I was staying with him when I met Sophie. I play music."

"What type of music?"

"Soul."

"Soul?"

"Yes, sir. Like James Brown."

Her father leaned back in his chair, considering Hunter's responses, clearly dissatisfied but unable to find fault.

"Who do you play with?"

"My music partner."

"Who's that?"

"Grape."

"Grape?"

"That's her name. We have a band, it's called Hunter and the Grape."

"You play soul music in a two-piece band called Hunter and the Grape?"

"Yes, sir."

"So Sophie didn't travel to Albuquerque and you didn't meet her then?"

"No, sir. If she had passed through there and didn't tell

me I would be quite upset."

"Why?"

"Because she's my friend, sir. I don't have many friends."

Sophie Durango's father cleaned his teeth with a gulp of water and stared at the wall.

Ryan lay back on the couch and closed his eyes. Hunter could hear Sophie Durango whispering to him gently, something about pains and sleep and not overexerting himself.

Hunter looked at his hands. His left index finger was trembling slightly. He made it stop.

Stacey had been watching the tense interaction between Hunter and her father with great interest. Now that it was over she filled the silence with a gurgling shriek of admiration.

"That. Was. Awesome!"

Her father swept his heavy eyes over her gently.

"What are you talking about, little one?"

"That was like a movie right there. Or television. It was like watching television. Ooooh! I'm so tense right now."

She shivered as if to shake off a cold tension that covered her body, then smiled broadly, her little teeth shiny white.

"Do it again," she said to her father.

"Do what again?"

"Ask him questions. Ask him why his clothes are so dirty."

"Shush now, Stacey."

"Please, please, please, please!"

Stacey bounced up and down on her seat. Sophie Durango hissed at her and she slowed her bumping until she was completely stopped. You could tell that it was killing her however. Her body trembled with energy.

Sophie Durango continued stroking Ryan's face like he was a war victim and addressed her father.

"Hunter can sleep on the couch."

"Fine. As long as he doesn't steal anything. You're not going to steal anything?"

"I hope not, sir."

Her father grimaced, not appreciating the sarcasm. He stood, took his blazer and strode through the alcove and up the stairs. There was something empty about how he left the room. Coldly ritualistic almost. Like he didn't even connect in his own house. Now Hunter's right hand was trembling. He slipped it under his thigh to calm it down. Stacey watched him but didn't say anything.

Sophie Durango pulled Ryan to his feet wordlessly and led him away without another glance at Hunter.

Stacey stared at him with a condescending little smile playing on her lips.

"Just you and me, I guess," she said.

"I guess so."

"Do you like games?"

"Sure."

"What's your favourite game?"

"I dunno. What's yours?"

"You can't answer a question with a question."

"Why not?"

"Cos it's a rule."

"Of course. Sorry. I like checkers."

"What's checkers?"

"It's a board game."

"I've never played. I'll teach you a better game."

Hunter nodded calmly at the energetic little sprite in front of him then closed his eyes. He felt exhausted. Every muscle ached against his bones and the seat knuckled into the small of his back. Stacey was still talking over the rules of her made-up game but he wasn't really listening. It didn't matter, Stacey only needed him to be there, as inanimate as a doll for her to babble to. She just needed some attention, it didn't matter who it was from.

Forty-Five

He wasn't sure where he was when Ryan woke him. The couch had pretended to be comfortable and then twisted itself into aggressive shapes. He couldn't remember falling asleep. It was still dark outside and for a moment he thought he was in Albuquerque. Ryan had his hand against his mouth. His hand smelled of tangy sweat and old soap.

"Follow me outside," he said.

Ryan took his hand off Hunter's mouth. He was already fully dressed and waited patiently for Hunter to drag himself into the world.

Hunter's left leg was dead so he shook it a moment, grimacing as sharp tiny needles shot him through. Ryan sighed as if he thought he was stalling but Hunter held up his hand and stiffly made himself upright.

Sophie Durango had never returned from her room, nor had her dad. Eventually even Stacey had grown tired of mumbling at him and pottered off to bed. Nobody had offered any bedding on the couch so he had eventually lain down without any and closed his eyes.

Ryan stepped quietly outside, holding the doors open for Hunter to follow. Then he walked out of the garden and onto the street. A red sky was gently illuminating the horizon, the dawn pushing back against the dark and there was a gentle dusting of dew on the lawn. Ryan walked ahead silently, each step a methodical mirror image of the last. There was always a sensible stillness about this time of night, when the dawn was near but not quite present. It held the appeal of a church. This was life in repose. A fake world.

When they had reached the crumbling wall that Sophie Durango had taken him to, Ryan stopped. Hunter was keeping a careful distance a few paces behind. Ryan kept his eyes downcast and waited until their shadows on the concrete aligned, the yellowing lights casting them in a murderous haze. He licked his dry lips before he spoke. Had Sophie Durango told him about what had gone on between them? Hunter waited for something to happen.

"She has done this before, you know," Ryan reluctantly offered.

"Done what?"

"Something like you."

Hunter didn't like why Ryan spoke of him like an object, but his tone suggested that the detachment was necessary for him. Fundamental to how he kept his misaligned world orbiting safely. He was now certain that Ryan wasn't going to hit him at least.

"I don't know what you mean."

Ryan's eyes remained locked on their shadows, so Hunter copied him, searching the black shapes on the ground for something that might help him understand.

Ryan titled his head to the side, and his shadow obeyed.

"There was Jake. He turned up about five months ago. I answered the phone and pretended that I was her brother. I told him the wrong address. He still found the house though. I was home when he turned up. He just knew Sophie 'from around'. Because he thought I was her brother he didn't even try and act like he wasn't searching for her, or else he didn't care. He was an ugly bastard, conniving face, eyes that would sell you. Even when I told him to leave he wanted to stay. He left eventually when her dad returned and threatened to call the cops."

Ryan paused in a trained manner, giving Hunter the time for this information to sink in. He had gone through this conversation before. He licked his chapped lips again, biting some dried skin off before continuing. They looked painful.

"Then there was Billy. I didn't even know people were still called Billy. He was smooth. Turned up in a beat-up convertible, muddy and used, but with a bit of flare to it. A Mustang. You like Mustangs?"

"Yeah, I always wanted one."

"Right. This guy stared straight through me. Sophie embraced him, told me he was her cousin. He went along with it. Stayed and ate with us, just like you. Her dad was away so I couldn't prove he was or wasn't a cousin. Stacey didn't remember him. After we ate he said he needed to drive up to Burbank to meet his uncle, took Sophie with him so she could catch up with some family. I stayed up all night until he dropped her back. He just pulled up, she got out, came inside like it was the most natural thing in the world and got into bed with me. I always know when she's guilty of something because she fucks me like it's going to be the last time. To make me forget. And I let her."

Their shadows were so close that they joined at the feet and then as Hunter shifted his weight from one foot to the other, at parts of their hips and shoulders. He moved from side to side, watching the melding with satisfaction. He had stopped listening to Ryan. He didn't want to.

"I don't blame you. I want you to know that. I want to be angry but I can't be. I love her, and I know she needs to work her shit out. Some day she will, and then people like you will stop arriving to see her."

Ryan turned to look at him, taking a step back as he did so that their shadows abruptly separated. Hunter reluctantly drew his eyes up into the reddening sky. He couldn't look at Ryan. He hated him, hated him for being here, hated him for being an obstacle, hated him for telling him something that was a horrible truth, but most of all hated him for knowing who he was and how he meant nothing to Sophie Durango. It didn't matter if nothing that Ryan said was true. She didn't care about him. He had known it all along but refused to admit it. The sky was a mixture of so many shades of red that he could never possibly count them all.

Ryan stood beside him for a while longer, then eventually left. His shadow receding with his footsteps until it was quiet. The yellow halogen glow began to get eaten up by the growing dawn. A slow suffocating war of light. Hunter stayed still, afraid to take his eyes off the brightening sky. If he didn't move then he didn't exist and then this had never happened. The reds turned orange and then almost yellow.

He had nothing to go back to Sophie Durango's house for. He could walk back in. Demand to see her. Question if was it all a lie. Try to avoid the wrath of Ryan and her father and attempt to rip her away from the bosom of her life. Or he could wait. Let the time of the morning pass until she was alone and then steal in to see her. Surely that was what he should do. He couldn't just leave. The journey had been too far. What if she didn't want him to leave?

But he knew. He had known from the moment her face had shrugged at him impatiently when she first saw him. Pretending not to recognise him. Ruefully aware of what she had to do to make him leave. Even if it wasn't true, and she could fall in love with him, where would he take her? Back to Albuquerque, to the prison of a house where his deceased mother lay dormant, her stench of death waiting to arrest them in her posthumous pain? No. He had nothing to offer her but the clothes on his back and even he didn't want those.

He turned to take slow heavy steps back to collect the bike but it was resting against the wall in front of him. Ryan must have brought it for him even as he stared at the sky. There wasn't even a reason to cast one final eye over her house. It was over. Sophie Durango was nothing anymore but a memory that he could twist and spurn and envelop and colour with whatever emotions he wanted, because she would never know, and nor would anybody else.

He didn't get onto the bike but walked alongside it. It felt right that he should walk. He turned back in the vague direction of Venice beach and the sea and began one step at a time. Each step taking him away from Sophie Durango. The air felt thick around him, cloaking his body in an extra skin. A few cars passed by, bleary-eyed owners too tired to be upset at the hour and no longer aware of what a red sky looked like above them or how many colours existed within it.

For the first time in what seemed like forever Hunter had nowhere to go. No purpose. The only person who knew or cared where he was had disappeared. Would Grape even want to see him again? Why should she? He had abandoned her. It occurred to him that he might never see Grape again, he might never find her. The thought punched him in the belly like a cane to a whelp. He stood astride the bike and began to cycle into the warm morning air. Buildings floated past him, each one the same. He could taste the beach, the sea azure in the distance. He had never been close enough to understand the ocean before but now it drew him to its embrace like an old friend. He knew instinctively that Grape wouldn't have strayed far from the sea. He knew her better than he thought.

As he cycled, a light muscular burning beginning in his thighs from the effort, he wondered what Sophie Durango could be thinking. Would she wake up and care that he was gone? Would she question Ryan, or just assume he had left of his own accord? Or was that what she had really wanted and she had feebly sent Ryan as her messenger? None of it mattered anymore, it was better to not think about it. He stood up on the pedals and pushed down on each stroke with a fierce aggression, flying through red lights and stop signs with the grave abandon of somebody who refuses to acknowledge the presence of anyone else in the world.

Forty-Six

The last time that his father walked away from him had been the last time that he had seen him alive.

It was a clear morning, flanked by a light air that was crisp and tasteless. The New Mexican skies usually draped languidly close to the earth, but now they eagerly scraped the heavens. He watched his father churn a ferocious stride away from the car. The engine was still running so his mother leaned across and switched it off. The car felt emptier once she did. His father's pace began to quicken still further.

"He'll stop soon. He'll get tired and come back with his ragged tail between his legs."

She sounded confident, sure in her ability to keep tabs on the man who so singularly loved and despised her. Cat wasn't so certain. He angled his body to look outside the window at the dwindling figure getting smaller and smaller yet still holding all the power of the world in his movements. He wanted to get out and race after him. To

341

force his hands around the man's heavy waist and drag him to a stop. But he couldn't leave her. He didn't know why but staying was more important, or at least it felt that way. So he stayed and watched his father get devoured by the desert. He never saw him alive again after that.

That morning, when he didn't return, his mother applied some make-up to her cracking skin, puckered like a Christmas Turkey in the mirror, turned the ignition back on and pretended like nothing had happened. It was all her fault of course. The argument. The refusal to forgive and forget or admit indiscretions. Trivial in the grand scheme of things but fundamental to their relationship. And then it ended. Her vitriol had spat in his face like a wave of dismissal and then there was nothing more to be said. Nothing except a walk into the bowels of the desert to forget the entirety of an unfulfilled life.

The boardwalk by the beach was almost empty, and despite the salt in the air it held the same heavy feeling as that day in the desert.

Hunter was tired and he reluctantly slowed his pace, scanning the few faces that ventured out across the sands for Grape's familiar lazy gait, hoping to see her staring back at him from any of the loose faces he looked into. The surf rolled into the worn Los Angeles sands as he approached the spot on Venice where he had last seen her. As he sloped along slowly he passed by the turn for the bike rental store where he had robbed the bike and stopped, the brakes forcing the rubber tires in protest. The shop was closed but there was some activity in the little stores opposite. The grating of a clothing store was lifted up from the inside so Hunter moved to it and waited patiently. The metal painfully travelled higher and higher until a face peered out, still mostly hidden by shadow, eyes half closed, mouth barely moving.

"Not open yet, go away."

"The bike place?"

"What?"

"The bike rental place, over there, when does it open?"

"When I fucking feel like opening it, kid."

Hunter paused, then the face registered what he was sitting astride. Cold pale eyes searched him.

"That my bike? The one that went missing yesterday?"

Hunter nodded his head apologetically.

"Why did you bring it back?"

"I don't know."

"Why did you take it?"

"I was trying to find a girl."

The translucent orbs of a man who has seen too much narrowed the folds of skin covering the eyes like an awning.

"You giving it back to me?"

"Yeah."

The man nodded. His body dragged through the space then a clammy hand clamped on Hunter's wrist.

"Is this a joke?"

"No, sir."

The man's mouth was gummy, lopsided on the left, with one eye bigger than the other. His pale skin was loose but stuck tightly to the bones in places.

"You eaten breakfast?"

"No, sir."

"Good. I'm making eggs."

The man shook the handle bars to encourage Hunter to step off, then he wheeled the bike to the side of the shop and left it against the wall.

"It'll be fine there. Come on."

He trundled into the bowels of the building, past pillars of towels and T-shirts. Hunter stared after him a moment then followed gamely. His hand brushed the soft cotton of the new shirts and he yearned for the feeling of fresh clean clothes on his skin. His shirt and pants had grown tired of the constant sweaty movement and the fabric was hanging together by inertia.

The sizzling of fresh eggs, followed by a heady smell of pepper and butter ravished his senses and he drifted to a small room at the back of the shop. The man's hands were covered in liver spots, which gave him the appearance of a skinless leopard, but they were nimble and quick, flipping the eggs with a trained eye over a small hot plate.

"How do you like your eggs?"

"Any way you wanna make them, sir."

The man grunted and tossed two sunny-side-up eggs onto a plate, ripped off the head of a baguette and shoved the lot under his nose.

"Sit down."

Hunter sat on a stool at a small table.

"Tell me about the girl."

"Huh?"

"I want to know about the girl, why you brought my bike back, and who this girl is. She must be quite something to make you steal one of my bikes."

The man scowled but the gruff dismissal was an act. He wanted to tell his own story first and so he continued before Hunter could reply.

"I'm Claude. Claude is a French name. I'm French. Or used to be. Now I don't know. I'm a boxer. Nobody touches my bikes from around here because they know what's good for them. Only a brave man or an idiot messes with the French boxer down here."

"You don't have an accent."

"I adapted. That's what you do in life, you adapt. Maybe now I'm French-American. Adapt. It's a form of intelligence, and don't you forget. Don't adapt and die."

"So nobody will take the bike outside?"

Claude laughed through his nose, a glob of mucous shooting onto the frying pan at the same time as he flipped his own eggs off onto a plate.

"No. No, they won't. We all know each other down here. The only people who steal stuff are tourists. I heard that a skinny kid had taken my bike, and I thought he was either stupid or not from around here. If he wasn't stupid then he wouldn't come back, cos if he did then I'd break both his wrists. That's what I did to the last kid."

Claude looked at Hunter for emphasis, his eyes hawkish and his mouth moulded into a heavy pout.

Then he screamed and leapt at Hunter.

"Aaaaaarggrgrrgrgh!"

Hunter's stool rocked as he jerked backwards. Claude let his body tumble forward in laughter. Bent double, he wheezed and chortled, then finished with a deep hawk of spittle to the floor.

"Relax, you brought it back so I forgive you. Not many people do that. The art of street-borrowing has been lost – people can't trust each other anymore. If I thought people would bring my shit back after they used it then I'd let them take whatever they want, but people are greedy and you can't trust them. The beach people, they're the only ones I trust."

"I'm sorry I took your bike."

"No, you're not. You're only sorry if you get shit for it. Instead you're getting breakfast."

Hunter wiped the last of the yolk off his plate and swallowed down the bread. Claude sat down on a stool in the corner and began mopping up the runny eggs, eyeing up Hunter as he did.

"Now tell me about this girl. Did you find her?"

"No."

"No? What kind of a fucking shit story is that? If you didn't find her then get out of here and stop wasting my time."

"OK, I found her."

"Good. What happened?"

Hunter hesitated. "I'm not sure."

"What?"

"I found the girl that I was looking for, but she was the wrong one."

"Where is the right one?"

"I left her here, on Venice, when I went to find the wrong one."

"Did you fuck the wrong one?"

Hunter held Claude's gaze, even as his weak eyes shivered with anticipation, his chest heaving with the constant struggle to breathe. The thought occurred to Hunter that Claude might die soon.

"Yes."

"Good. Always fuck the wrong one. Make love to the right one."

"I guess ..."

"Are you sure the other girl is the right one?"

"I'm not sure about anything."

Claude shovelled some wet eggs into his mouth and

gestured for Hunter to continue.

"Tell me everything and I'll decide."

The sun was streaming through the store front, casting a sharp glare on the white walls that made Claude squint. Hunter told his story in a fashion that made him squirm with self-conscious unease. Claude's eyes never left him, his cloudy pupils devouring every movement. Hunter began telling him everything: things he had forgotten, moments that had been important but previously ignored, the old man, getting robbed, Sir Will, Grape's uncle, Delilah, even finding his mother dead, then finally discovering Sophie Durango, sleeping with her and then leaving at Ryan's behest.

Claude's expression was inscrutable and by the end he hardly seemed to be paying attention. After a while he puffed out his cheeks and spoke seriously.

"What's your name, boy?"

"Hunter."

"The girl, what's her name?"

"Grape."

"Your names are Hunter and Grape?"

"Well no, my name was Cat, and she was Star. We, well, Grape, she changed them."

"She changed your names?"

"Yeah."

"Why?"

"I dunno. I guess it's a thing she does. She changes her name to remind her of the last nice thing that happened to her in the world."

The old Frenchman closed his eyes, the lids touching gently like a butterfly's wings. When he opened them there were tears hovering on the cusp.

"I had a girl."

He stared at the wall if it held all the answers. Hunter waited.

"I left her in France."

"Oh."

Claude nodded his head gently, his eyes in the past.

"Polina. She was beautiful. Fiery. She refused to leave France. 'Come to America,' I pleaded with her. 'No, stop asking me.' 'But please,' I said, 'we will have a great life together.' She loved France too much. She lost her temper and said to me 'Claude, stop asking me or I will leave you.' I didn't believe her. I knew that I could convince her. So I stood outside her apartment in Paris and begged her from the street. I slept outside her door, sang songs, performed theatre, sat in the rain. Waiting for her to change her mind. She never came down. After two days her neighbour told me that she had gone to her parents in Marseille. She never even told me. I was so proud. Imagine, a proud Frenchman. So I thought if she could leave then I could also. So I did. I left for New York within a week."

Hunter's nose was itchy but he didn't want to scratch it in case he distracted Claude from his thoughts. He felt like he should offer something.

"Maybe she was afraid?"

Claude's doleful eyes floated over to rest on Hunter.

"Afraid?"

"Of leaving France?"

Claude made a noise, something like a soft laugh. His lips were wet misshapen things.

"No. I thought so to. I thought that after a while I would come back for her and she would change her mind, that the pain of my absence would convince her to move past her fear and to take the leap into the unknown with me. An adventure I called it. So after six months, when I had found a job and an apartment, I returned to France for her."

Claude fell silent again, seeing everything play out in invisible scenes before his eyes. His eyes flickered back and forth, observing the imaginary actors float about their business.

"What happened?" Hunter said.

"She was living with another man. She came back from Marseille and I was gone. I tried telling her my reasons but she fought with me. She was fiery. 'Claude, you left me!' she cried when I shouted and stomped my feet. She thought that I had gone to America and forgotten about her. It didn't matter, she had moved on. 'But we are in love,' I said. 'What happened to being in love?' She stopped shouting then and kissed me gently. 'Oh, Claude,' she said, in that tone she would use when I didn't understand her. 'Oh Claude, we are in love, but you don't need me enough. If I was enough for you then you would never need to leave Paris. The world here is too small for you.' So I cried a little, drank a lot of wine, and returned to New York, convinced that she was right, that she was setting me free, that I didn't need any woman, or that if I did then she would come to me when life determined it should be so. Polina. Unfortunately, there are not many women like her in the world and I never found anybody else. And she never came to me."

Claude closed his eyes, preferring to watch the final dance of his past in the darkness. Hunter took in the constraints of the tiny box room they were in as his loneliness became apparent. This was a broken man hanging on to the vestiges of a past life. The headache returned to Hunter with a nauseous raping of his senses and he had to close his throat to stop from retching.

Claude opened his eyes with a great effort, deep breaths quivering his slender frame.

"I think that you should find this girl."

"I will."

"You have no choice. You cannot lose her like how I lost mine." Claude was insistent.

"I don't think it's quite the same."

"Love is all the same."

"I guess."

"Of course it is. Polina. Grape. It's the same. You can't make the same mistake that I did."

"I won't."

Claude suddenly rose to his feet to emphasise his point, his hands animating in circles around his figure like a conductor. He swung around the room impatiently as if there was a presence threatening to disrupt the clarity of his newfound purpose.

"Do you understand what I'm saying? The importance?"

"Yeah, sure."

"But do you really?"

Claude pressed his eager face against Hunter's so that their noses touched. He was aggressive now. The feeble figure with the matchstick memories morphed into something harder. As if his physicality could change anything. Hunter pushed back at Claude, a little irritated and his headache pounding, but the old Frenchman leaned back into him, his tepid frame relishing the angst. He jabbed his finger into Hunter's chest.

"You are too young to recognise an opportunity. I will not let you pass it by like I did. I made the mistake once and it haunts me. Now is my time to prevent you from repeating mine.'

Hunter was forced back against the wall and held his hands up reflexively against the rising tide of Claude's exuberance.

'OK, calm down. I want to find Grape.'

'No. Not 'want', but 'have to'. There is nothing else in this world for you but to find her.'

'OK.'

'*Tell me that you understand!*' Claude suddenly screamed at him, his face constricting in upon itself like a vacuum sucking the energy from the air. 'Your mother is dead. Your father is dead. You found an old man, and he is dead. Her uncle is dead. Sir Will has gone. Sophie Durango doesn't exist. Polina is gone. Polina is dead. Everybody is dead or gone!'

The sun's glare from the white walls pressed angry white spots into Hunter's eyes. Claude was one of the white spots, dominating everything. The pain in his head was unbearable. He needed some space. He needed Grape – she would be able to relieve the situation. He stepped away from Claude but kept his hand against the cool surface of the wall for reassurance.

Claude was repeating Polina's name to himself.

'Polina. I know things. I don't know much, but I know some things. I made wrong choices. It was my fault, Polina. But I know things about love. I'm French. I know when not to let something go. Sometimes you just know, even if you want to fight it.'

Hunter nodded again, then grabbed the water tap by the small sink and dragged his mouth under the font. He drank crazily, hoping the water would quash the rising pain in his

351

head. Grape. He had to find Grape. He had pushed her from his thoughts when he was with Sophie Durango. He had to do that otherwise nothing would have made sense, but now there was nothing else. Claude was right. Claude was definitely right.

Claude was watching him. Hunter wiped his mouth. It seemed like Claude was waiting for him. To acknowledge Polina maybe, or to thank him for his wisdom. Anything was better than nothing.

"When did Polina die?"

"A long time ago."

"I'm sorry."

"It's OK. It was a long time ago. I try not to think about her. When I do I get upset."

"Yeah, I noticed."

"*Oui.*"

It was the first French word that Claude had said and even he seemed surprised.

"I haven't spoken French in a long time. Not since Polina died. I never went back to France."

"How did she die?"

Claude wrinkled his face into a tiny ageing ball and shook his head. The conversation was over.

"I didn't mean to ..." Hunter began.

"It's all going to be alright, Hunter."

"*Que sera sera?*"

"Something like that. Now let's go and find this Grape."

Claude placed his gnarled hand on the teenager's shoulder, tipped his head in solidarity and walked out into the sun, a shadow of a man ready to take on the world.

Forty-Seven

They had walked up and down the boardwalk at least five times, Hunter traipsing in the crazed Frenchman's wake as he badgered and cajoled anybody who would catch his eye and babbled about a 'Grape'. He had clearly overstated his importance and people turned from him with the casual self-conceited shrug that they give to tired crazies. Claude had overestimated his place in this world but refused to acknowledge it. He had drawn a shroud of protective ignorance around him and wasn't going to relinquish it easily. The day was half over. Hunter was weary and ready to call for a time out and a regrouping, when Claude spun back into him and placed his life-stained hands upon his shoulders. He was surprisingly strong when passion took him.

"I know," he whispered reverentially.

"You know what?"

"Where she is."

"Where?"

"Where else?"

"I don't know, that's why I asked you."

"Follow me. I know where she has to be."

Claude skipped off into a scurrying scamper, his skinny legs moving across the ground furtively. Hunter strained to keep up as Claude skipped around the corner, down a side street, across Pacific Avenue heading for the canals, then at the last minute doubted himself, turned back upon his tracks and into a small alleyway. Huge graphic murals decorated the walls, chipped and exposed to the naked brick where the paint had fallen away. At the far end of the alleyway there was a half-finished mural of Charlie Chaplin playing cards with what could have been a depiction of Bob Marley and David Bowie but it wasn't entirely clear.

Claude didn't stop until he got to the mural, then swung his head from side to side, searching for something. There was nobody else in view. Hunter caught up to him and examined the mural. It had been started a long time ago and never finished, the paint fading into the fabric of the wall like a cheap tattoo. The alley stank of piss and the air was stale without the sea breeze filtering it. Claude meandered towards a doorway on the right where a figure was bundled up in a sleeping bag. Claude pressed his foot to the ribs of the sleeping body but there was no reaction.

"Grape? Is that you?" he queried.

Claude rolled the body over and a dark face stared out. The man's eyes were open but he was unresponsive. Claude kicked the man harder this time, looking to Hunter for support. The eyes didn't blink. A third time and the eyes widened in pain. The homeless man yelped out in feeble protest.

"What the fuck, man, come on?"

He had been sleeping with his eyes open. Now he rubbed

them together, getting the wet back into the dry holes in his face.

"You're not Grape?" Claude demanded.

"Not what?"

"You're not Grape?"

"No shit, I'm not."

"Where is she then?"

"Leave me alone."

"Where is she?"

"Claude, just fuck off, man, I've had enough of your shit."

"Listen, Jackson, I know you know where she is. Or Alexa, she should know. Why isn't she here with her?"

"Fuck you."

The homeless man known as Jackson gathered his spidery body out of the sleeping bag and rose to his feet, face hanging to his chest groggily. Claude stared at him then looked back at Hunter.

"Grape would have been here with Alexa."

Hunter nodded calmly, as if that made all the sense in the world. Jackson ambled towards Hunter, sleeping bag trailing around one foot. He had big wide eyes, like a child who had never grown up because he didn't like how the world looked.

"Who are you?"

"Nobody."

Jackson grimaced and clutched his hip where it clearly ached. Claude came behind him and jabbed a skinny finger into his back.

"Did you see them?"

"No."

Claude pushed Jackson harder, looking to Hunter to

support him as if this was a police interrogation. His finger was a weapon.

"Describe Grape to him. He will have seen her."

Jackson settled his weary eyes on Hunter, challenging him to expose him to something other than his life.

"She's pretty," Hunter said lamely.

"There's a lot of pretty girls."

Hunter didn't know how to describe Grape. Closing his eyes he saw her gentle face looking thoughtfully back at him contentedly.

"She has nice eyes, big, round, always looking, seeing everything. She doesn't speak much, but when she does it's calming. She has a gentle smile. She's kind of like the wind, a nice breeze that makes you feel good about yourself. A breeze that doesn't really know where it wants to go but you want to find out where it ends up."

Hunter opened his eyes slowly to find Claude and Jackson staring at him, unblinking. Jackson nodded and looked at Claude.

"She sounds like Alexa."

"I know," Claude agreed.

"Who's Alexa?" Hunter asked impatiently.

Jackson snuffled and coughed, hawking a large globule of yellow gunk onto the ground, then turned back to his corner. He motioned for Claude to carry on.

"I ain't seen any new girls, but she sounds like Alexa."

Jackson settled himself back against the wall, resting his head against the stone. His wide eyes seemed heavy and he had a winding cut down his forehead that looked to have been there for some time and never quite healed.

"Claude, when you gonna let me stay in your shop again, man?"

"When you find Grape for me."

"Fuck you."

Jackson turned his cheek against the cold wall and looked into the shadows so they couldn't see his eyes anymore. Claude shifted from one foot to the next uncomfortably, having expended his options.

Hunter should have kept the bike. Claude had tried his best. Maybe the Russian was wrong.

"You don't know where we can find Grape, do you?"

Claude shook his head with the morose air of defeat.

"I thought she might be here."

"Why?"

"Alexa was supposed to be here. She never came back. Grape sounds like Alexa. I guess I hoped that maybe they came together. Magnets."

"Thanks for trying to help me."

Claude looked up at Hunter with pained eyes, thin red veins streaking his pale irises like a tearing sky. It hurt to look into his eyes too long but Hunter held his gaze even as the hurt poured out. His body sagged in on itself, as if not finding Grape was a physical weight pressing down upon every fibre of his being.

"I'm no use to you, Hunter. I can't help you. I'm an old Frenchman who can't speak French anymore, who nobody respects."

Claude began to walk out of the alley, giving Jackson a cursory glance as he left. Jackson didn't say a word but kept his head facing the shadows in protest.

"I'm sorry for kicking you, Jackson."

"Fuck you, Claude. Fuck you."

Jackson's words hit Claude hard and he bent a little lower to the ground as he walked, feet dragging on the ground like a brush picking up detritus. Hunter followed him out of courtesy and they gradually melted back towards the beach. Behind them Jackson's voice rang out.

"*I didn't mean it, Claude! I'm sorry!*"

Claude didn't reply but he heard and it seemed to make him feel better. He walked a little faster.

Maybe if Grape didn't want to be found then she wouldn't be.

The bike was where Claude had left it, even as he had closed his shop. A good-looking young man in a ripped T-shirt stood a few feet away, advertising parking. He nodded at Claude as they approached.

"Kept an eye on your bike, Claude."

Claude didn't respond so Hunter gave the guy a nod on his behalf then waited while Claude pulled the shutters up, fumbling with the key like it was a heavy brick in his hands. The shutters rolled halfway up with a grudging whine and Claude stooped to go inside. Hunter caught Claude's arm and he turned back to look at him, face pained.

"Thank you for helping me," Hunter offered.

"I didn't help you. I thought I could."

"You did."

Hunter was unable to think of anything of solace to say to the old man and was hungry with desire to leave and continue his search for Grape. Claude's thin knotty hand grabbed his wrist and he pulled him closer.

"Find that girl, and bring her here. Bring her here so I can see her. That would make me happy. I'll make eggs. Everybody loves eggs."

"I will."

Claude dipped his head to go inside.

"Will I bring the bike in?"

"No. You take it. Or if you don't want it let somebody else take it. Maybe it will help them find somebody."

Hunter pried his wrist free of Claude's eager grasp and let the old man disappear into the store. The shutters rolled down and then he was left standing there, alone again. After a moment he went to the bike and wheeled it away from the shop and out onto the boardwalk. The good-looking guy gave him a look but then turned back to his own business, waving down an approaching car with a benign enthusiasm. Hunter watched him a moment, seeing the rippling muscle under his skin and wondering what he had dreamed of when he was younger, what yearning had sent him on his way through life that had ended up here on the beach selling parking and friendly with a regretful old man who rented bikes in the hope that other people's happy stories would help him forget his own tragic one.

Casting all these thoughts from his mind Hunter began to walk along the boardwalk again, the wheels of the bike squeaking for company, and he searched for Grape. He was going to find her. He wasn't sure if she wanted to be found, but he was going to find her no matter what.

Forty-Eight

The sky was peeling back the day, beating the last hints of sun into retreat. The beach had earlier been a hive of frenetic activity, people screaming, laughing, selling, hoping, loving, living. Obscure faces regaling the world with florid tales of their own importance. Now it was beginning to empty. Stalls were slowly packed up on the boardwalk and tourists drifted away like dying smoke. Hunter had long given up his search. He had caressed the outskirts all day, up and down, retracing his steps over and over, considering the same faces over and over again as if they would somehow morph into Grape's and mock him for not seeing through her initial disguise.

He sat on a pile of grass near the skateboard park, close to where he had originally left Grape and stretched his legs out. If she wanted to be found then she would find him, so all he could do was wait, and hope that she would come back. He almost believed that. But Grape had a strong will and didn't seem to want to have ever dwelled in the past.

For her the present was all-important, and if he had exited her orbit then he was now a part of her past. He thought about going back to Claude and admitting defeat, maybe alleviating some of the man's quiet solitude and allowing him to impart more of his pain about Polina. But he couldn't. He had to wait here just in case Grape came by. He didn't really know what else to do.

The light filtered away behind him, a tepid red cloak enveloping the sky and casting covetous glances onto the sea below, trying to bury colour into its depths. The horizon echoed into the distance forever and Hunter felt small and irrelevant. What importance had he to the world anyway, what importance had anything for that matter? An overwhelming heaviness filled the hollow cavity of his bones and his body stuck to the earth like a weight. He was tired. Before when he had been tired he would remember what it felt like to be close to Sophie Durango. Now when he thought of her there was only a blank face and gaping void. Maybe it had always been that way but Grape had pulled him out of the memories before they became grey and tasteless. Sophie Durango had placed a veil over his mother in the way that Grape had followed suit over Sophie Durango. Who would take the place of Grape, or would anybody? Would he become like Claude, alone and filled with regret? His hands drew a slow pattern in the sand at his feet like a thousand had before and he focused on the tiny grains spilling off his skin. So many, none of them the same. Like people. Shapeless until events cast them into something more than they were before. The red in the sky was almost gone and the night was closing around him.

He must have fallen asleep because he suddenly realised

that he was cold and his arm was numb from lying on it.
He shook his body out and got to his feet. The beach was
empty, the boardwalk quiet. Apart from the distant hum of
the city beyond, there was nothing but the crashing of the
waves breaking on the beach. He walked towards the
sound, tasting the cold salt air on his tongue. He shivered a
little but kept walking until he was at the edge. The moon
cast little slivers of light across the ocean. It seemed even
bigger at night when all the blackness of the sea held
unanswerable depths. Claude would have gone to sleep by
now. He was alone on the beach.

Not alone. There was the almost imperceptible
movement of sand against feet behind him. Then there was
a body behind him. It stopped and he waited. He didn't feel
afraid. The sea was so close that he could fall into her
protective bosom in a heartbeat and that made him feel
safe. He was defeated anyway.

"What are you doing?"

He knew that voice. Of course he did. But it was night
and he was tired. He didn't want to turn around. He
wondered was the Russian always right. Despite his hard
edge there had been a sharp romanticism within him that
he protected.

"Waiting," he replied carefully.

"For what?"

"For somebody."

The voice snorted in derision. There was the sound of a
body lowering itself, feet shuffling through the sand
awkwardly to get comfortable.

"For who?"

The voice was gentle even though it was trying to be
rough. He shivered again. He was afraid to look at her in

case she didn't exist or bolted from him like a tease.

"A girl."

"Did you find her?"

"I don't know yet."

Hunter's hand still held some of the grains of sand rolled around under his thumb and he let them fall. He cleared his throat, the sound hard and uncomfortable in the quiet. The breaking waves were methodical.

"How will you know?"

He knew this voice, the soft dulcet tones were calming. Grape. He could feel her gaze rest languidly against his neck, watching the veins as they slid under his skin and brought him life. He didn't know what to say back to her. He would say anything just to keep her in conversation. He hadn't lost her for very long but it already felt epic. Maybe this was how things felt when they were important – they were magnified until the reality was obliterated. His mind closed its doors and shut him out so there was just a blankness. He wanted to see her face again. Grape.

He turned to her through the air but keeping his eyes on the ground. When he was facing her, he allowed his gaze to drag across the sand, then up along her naked calves, her round pale knees, across the hem of her skirt, and up over her hips, along the side of her chest and over the curve of her neck and then through her brown hair and into her large blue eyes. He had never looked into her eyes properly before. Now he did and he was astounded. They challenged him and he struggled to stay afloat. What would Claude do if he was faced with Polina again, would he wither in her presence or be lifted into something euphoric? Or did it matter what you did in those first moments?

The waves continued their endless breaking on the shore.

No matter what happened on the beach they were certain to continue as before.

"Hi, Grape."

"What happened to the girl?"

Her face was impassive, her body relaxed in on itself, but there was a gravity to her tone. He swallowed, afraid to lie because she would know if he did.

"I found her. She wasn't anything."

Grape scrunched her face, maybe not expecting him to have been honest. Taking a moment to consider, she smacked her lips together loudly.

"I'm glad you reached her. That was important to you."

"Yeah."

He spoke slowly, the words slurring in his mouth. He felt like an idiot. His entire presence was an apology.

"What happened?"

She wanted to know that he missed her. She wanted to hear him say things to her, but he couldn't be dishonest, he owed her his honest truth. He owed it to both of them. Even if it tore her apart. If it tore her apart he would find a way to fix it, he decided, and the need to protect her emboldened him.

"I meant nothing to her. She didn't care."

Grape let her head nod like a small bobblehead-doll, gently going up and down thoughtfully. He noticed that her hands were balled up and her body was tense and straight as if she had expected him to fight her over the truth. He looked into her eyes with what he hoped was a candid openness but he couldn't read her. Only a small vein above her left temple that he had never noticed before gave any idea of her feelings, throbbing away impatiently with a quiet fervour.

"Did she mean anything to you?"

"I thought that she did. I was wrong."

"Why?"

"I thought I loved her."

Grape's head snapped forward abruptly in a gesture of butting him, her nose grazing the air ferociously.

"I know you did, you always spoke about her like that."

"I guess."

"Tell me what happened."

She spoke aggressively. He had never seen her this passionate. Her chest heaved and she swallowed deep gulps of salty air to control her breathing. He spoke quietly, as if the tenor of his voice could calm her emotions.

"I found her, but she wasn't who I thought she was. I had made her into something that she wasn't."

"I could have told you that."

"Yeah."

"But you wouldn't have listened to me."

The moon cast an ethereal glow across Grape's face and the reflection from the waves rolled over her skin. Her face was couched into a hard frown. She was beautiful when she was angry. She was always beautiful. Hunter had only seen what he had wanted to see. Her eyes were brilliant in the sea of cold blue that shadowed her face.

"I wouldn't have listened to you, you're right. I'm sorry."

"Sure."

She wanted to make it hard for him, and he wanted her to.

"And I realised that I missed you."

"*Harumph!*" Grape snorted with what was supposed to be mocking condescension but came out like a pained gasp.

She rose to her feet, and began to walk along the break of the sea. Hunter watched her ass sway, buttocks outlined by the light fabric of her skirt. Then he followed her dutifully, staying just a few feet behind her like he knew she wanted. The waves parted respectfully just before they touched her but swept against Hunter with precision.

Grape took off her shoes and left them on the sand then stepped into the foaming wavelets and stood still, staring out at the ocean. Hunter stopped beside her. Her face was impassive. Everything felt important.

"I watched you today. I watched you with that old man, I heard him ask about me. Who was he?"

"Just a friend. He was trying to help me find you."

"Why was he helping you?"

"Because I told him about you."

"Why?"

"Because you're important to me."

"I'm not sure if I believe that."

Her eyes swept past the glistening waves deep into the horizon and considered where the blackness began. She was making a decision. He took off his own shoes and placed his naked feet into the cold waters, letting the sea swirl around his ankles adventurously. He wanted to put his arms around Grape, to pull her warm body tightly into him. As if hearing his thoughts her body visibly tensed, shoulders lifting up to her ears in a definite show of unease. She stepped deeper into the water until it was at her knees, the water sloshing just below the hem of her skirt. He followed slowly, not bothering to lift up his jeans. Her lips were set so tightly against her jaw it looked sore.

"Did you have sex with her?"

"Yes."

"You shouldn't have done that."

"I know."

The skin pulled across the smooth bones of her face so aggressively it seemed it might crack.

"I don't know if I could ever sleep with you now. Knowing that you had sex with her."

"She's not important anymore."

"But I hate her."

"You shouldn't."

"Don't tell me what to feel."

Grape walked deeper into the water, letting the sea pull at her until it was at her waist. The dark water gripped at her skirt and pulled it out and around like an unhappy umbrella. The sky was darker out here, the air thick with night and Hunter couldn't see that far in front of him. He shivered reflexively and followed her. He was taller than Grape but the water still hit his balls and sent tremors up his spine. Finally he stood beside her. Her body swayed from the strength of the water and he held his hands out ready to grab her. Her expression was unreadable in the darkness and she kept her face forward. When she spoke again it trembled with rage.

"You shouldn't have gone to find her!"

"If I hadn't been looking for her then I would never have met you."

"But you did meet me."

"And I'm glad that I did."

"It's different now. Because you had sex with her, and she rejected you. So you come back to me. Is that how it is? I'm the only thing that you have left?"

"No."

"How do I know that you're not lying to me?"

"You have to trust me."

"Tell me it's not because you have nobody left in the world. Tell me it's not because you have nothing to go back to, nothing to go forward to, and I'm the only thing that you know. Tell me that's not the truth?"

Hunter stared out to the darkening horizon where the suede tailbone of the sky merged with the black sea to become one wall. Grape was right.

She stepped deeper into the ocean, the swell of the waves enjoying the challenge of skirting higher and higher up their bodies. She stepped forward until the waters were covering the bottom of her breasts, then swelling forward up and above her collar bone. Hunter stayed close, hands held behind her back protectively. It felt dangerous being out this deep and not being able to see what was under and around them. They were at the behest of the sea now. The dark-blue wet rode up his chest and some spray hit his chin. It was a gentle swell though and a quiet evening, the sort that surfers hate but that Hunter was glad of. He felt like he knew what she wanted to hear but he wanted to be honest.

"You're right. I don't have anything. That's the truth. I don't know where to go, and you're the only one left in the world who gives a shit about me. So maybe I do need you because I don't have anything else. Or maybe it's not and it's the way it's supposed to be. Maybe you have nothing either and you need me. Maybe I've realised that I do give a shit about you. The world doesn't give a shit about either of us, but it threw us together and that means something. At least I hope it does, but I actually don't know. I don't really know anything."

"How do you know that I give a shit about you?"

"I don't. I just hope that you do. Do you?"

"Yeah. I guess, but maybe that's not enough. Maybe it's too late."

The water splashed up onto their faces and made it harder to speak so they had to raise their voices before the wind and the sea carried them away.

"I don't think that it is," he said.

"You don't think about anything properly until you have no choice."

"Maybe. Is that so wrong?"

Grape stepped forward again without taking her eyes off the horizon. It was getting hard to stand now, the current pulling at their legs eagerly, trying to whip them upside down. The swell was bigger and louder but Grape ignored it and stepped up to her chin, the water hitting her eyes so that she had to bob on her toes with it to keep her mouth and eyes above the water. Hunter followed but caught a large splash of water in the face. It was almost time to turn back or begin swimming. But he couldn't swim. It was dangerous with the current now. Once they lost contact with the bottom they could be carried off into the depths. He pretended that couldn't happen to them. Grape still didn't look at him, keeping a stony hardness in her voice that would have unnerved him if he wasn't so focused on keeping his head up and his toes down. His shirt was stuck to him like a second skin and he couldn't breathe properly, the cold tightening his chest like a vice.

"So you give a shit about me?"

"Yeah, yeah, I do."

Grape shook her head, fighting to turn it against the confines of the sea. She was almost shouting. Her feet weren't touching the ground and one swell almost carried her away from him but he grabbed her arm and kept her close. She still refused to look his way.

"What's your name?"

"You know my name?"

"I want to hear you say it?"

"Hunter."

"Did you tell her you were called Hunter now?"

"No."

"So you never slept with her when you were Hunter?"

"No. I was only Cat to her. Now I'm Hunter."

"Am I still Grape?"

"I hope so. I'll call you whatever you want me to call you."

"I'm Grape. It has to be Hunter and Grape or nothing."

"OK."

"OK."

"Grape?"

"What?"

"I'm cold. We should go back."

"Why?"

"I can't swim."

"Then go back."

"You know that I won't without you."

"Why?"

"Because I don't want to lose you again."

Grape turned to him. Her face was covered in the sea but her eyes burned fiercely. She might have been crying but it was too dark and her face was too wet to tell. He wasn't sure if he was crying or if the salt was just stinging his eyes. He made what he hoped was a caring face but the sea hit him hard and it was a struggle to keep his eyes open. He couldn't let his toes leave the bottom. His struggle made her smile, eyes lighting up her face. He smiled back as best he could, his body sliding along now with the drag of the all-powerful ocean. He couldn't let his toes leave the bottom. He couldn't swim but it was only when he said it out loud that it became a reality. Now he was afraid.

He was about to reach for her when a huge wave smacked her head, pulling her under and into its embrace. The same wave cascaded over him and he was thrown back, losing his grip on the sand at his feet. He pushed his hand out against the cool pressure of the sea and found the wet cloth of her skirt, dragging her towards him. The sea swirled him around like a plaything. His head went under the water and everything was black. He was lost. He wanted to flail about, panic taking over, but his grip on her skirt kept his focus and he didn't waver. His other hand grabbed her arm and pulled her towards him. Her body crashed into his and they spun a little, gasping for breath and pulling towards the shore. She was swimming and he was turning but he kept calm for her. He kicked into the emptiness and hoped that he would be able to breathe again. How easy it was to ignore the taste of the air until it was taken away. Grape kicked and pulled him and then he could feel the sand again. Once they had found some leverage on the bottom and he could stand properly Hunter embraced Grape tightly, burying his nose in her wet hair. She clutched at him feverishly, hands raking into the bones of his spine and they held each like that for a while, the sea lifting them off their feet intermittently, but it didn't matter. They stayed wrapped around each until they could feel the other begin to shake and then Hunter led Grape out of the sea and onto the beach, hands clutching her waist like he might lose her and never see her again.

Forty-Nine

"You found her?"

Claude's sombre eyes lit up on the bedraggled kids standing before him in the dark. Grape was shivering heavily, her body shaking aggressively, water dripping down her pale skin. The halogen of the street lights made everything feel special. Claude had been awake when they knocked on the shutters, maybe even waiting.

"Yes. This is Grape."

"The Grape?"

"Yes."

Claude took her light hands in his and kissed the tops of them with his weathered lips.

"It is an honour. I know everything about you."

Grape looked at Hunter but he simply shrugged.

"Can we borrow some warm clothes, Claude?"

Claude smiled and opened his arms to Hunter with a dramatic flourish as if he had been waiting for this moment his entire life.

"Of course. Please, let me take care of you both."

He ushered them into his little shop, making sure that they ducked their heads under the metal grating. Then he pulled Hunter into a hug that belied the short time they had known each other. When he released him Claude turned to Grape, tired eyes lucid with significance.

"I'm so glad that he found you. It was important."

His eyes began to fill up and Grape smiled at him with that knowing smile that she had.

"I know it was."

Claude looked at her proudly, taking in her curved frame and soft eyes. Her wet hair was scraped behind her ears and her face was red with the cold, lips light blue which only served to make her more beautiful. She embraced him, encircling his meagre frame with her arms and he let himself be free in her bosom. His body collapsed into hers and it appeared like it had been a long time since Claude had been that way with someone. She held him and he closed his eyes and let it happen. Hunter was thinking he might have fallen asleep when he quietly opened his eyes and lifted free of her grasp. Grape kissed him on the cheek and it seemed for a moment that he might cry.

Raising his hands apologetically, he stepped back and announced like a Grand Vizier: "You're both so wet, and cold, I am so rude, I have towels, of course I have towels, I sell towels! Come in and let's get you warm, I'll make coffee and warm whiskey."

Claude dragged the shutters to the floor behind them to keep the heat of the shop in and threw some towels at them in a flurry of enthusiasm.

"Get dry, please get dry quickly or I'll never forgive myself."

The shop was dry and welcoming, a sanctuary from the chaos of the outside world. The skinny Frenchman busied himself to try and contain his excitement, drinking in Grape's presence and flicking his eyes to his young friend often. Their presence seemed to inject him with a fire and he was determined to fan it further without making a fool of himself.

Hunter picked up the largest towel that he could find and smiled as he curled it around Grape, her big wide eyes filling the room and seeing nothing else but him. And for first time in a long time he needed nothing else. Claude watched the two of them and it reminded him of something that he had forgotten and thought he would never be a part of ever again. They saw nothing but each other.

Fifty

"How does it feel?" she asked.

Hunter touched his nose to Grape's and let it rest there. Her face was so close that she was blurry and out of focus, almost a mirage.

"I don't know yet."

Grape giggled and hit him playfully on the cheek then squirmed away from his grasp. Sitting up, she threw the coverlets off her body and got to her feet. Claude had made them a bed amongst the towels and shirts in the storeroom below. It was small but cosy. He had insisted on having them sleep in his room but Grape had politely refused. Claude was so smitten that he couldn't argue with her. He had bid them goodnight with a warm smile and a hug for each. Hunter had been worried that Claude might cry but he kept it together.

"Tomorrow I will close the shop and we explore Los Angeles together," he had said.

Grape had kissed him on the cheek again and stroked his face softly before he left.

"He's a kind man," she said.

Now she stood above Hunter in just her underwear and an oversized Venice Beach T-shirt and glowered impatiently.

"Tell me how it feels, Hunter, or I'm leaving and I'm taking Claude with me."

Hunter sat up with a straight face and pretended to be upset with her but a smile trembled on his lips.

"I can't tell you if I don't know yet."

"Well, if you can't tell me what it feels like to be in love then I can't tell you either."

"Fine."

"Fine."

They smiled shyly at each other.

Grape relented and slipped back under the covers. She curled into his arms and they held each other, for that was all that they needed to do right now. Just feel the comfort of each other's presence and for the first time know that neither was leaving. Grape's breath was hot against Hunter's neck and he felt himself melt into her body, that seductive feeling of contentment and desire for sleep mixing with the need to be awake and hold her to his chest. Grape's body softened in his arms and her breath became heavy. Her eyes flickered.

"Can we find them again?"

"Who?"

"Sir Will. Sir Will and Delilah."

"Yeah."

"We should bring them to the beach. They would like it here."

"Yeah."

He would like to see Sir Will again, it seemed important.

But now he needed to sleep. He could think about everything else tomorrow. Everything began to slow down but Grape was still quietly talking.

"First we have to explore with Claude."

"Uh huh."

"It would be rude not to."

"Uh."

"How do you think we will find them?"

"Mmmh."

"Hunter? Hunter?"

"Huh, what?"

"Are you sleeping?"

Hunter opened his eyes and looked at her, expecting to see her shining face peering into his but her eyes were closed, her face smooth and calm in those moments just before dreams take over. Those were her last words – she might not even have been aware she had said them. He said nothing but watched her until he felt his eyes were heavy on his head and nothing else mattered but holding her close and drifting off into fantasy.

Tomorrow would be different, and the day after and the day after that. They were still two little travellers orbiting a huge universe, but there were always possibilities and "together" was something he had never been able to say before. Together they would figure it all out.

Then he closed his eyes and let it happen.

The End

If you enjoyed *Hunter and the Grape*
you may also enjoy *Kingdom of Scars*.

Here's a chapter sample as a taster . . .

Kingdom
of Scars

Chapter 1

Schooling with Don

He had always enjoyed the walk from the DART up to school. It didn't really make any sense because half of the time it was cold and dreary and his feet hurt. But there was something that excited him about walking past the council flats from Connolly Station up through Summerhill to Mountjoy Square – the sense of danger. He had a physical routine that he used to slip into when he approached. He'd knit his eyebrows together like he'd seen on the television – it made people look very intense and dangerous, he thought. He would bob his head and his hips from side to side, adopting the 'walk' of inner-city Dublin, a little like the lads who had approached him at the station. Safety in replication. Lastly, and most importantly, he'd stare at everybody who passed with malice, as if he wanted nothing more than for them to attempt to start a fight with him. He always felt empowered when he did this, so much so that on odd occasions he actually resented having company to walk to and from school with, as it meant he couldn't do his act.

The school was right in front of him. The big black gates confronted him, with all that separated him from the dark castle being a tidy moat of a tarmac road with cars streaming across it. He crossed the road and slipped in past the gates just as they began to close behind him.

Lessons dragged that morning and at the allotted time he eagerly skipped class and made for his appointment with Don.

Don's room always stank of heavy smoke which hung in the air like a blanket, warm and suffocating. It permeated every pore in Sam's exposed skin and coated them in a thin layer of dark yellow nicotine. Yet it was strangely comforting.

Don sat across from Sam behind that massive oak desk of his that was covered in stacks of papers, folders, files, books, photographs. Sam was convinced half of them had never been moved since he first came to the office but it was hard to tell through the haze of smoke.

"How's class?"

"Fine."

"Home?"

"Yeah, good."

"Anything new?"

"Not really, no."

Don took a long drag from his cigar, but it didn't respond satisfactorily so he relit it.

Sam was fascinated by the flame as it flickered for a moment, testing the foreign air around it, then growing in confidence wrapped itself around the cigar with gusto, burning it quite brutally before abruptly disappearing.

Don's fingers were long. The digits of an artist. He would most likely have been involved in the arts if he hadn't been a priest. But the scholarly profession suited him, as did the less rigorous demands of being mentor to the young men in the school.

Blowing a perfect smoke ring, Don finally turned and looked Sam straight in the eye.

God, for a priest he was damn cool, thought Sam. He realized that he was staring and as covertly as possible shifted his gaze to the window above Don's head, searching for a pigeon. They liked sitting on the windowsill and crapping down onto the courtyard below where they would regularly catch an unfortunate student.

"Are you with us today?"

Sam snapped back to reality, fixing his gaze back on Don's piercing eyes that gleamed through the smoke.

"Sorry, yeah, just drifted there a little bit."

Don watched him for a moment, nodding his head gently. Then he inhaled another deep long drag and allowed his eyes to wander around the room, feigning interest in the heavy books lining the shelves all around.

"You've been doing that a bit in class lately, haven't you? From what I hear."

"Who said that?"

"I have my sources, but I can never reveal them." Don smiled as he spoke.

With Don there was never recrimination, only warm comradeship and a search for understanding. That was his secret: you liked Don so much that you never wanted to disappoint him. It was a Jesuit trait. They were clever, these old Jays, wily like magpies. You were always wary when you saw more than one – it usually meant trouble – but when they weren't around you found yourself yearning for them and wondering why you weren't worthy of their attentions.

"I've just been a bit distracted lately, that's all."

"Why?"

There was a long pause. That was the beauty of talking with Don: he would let you take your time. If you were really lucky you might get to spend two classes in a row in that homely office of his, just talking about whatever came to your mind. Don fancied himself as some sort of amateur psychologist and to him every detail was important. Including the fact you'd made the choice to skip maths. Nothing was irrelevant.

"I guess I'm finding it all a bit boring lately, finding it difficult to concentrate."

"What have you been thinking about instead?"

"Nothing."

"That was a bare-faced lie."

"No, it wasn't."

"You looked away."

"That's beneath you, Don – too cheap."

"It's in all the books."

Sam laughed out much too loudly, but he couldn't help it.

"What have you been thinking about?"

Sam stared Don in the eye. Don stared right back.

Sam knew that this was the point where Don would decide if he was telling the truth or not, and if he thought that he was jerking him around then he'd be heading back to class within minutes. Equally, if Sam had nothing of note to say he would be sent back anyway. He really wanted to miss another class.

What was the truth though other than somebody else's lies?

"I went to a concert at the weekend."

"How nice – who did you see?"

"The Chemical Brothers."

"Who?"

"Hardcore dance and raver band, you wouldn't know them."

"Ravers?"

"Yeah, it was pretty mental – got home late."

Don's interest was piqued. He tried to hide it, but he failed.

Now that Sam had started he wasn't going to stop, but he mightn't give out too many details – just enough to keep Don hooked. He wanted to tell him everything that was really going on – there was something very comforting in knowing that he could say anything and most likely not be judged but actually offered advice. What did priests know about life though? This story was better.

"Any drugs in those kinds of places?"

Sam hadn't expected him to say it straight out, but he had. He might as well have nailed the point to the wall, written on a white flag with heavy red paint. Sam felt a tiny bit less respect for Don than he had moments before.

"Of course – it's that kind of place."

Sam let that hang in air, teasing, just out of Don's reach, unless he really wanted it.

"Sure."

Don looked at him and inhaled from that impressive cigar again without commenting further. Fuck, he wasn't playing the game the way Sam had expected – he probably knew exactly what he was doing and wasn't going to be led in.

Sam wriggled in his seat to make himself more comfortable. There was silence and he felt the need to fill it.

"It was a good night."

Don nodded. But that was it. He didn't pursue it any

further. If Sam wanted to tell him more then he'd have to volunteer.

"Your marks are slipping. All of your teachers are reporting that."

Don came straight out with it. So that was why he had no further interest in the concert.

"And the Chemical Brothers aren't playing until November."

Sam stared at Don. How the fuck did he know that? He could feel the blood swarming up through his capillaries and flooding his cheeks, propelling hot air around him like a visible force field. This was trouble. Don was not to be lied to.

"Is that all?" Don continued, a bored tone in his voice.

"Yes."

"OK."

Don spun away in his chair, swivelling to face the window. At his movement two pigeons on the sill were startled and they jumped off the ledge in a bustle of feathers and cat-like purring.

It was all so seductively relaxing in this office. But right now Sam wished he could leap off the ledge with the pigeons and fly somewhere. Being caught lying hurt because of the pride involved.

"How did you get the swollen nose?"

Shit. Was it that noticeable? Sam had figured it looked fine. Fuck. He had wanted to tell him but he hadn't.

"Football. Ball hit me in the nose."

"Your answer was too quick. Come on?"

"You can't judge that."

"Am I wrong?"

"Yes."

"OK."

Once you start lying it becomes habit very quickly. Sam had heard that once before, probably from Don during one of their more productive conversations.

Don stiffly kept his back to him, indicating that the conversation was finished, so Sam reluctantly pushed out his chair which scraped across the floor with a petulant squeal. Don's shoulders shook a little from the grating noise. Sam immediately wanted to explain that it hadn't been a childish gesture on purpose but the damage was already done so he didn't bother.

Making sure to close the door behind him as respectfully as possible, he walked back to class with leaden feet, replaying the conversation with Don in his mind over and over as if adding guilt to the past might somehow reveal a reprieve hidden in their words. There wasn't one.

THE END.

If you enjoyed this book from
Poolbeg why not visit our website

www.poolbeg.com

and get another book delivered straight
to your home or to a friend's home.

All books despatched within 24 hours.

Free postage on orders over €20*

Why not join our mailing list at
www.poolbeg.com and get some
fantastic offers, competitions,
author interviews, new releases
and much more?

*Also check out our Facebook and Twitter pages
for updates on book events, reviews, new and
forthcoming releases.*

@PoolbegBooks

www.facebook.com/poolbegpress

*Free postage over €20 applies to Ireland only

Made in the USA
Middletown, DE
09 December 2019